INSIGHT

Fact or Fiction? You Decide.

By

Gary Davies

DEDICATION

Dedicated to everyone who wonders if I'm writing about them.

I am. *(Anonymous)*

CONTENTS

ACKNOWLEDGMENTS

To the proof readers who have and continue to follow me on my journey. Many thanks for your honesty, suggestions and guidance. Your input was invaluable.

ABOUT THE AUTHOR

Gary Davies was born and has lived most of his life in Cwmbran in South Wales. Having served in the British Army, most of his working life has been in the manufacturing industry.

Insight is his first novel covering a subject that touches most of us. Having spent many years as an avid reader he decided it was time to dip his toe into the vast ocean that is writing.

CHAPTER 1

Hello, my name is Gary Channing, I'm 38 and my life is about to change drastically! Kind of like *The X Factor* but without the singing, from being a nobody to the most sought after person on the planet. Hopefully I now have your attention?

My wife, Sue, and I decided to go on one of those ghost weekends. You know the kind, you pay 3 times the price you would normally pay to stay at the place because you're on a haunted weekend. Yeah right, like ghosts only work certain weekends and charge more to haunt you because of it! But the wife thought our lives needed some excitement, having fallen into the usual midlife monotony, work, home, home, work. She had a point, after 12 years of marriage and 2 kids things weren't exactly what you'd call exciting, but boy oh boy was she going to get her wish, by the bucket load.

So the kids were sorted and off we went on our ghost hunting weekend, 2 hours later we arrived at the unusually named 'Hope Hall', it looked like your typical stately home, all windows and ivy, plus the must-have gravel drive. We parked up and walked into the reception, which to be honest looked like it had been knocked together by a 3-year-old. The young lady behind the barricade, (for want of a better description) took the usual details off us, booked us into room 12 and sent us on our merry way with directions, "Have a nice stay" and a rather forced smile. Good start.

Our room was on the second floor, at the end of a long corridor, filled with potted plants and ancestry paintings, which gave you that, you're being watched feeling, spooky! As we entered I glanced back down the corridor and noticed a group of about 5 people, all watching us enter our room! The weird meter started to twitch! By the time I shut the door Sue was unpacking and organising toiletries, nothing like good organising to make you feel at home and make your teeth itch. Having had a look around the room, I found the 'Planned Events' sheet, detailing events from ghost walks to table tipping! (Is that like cow tipping only with tables?) I know, a bizarre sense of humour, you're not the first!

Looking out the window, I finally found something to make me smile, one of the most beautiful views I had ever seen, I turned to mention it to Sue and looking back at me were about a dozen people! This was one of those close your eyes and shake your head moments, it worked, I opened my eyes and thankfully they had all gone, but were they really there in the first place?

Both myself and my wife shared a healthy interest in the paranormal, enjoying all the Ghost Hunting programmes and having our fair share of 'incidents' shall we say. A previous home had caused us to get help from a local paranormal group who worked their magic as their leader explained it. To be honest he was a little premature in his grand statement, but that's another story. So we were not novices when it came to unusual incidents. I decided to try out the bed whilst Sue busied herself, it really was comfortable, I closed my eyes and relaxed, I must have dozed off as I was startled by a male voice saying, "Welcome to our home."

Thinking we had a visitor I shot up off the bed and was startled to find the room full of people, males, females and children! I froze, what the hell was happening? Who were all these people? And more importantly what were they doing in my room, (well it seemed important at the time). Then a sense of calm came over me, a feeling of being in the company of friends, people I knew, although I did not recognise anybody, then I could hear Sue calling me, but I could not see her, a sense of panic started to wash over me and just as it seemed to peak I woke up! Bang, like being teleported from one room to another, no people, just Sue stood over me, calling me a lazy shit! Had it really been a dream? Had I really fallen asleep and dreamt it? I pondered it for a while whilst carrying out the 3S's, an old army saying, carried out before any social event, Shit, Shave, and Shower! In that order. The minds of men and there was me worrying about my 'Power Nap' dream!

So, suitably cleansed and attired, we left our room and headed for our first 'event' on the list, which was a social gathering of all the guests there for the haunted weekend. I couldn't wait, loads of false smiles and small talk, just my cup of tea. As you can tell I am one of life's great socialisers, not! So this was going to be one of life's little tests, which I had to pass otherwise Sue would kill me, no really, trust me. So deep breath, best smile and in I plunged.

The first person we met was Ian, he was as he described it our Event Organiser. I thought he was a cock and he'd fail miserably over the weekend to prove me wrong. Having navigated past him with minimum fuss, the next to invade my personal space was Jeff and Sally, amateur ghost hunters as they introduced themselves and happy to tell the world and his dog how good they were. They would prove to be the Yvette and Karl of the weekend, (*Most Haunted*) her screaming and frightening the shit out of everybody with it, and him swearing and talking to himself at every opportunity. Fantastic viewing, well for me it was. Next was Bill and Mary, nice people if your preference was OAPs who smelt of fags and piss! I kid you not, it was enough to curdle milk, but I think they knew as they kept pretty much to themselves after that.

Next was Phil, 40-something and his 'friend' Clare who appeared to be attached to him by an invisible leash about 3ft long, pretty girl and I mean girl. Phil was a successful car salesman who used to have his own business! Begs the question if he was so successful why 'used to have?' The one question 'Mr I could sell sand to the Arabs' failed to answer all weekend. Next up on our radar was Evan and Beth, both appeared to be in their late teens and introduced themselves as brother and sister, both were students, (tax dodgers I thought) although both for no apparent reason sent a cold shiver down my spine, Sue decided she was going to mother them all weekend, suited me fine, that left me to do as I pleased to a point. Ian then introduced Rob, our medium or not as it would later turn out, who was to guide us through our paranormal weekend, by this time my smile muscles were beginning to cramp, this was going to be tough, if only I knew how tough.

So our first event was a guided tour and history of Hope Hall, built in 1840 by Henry Hope, wealthy land owner and businessman who left his fortune to the upkeep of the hall. He never married and had no children, but, it was claimed, he had the Midas touch when it came to making money. He died in 1875. So my first question was if this was the case, how come the Hall was supposed to be haunted and if it was then it would be safe to assume that it was the ghost of Henry Hope, not so was the surprising answer from Rob, he then proceeded to impart with the biggest croc of shit story about devil worship and human sacrifice etc, etc. This guy should have been working for *The News of the World*, but it appeared that everyone else had taken it hook, line and sinker, Suckers.

We continued with the guided tour, from downstairs to up, I will say one thing for Rob, he put plenty of passion into his delivery. If I hadn't been such a cynical old git I might have enjoyed it. As we moved from room to room there seemed to be other guests wandering around, taking an interest in our group, but for some reason nobody in ours seemed to notice them! I put it down to Rob's Oscar winning tour.

Having completed our tour, we ended up in a large

dining room on the ground floor; I took this as an opportunity to vanish off to the toilet, more for a break from the group rather than a need to Pee! Having dragged it out for as long as I could, I made my way out into the hall pretending to adjust myself, as I looked up people were lining the stairs on both sides and along the landing, they appeared to be waiting for somebody. I thought, just my luck, I've walked out on a wedding party or some other formal occasion. Having given myself the 'double check' to ensure my fly was ok, I glanced towards the stairs and to my surprise the 'Honour Guard' had vanished! Things were becoming weird, very weird, I decided the first chance I got I was going to mention it to Sue; a "Gary, stop being a cock" response was just what I needed at this moment in time and I was sure my darling wife wouldn't let me down. Having arrived back in the dining hall to find, one I hadn't been missed and two, Rob and Ian were setting up the next event, I was so excited I thought I was going to fart! Thankfully I didn't, well not then!

Rob, announced that the next event was ready, he was going to lead the group through 'Table Tipping'. He explained that the plan was to communicate with one of the spirits and get them to lift and tip/tilt the table. Jeff and Sally took this opportunity to inform the rest of us of the last time they had been involved in this, surprisingly it involved the table moving, Sally screaming and Jeff swearing, no surprises there then.

So Rob got Phil, Claire, Bill and Mary to sit with him at the table, the rest of us picked a spot where we could view what was going to happen, suffice to say mine was a little further away than the others. So Rob got everybody sat at the table to form a circle using their hands and to concentrate, Rob called on any spirits present to communicate with them by moving the table, nothing happened, again Rob carried out the same request, again nothing happened, Sensing a little disappointment Rob asked the group to concentrate more, again Rob requested for any spirits to move the table, again nothing, I then noticed two females appear from the shadows behind Rob and they made their way to the table, it appeared I was the only one who had noticed them, they got to the table and started to rock it gently at first then lift it slightly, everybody seemed genuinely startled by this and I'm thinking are we not supposed to see them?

You could feel the excitement rise as the table moved more and more, I thought to myself, they're taking the piss. I stepped forward to say something and as I did the table dropped to the floor and the younger of the two females looked at me and with some venom put a long thin finger to her lips and just glared at me. Startled by this reaction I took a step back to my original position and, feeling like a naughty schoolboy, I looked up and the same female was giving me the most beautiful smile I had ever seen! The weird meter was now off the scale and the hairs on the back of my neck were stood to attention. The 'activity' carried on for a couple of minutes, much to the delight of the group, as both females disappeared back into the shadows they turned and smiled at me, which made me feel even more scared.

The lights were turned back up and Ian announced it was time for tea and biscuits, I was thinking of something a little stronger than tea and this was from a man who did not drink! I managed to get Sue over to a quiet corner of the room and proceeded to tell her about what had gone on so far, the response was predictable and kind of comforting, well as comforting as being called a 'cock' can be. But I did feel better for having spoken about it and made Sue promise not to tell anyone about what had happened.

Ian appeared from nowhere and asked if everything was ok, we confirmed it was, he then asked what we thought of the table tipping? Sue answered with enough enthusiasm for both of us and seemed to have the desired effect on Ian, as he buggered off to annoy someone else, me? I could feel my smile muscles starting to cramp again.

Next on the agenda was group experiments, we were split into teams of two and allocated a room in the hall to carry out a vigil, I was paired with Claire, much to the disgust of Phil, who was paired with Mary! Now that brought a smile to my face and Sue got paired with Evan. Claire and I were given a camcorder, a motion detector, plus a digital thermometer and sent to Henry Hope's bedroom, wonderful. Claire seemed overjoyed by the decision and seemed a changed person even in the short space of time after being surgically removed from Phil, who by now was well pissed. So off we went to old Henry's room for two hours of paranormal fun, Ian's words not mine, I can assure you. Claire was like a bottle of pop and couldn't seem to stop talking all the way to Henry's bedroom; my teeth were beginning to itch again!

We entered Henry's bedroom and set up the motion detector to cover the floor, we sat on the bed and I gave Claire the camcorder and told her not to film me, at all, which didn't seem to dampen her enthusiasm at all. I did manage to convince her that being quiet was a good idea. After about 15 minutes the detector went off and frightened the crap out of both of us, Claire managed to drop the camcorder in my lap which only added to the embarrassment of me squealing like a girl. I picked it up and gave it her back, got off the bed and reset the detector, as I returned to the bed I noticed that Claire looked as if she was asleep, I shook her by the shoulder but she remained, for want of a better description, fast asleep. Just then I heard a deep male voice say, "You won't wake her, she's in a kind of psychic sleep, it will do her no harm but will allow me to communicate with you!"

At this time the fart I told you about earlier was well and truly out! I turned to the sound of the voice to see Henry Hope sat in a chair in the far corner, I recognised him from his portrait. I tried the close your eyes and shake your head trick, but this time it did not work, I thought to myself, you cock, you've fallen asleep again and you're dreaming.

"I'm afraid you're not dreaming," stated Henry. *Fucking great*, I thought, with all rational thought out the window by now, I decided to go with it, so to speak.

"Come on then, Henry," I said, "what's this all about? Let me guess, we're in the twilight zone, or I have a brain tumour that makes me fall asleep and have weird dreams?"

"Close," he said. The man has a sense of humour, I thought! A sense of humour? He's a bloody ghost or a figment of my imagination what the hell was I on about?

Henry, or rather Henry's ghost, proceeded to explain to me that I was here for a purpose, which would be made clearer in the coming months and that I was being "prepared" to carry out what was required of me. Very cryptic, I thought. Henry explained that all that had happened tonight had been real; I was not going mad, although I felt like it, it was part of the preparation process to help me understand. He also explained that over the next couple of months I would receive visitors who would supply me with information to help me, but now was not the time to reveal it all. He asked me not to discuss what was happening and that I needed to try and keep a clear mind to allow 'things' to happen.

I looked at the floor to try and understand what was happening; my thought process was interrupted by Claire asking if she had fallen asleep. I looked at Henry's chair and it did not surprise me to find no one sitting there, I told Claire she must have dozed off for a minute or two.

The rest of the vigil passed without incident, so we preceded back to the dining room, with all pairs back, Ian asked each pair to share with the group any experiences they had. Bill and Sally were the first to pipe up; they claimed to have captured orbs on film and heard voices! Also Sally claimed she had been touched, brave ghost! This was naturally accompanied by the obligatory scream. Bill stated he nearly pissed himself, which I found highly amusing considering my previous description of him, but I did get the stern teacher look off Sue which made me feel like a naughty schoolboy. Ian planned to review everybody's video and share any findings with us all during lunch. This was the first time since my little chat with Henry that I'd thought what might be on the camcorder, Claire was clutching it to her like it was a prized possession, no chance of getting my hands on that then I thought to myself.

Jeff and Beth were next to contribute. I thought, this is going to be fun, if it's down to Jeff to explain we're all going to spend the next 10 minutes listening to him effing and blinding! But to my surprise Jeff seemed very subdued and it was down to Beth to explain, she claimed Jeff had been possessed! Now under normal circumstances a "bollocks" under the breath would have been my usual response, but after what I had been through so far, this was quite believable. Beth claimed that as soon as they entered the attic room Jeff started "acting weird," now I know what you're thinking, how could she tell? She claimed that the spirit of Henry Hope had possessed Jeff! This would have been around the same time I was having my conversation with Henry. Now I know he's a ghost, so does that mean he can be in two places at once?

"No" was the response whispered in my ear. This convinced me that Jeff was pulling a Derek Acorah episode. But, as before, the rest of the group were hooked, this was one piece of video I couldn't wait to see. That was pretty much it as far as the experiences were concerned, Ian called an end to the proceedings announcing to my surprise that it was 5am and time to get some sleep; he asked us all to meet back up at 2pm for lunch for some camcorder classics! Boy, that man kills me, so witty and funny!!!! Again, NOT!

To say it had been a strange trip so far was an

understatement and certainly not what I expected. I sat on the edge of our bed trying to make sense of all that had happened, what worried me more was the fact that I didn't really seem that phased about what had happened, curious yes. My thoughts were interrupted by Sue coming out of the bathroom, a quick pee and a brush of the teeth then bed, good plan! You know what they say about the best laid plans?

Having done the business I left the bathroom ready for bed, Sue was already asleep and I was planning to join her very soon! So it came as no surprise to find you know who sat in the chair next to the bed.

"Come on Henry," I said, "you're taking the piss, I'm on my chinstrap here, and I need to sleep."

"All in good time, Gary. We need to make plans, you need to understand what this is all about before you leave, later your friend, the medium, plans to show everybody his talent, he does have a talent but not for talking to the dead! Reading people's thoughts? Yes, but communicating with the dead? No. So you need to understand how to "draw out" the thought readers and learn how to expose them for what they are, so listen very carefully and no falling asleep!"

"Yes, Dad." A smartass ghost to boot, lord help me.

So Henry proceeded to explain it all to me. "People like Rob read people's thoughts, they cannot communicate with the dead or ghosts or spirits, they get snippets of what people are thinking hence the, 'I've got a Bill or a Bob here, someone's dad or grandfather' and so on. They don't get all the information, then as the people who this info relates to think harder, and those who it doesn't relax, then they home in on their thoughts until they have narrowed it down to one or two people, then they are able to get more information as they think more about Bill or Bob, basically they tell people what they are thinking and they don't even realise it, as simple as that. So they're not telling them anything they don't already know. Now to prove this, later I want you to think of a name, someone you don't know, and concentrate really, really hard on it. You're going to need to be picked out, then once he's taken the bait you need to reel him in so to speak, all of it needs to be false information then you'll know for sure that I'm right. Mind you, you should already know that because people who communicate with ghosts do it just like we are now, it's as simple as that, they see them and they can hear them, but also the ghost must want to be seen and heard also. Have you got all that?"

"Yes, I think so."

"Good, now time for sleep and keep an eye out for some of my guests."

I put my head in my hands and said, "Thanks Henry." I looked up and he was gone. Thank fuck for that. Boy did I need to sleep.

CHAPTER 2

I awoke at midday to the sound of Sue showering. I felt strangely refreshed and full of energy, which was very unusual for me. Sue and I swapped places in the shower, I really did feel great, having showered and dressed we headed downstairs for some food, I was starving. Everybody else was already there, some looking a little worse for wear to be honest, much to my amusement, which was swiftly curtailed by an elbow to the ribs from Sue. We grabbed some food and coffee, found a table next to Phil and Claire, now he really did look like shit! With pleasantries exchanged I proceeded to work my way through the equivalent of a small banquet that I had on my plate.

Having finished my food, I looked across to Phil and he really, really did look like shit, it turned out that he'd had the room from hell to sleep in. Again, Claire had heard nothing, but Phil had been pulled out of bed, had the quilt pulled off, he'd seen shadows and heard voices, he was not a happy camper at all, Claire was gutted she had missed it all, which cheered Phil up even more. Everybody else had seemed to have had an uneventful sleep, suffice to say I included myself in that category.

Ian arrived like Dale Winton on acid, all smiles and fake tan; he asked us all to make our way to the dining room where he had set up the equipment to review everybody's 'evidence' from last night. First up were Phil and Mary, they had been sent to the kitchen. They had captured a couple of orbs, which Ian kindly explained were spirits! This was met with a loud bang from the room above, which made everybody jump, including Ian. And that was pretty much all they had. Mary explained that their battery had run out after 10 minutes and the spare didn't last much longer, she tried to get Phil to agree with what she had said, but he was definitely 'off planet'.

Next up were Sue and Evan, they had picked up some strange temperature readings in the library and caught on video what looked like someone walking through the closed door at the other end of the room, the cameras weren't the best and had seen better days so the footage could have been better, but even so it was pretty good, neither of them had seen it at the time so the footage came as a bit of a shock. Bill and Sally had been given the wine cellar, they had nothing to show for their night's work apart from Sally screaming at everything and anything, which frightened the crap out of Bill every time.

Jeff and Beth were next, they had been given the attic space, I wanted to see how long it took for Jeff to swear on camera and I didn't have to wait long as he tripped up the stairs leading to the attic, classic.

Now I did say there was something about Beth and Evan, well Beth to be precise, as soon as they were in the attic she changed, Jeff had set up the camera on a tripod so they could walk around, they had been given a digital audio recorder to try and get EVPs, (Electronic Voice Phenomena). All you could pick up on the camera was "muttering" no real words as such, you could hear Jeff asking questions in the background. As Beth passed the camera the picture seemed to distort and the camera shut off. The next thing you see is 55 minutes later and Jeff looks like he's been dragged through a hedge, Ian stops the video and asks Jeff and Beth what had happened, Jeff was about to answer when Beth announced that the battery had run out without them knowing and Jeff had fallen over some boxes!! Jeff seemed a little surprised by this explanation and was about to respond, then Jeff fainted!! I kid you not; he just passed clean out and fell off the chair he was sitting on, followed by the customary scream from Sally.

Jeff came round after a couple of seconds, no real harm done apart from his male pride, Beth on the other hand had a strange look of satisfaction on her face, very bizarre I thought. Anyway, drama over and back to the show. Last up were Claire and myself, this brought me back to reality with a thump, I was quite worried what Ian had found on our video, my fears were unfounded, it showed the motion detector going off, Claire falling asleep, the battery running out and that was it! Thank god for that. Ian asked if anybody had any personal experiences that had not been recorded on video that they wanted to share with the group. Phil put his hand up and proceeded to explain what had happened to him in his room, he had decided to 'ham it up' a bit from the version he had told us earlier! Any glimmer of sympathy I'd had for him vanished instantly, the word cock sprung to mind again.

So with the evidence review over, Ian explained the plan for the rest of the day, we could review all the evidence for ourselves and chat to Rob about anything that had happened, otherwise it was a meet back here at 7pm after evening meal to do the séance with Rob as a group and as couples, or one to one if Rob had any messages to convey! After that it was another night of vigils with a view to finish at 4am. I was pissing myself with excitement as Sue and I looked at each other!

"Don't start," was her stern reply to my excited expression, oh she knew me so well.

I said to Sue, "Let's get some fresh air, let's go for a walk, I need to talk to you."

We left via the French doors into the beautiful landscaped gardens, I explained or tried to explain all that had happened since we had been here, concentrating mainly on the conversations with Henry!

She looked me in the eyes and much to my relief she said, "I believe you."

I explained about the planned séance later and what Henry had said to do, I told Sue to come up with a name and just focus on it as hard as possible. We agreed a plan of attack for later and started to make our way back towards the house, I asked Sue what she thought of Beth and Evan?

"I'm not sure," she said, "at first I thought they were your typical young students, here for a bit of a laugh, but I've been watching them and they do act quite strange at times."

"What do you mean?" I said.

"Well sometimes it seems as if they are having a conversation with a third person. Also they don't appear to have mobiles! I mean teenagers without mobiles! Never happens, also when I did the vigil with Evan he wouldn't use any of the equipment, he just plain refused, which I thought was strange at the time, but now after what you've told me, it seems even stranger. I'm going to keep a very close eye on them pair at this séance. Don't make it obvious, they'll suss you out otherwise."

We arrived back at the hall and entered the way we came out, only Phil was still there, he seemed totally engrossed in the video footage that was playing.

"You ok, Phil?" I asked, which was met with a wave, his eyes never left the monitor, "Let's leave him to it," I said.

As we left the dining hall we saw Evan and Beth deep in conversation by the door to the cellar.

"Everything alright, guys?" Sue asked. Either they didn't hear her or they chose not to. Anyway I was more interested in the couple at the top of the stairs gesturing me to follow them, I grabbed Sue's hand and pulled her to follow me. We got to the main landing and the couple had disappeared, nothing unusual with that the way this weekend was going.

I said to Sue, "Go to the room and I'll have a look around." It came as no surprise that as soon as Sue had left that the couple "reappeared." They gestured me to follow them, I followed them to the attic and found them sat on an old sofa. They appeared to be in their late 60s.

I asked, "Are you ghosts?" I know, stupid question.

"Yes," they said, "our names are Gwen and Albert. We met Henry when we were alive, we died within a couple of weeks of each other and found ourselves here!"

"Ok, so why have you brought me up here?" I said.

"We need to explain some things to you to help you understand what's happening. You're on a very important journey and we are here to kind of give you directions."

"So you're my spiritual sat nav then?" I asked with a smirk, I thought it was quite funny under the circumstances, suffice to say 'George and Mildred' didn't see the funny side, wasted!

"Ghosts or spirits need energy to communicate or show themselves, hence the reason why batteries run out quickly and the more energy around the more we can do. Henry built this house here for a reason, a high source of natural energy lies beneath the hall, that's the reason why we can pretty much do what we need to do. Not all ghosts are spirits, some are 'recordings' of people, light is energy, light allows us to see. That energy has to go somewhere, it's kind of stored in its surroundings and can 'playback' at any time, so not all paranormal encounters, as you like to call them, are caused by spirits like us. Yes sometimes we are seen, but usually for a reason and to the right people, but in death some spirits retain the evilness they had in life and can cause chaos, but it is unusual. Ok, time for you to go before you're missed.

Remember, Gary, not everybody you see is real, especially here, bear that in mind and good luck with your journey." And they were gone, so I made my way back to our room, Sue was lying on our bed reading, she glanced up as I entered.

"Find anything interesting?" she asked, so I relayed what had happened in the attic. "You're becoming a right little ghost magnet, aren't you?" The hint of sarcasm didn't go unnoticed.

"Everything ok?" I asked.

"I'm sorry; this weekend was just meant to have been a bit of fun and has been hijacked by the spirit world it seems!" At least this statement was accompanied by a smirk.

"I know, it's not like I planned it, well apart from Jeff fainting!" I returned the smirk. "Mind you, who would believe us? I mean, what spirit in their right mind would pick a sarcastic, anti-social prick like me to spread the word?" Now that was met with a full on laugh, which cheered me up also.

We had a quick shower, changed and left for tea; downstairs we met Claire, who looked quite worried.

"Is everything ok, Claire?" asked Sue.

"I can't find Phil," she said.

"Is that such a bad thing?" I asked. Sue scowled at me and Claire didn't seem to hear.

"Where did you see him last?" Sue asked. "I left him in the dining room; he wanted to have another look at his and Mary's video footage."

"Why?" I asked.

"I'm not sure, he thinks he's being haunted! I know what you're thinking, what's so strange about being haunted in a haunted house?" To be honest, Phil had been singled out for some rather 'personal' attention.

The others arrived and Claire asked them about Phil, most of them had the same response as me and Sue, apart from Beth, she replied with what can only be described as the most malicious grin,

"Who cares?" Now that did get everybody's attention.

"That's not very nice, Beth," said Mary.

"Who cares what you think? You old bag!" It appeared it was time for Beth to show her true colours. "What a sad bunch of people you are." This outburst really did take people by surprise, well apart from me, I had a feeling there was more to Beth than we had seen and, boy, how right I was.

"Why are you being like this?" asked Sue.

"What the fuck has it got to do with you?" was Beth's reply. Enough was enough. I stepped forward and grabbed Beth by the elbow with the intention of moving her away from the group and having a stern word. As my fingers made contact with her, it was like being electrocuted, I was frozen to the spot. Beth's facial features seemed to change to what I can only describe as demon like! She turned and faced me.

"Don't fucking touch me!"

Now I don't claim to be the bravest of men but the change in this woman frightened the crap out of me, apart from the facial change, her voice seemed to deepen and the smell from her mouth made me gag, all this made me stagger back holding my hand. Beth and Evan stormed out the main doors leaving us all stood there open mouthed.

"What the fuck just happened then?" was Jeff's response, we were all stunned and for once we all seemed to have experienced Beth's outburst.

My whole arm was tingling, confused was an understatement, Sue asked me if I was ok. I just nodded, I was quite shocked by the whole incident. As I was stood there I felt this hand on my shoulder, as I turned to see who it was, a wave of calm seemed to wash over me and the tingling stopped in my arm. As I looked, Gwen who I had met earlier breezed past me, this was fast becoming the twilight zone on acid.

The silence was broken by Ian's arrival. "Did I miss something?" was his opening statement. Fuck me. If only he knew! It did seem to bring everybody back to reality, Sue took charge of the situation.

"Phil's missing and Beth's just flipped and insulted everybody before storming off with Evan."

"Oh right, I really did miss something then. Phil's fine, he's sleeping in my office, he came to see me and Rob about the problems he'd been having - of a spiritual kind before you ask!"

Claire left with Ian to see Phil. I guided Sue out earshot of the others so we could talk.

Sue asked, "Are you ok?"

"I think so, what the hell was that all about?" Sue gave me that look of *spill!* So I told her everything including Gwen's appearance. What concerned me more was Beth's outburst, now I know we had our suspicions about Beth but the image she had left me with was one of pure evil and a feeling of "don't fuck with me or you'll pay." Just thinking about it gave me the shivers, I didn't mind telling Sue that the whole encounter had really freaked me out. I was, for the first time, struggling to get my head around it.

"Do you think they'll be back?" asked Sue.

"I don't know, but I hope not," I said with a nervous smile.

Tea was unusually quiet, not that there were many there, I had a stomach that really needed feeding and I mean feeding. Sue just looked at me shaking her head which made me feel like a naughty child. Mind you, I was eating like one so it came as no surprise really.

With my stomach full, my mind was back on an even keel, well sort of, I wanted to discuss with Sue our plan of attack with Rob later. For someone who didn't even want to come on this weekend I was like a dog with a bone, my mind seemed to have processed all the crazy shit that had been happening and accepted it. I was a man on a mission and if I was honest with myself I was really up for it, hook, line and sinker.

After a quick shower and a change of clothes we made our way to the dining room for the highlight of the weekend! (Ian's words not mine.) Ian was there like a puppy needing a pee, Bill, Mary, Jeff and Sally were already there. Ian explained that Phil and Claire wouldn't be joining us, he made no mention of the Devil's spawn, Beth and Evan, which suited me fine. Ian told us that Rob would be waiting for each of us in turn in the library, Bill and Mary wanted to go first, real eager beavers, so Ian escorted them to the library and returned a couple of minutes later. Much to my annoyance he decided to make a beeline for us, having sat down he looked me in the eye and asked,

"Do you think Phil is possessed?" We just looked at him, I thought he was joking but the look on his face told me he was deadly serious.

I asked, "What makes you think that?" Ian explained that Phil had come to see himself and Rob this morning; he'd explained that he'd be woken during the night by a woman's voice telling him to go to the attic, he remembered going up to the attic and that was the last thing he could remember until he found himself wandering around the grounds but couldn't remember how he'd got there from the attic. So he'd gone back to the hall to explain to Claire what had happened, as soon as she saw him he could see the look of horror on her face. When he asked her what was wrong, she just took him into the bathroom. There he could see his bloodshot eyes and what could only be described as hand marks around his neck! Claire was naturally shocked, even more so when Phil explained that he could remember nothing. It had been Claire's suggestion to Phil to go and speak with Ian and Rob. The cynic in me was thinking, that wasn't a good move. I turned the question back on Ian.

"What did Rob think?"

The answer was kind of predictable; Rob had said it wasn't his area of expertise! I was like, what a cop out.

I said to Ian, "Then why ask me what I think? I'm

no expert either." His answer completely threw me.

He said, "Rob thinks you have the gift." I just looked at him with a stunned look on my face. Thankfully Ian's reply kind of dug me out of my own hole. "I told him he was talking rubbish," he stated with a kind of nervous, *I believe him but don't want you to know* look on his face. Thankfully the awkwardness of the conversation was broken with the return of Bill and Mary, both of them had tissues in their hands and had obviously been crying. Jeff and Sally were then ushered out by Ian as the next to see Rob, Ian didn't come straight back which gave us a chance to ask Bill and Mary how it had gone, I left the questioning to Sue, being slightly more tactful than me!

They explained how their son Steve had spoken to them through Rob! They told us how Steve had been killed in a motorbike accident 3 years ago on his way home from work and that he'd told them he was at peace and that he hadn't suffered at the time of the accident, all good, consoling stuff and the kind of things you would want to hear in their situation, I was thinking to myself.

Before we knew it, Jeff and Sally were back wittering excitedly to each other like a couple of school kids, followed closely by Ian. It was our turn next. We followed Ian into a small study like room where Rob was sat behind this massive desk, to me he just looked like a dick! But maybe he thought it added to his drama. Anyway, Ian sat us down and scuttled off. Rob asked if we were happy to have a reading as a couple, to which we replied "yes". He explained to us that he was just a messenger for the spirits and sometimes the messages might not make sense straight away! I was doing my best to keep a straight face. He asked us to think of the name of the person in the spirit world we wanted to speak to, this was where our plan came into effect.

Very soon I could see him frowning, which distracted me a little. Straightaway he blurted out the name Michael, who was the son of one of Sue's friends, who was, I might add, still alive. I had been thinking about our neighbour's dog, Sabre, which I think had thrown him a little. Me getting distracted had allowed him to pick up on Sue's thoughts which was her friend's son Michael. Again, he proceeded to come out with this story about how our 'son' had died in a swimming accident and gave us the usual he was at peace and with other family members in the spirit world waiting for us! All this was confirmed by Sue when I questioned her later, She told me that her friend, Deb, had a son called Michael who had nearly died in a swimming accident on holiday a couple of years ago. Rob was nothing more than a very clever thought reader, as explained to me by Henry and confirmed by Rob's performance, and with the reading concluded we joined the rest of the group. Due to the events of the past 36 hours Ian had decided to cancel the last set of vigils, which was fine by me, he explained that there would be a small refund due to this and asked us to "Like" their Facebook page! I thought, you cheeky sod. Ian gave us his end of event speech, we all said our goodbyes and thankfully left. As we left I glanced in the rear view mirror to see not Ian and Rob but Henry, Gwen, Albert and a whole host of others waving goodbye, now that really did give me a 'piss shiver'.

CHAPTER 3

The trip home was quiet to say the least; Sue seemed to spend the whole trip deep in thought, not that it surprised me, we had our money's worth that's for sure and there was a lot to take in for her also. I mean, having your husband "outed" as a physic or whatever I was supposed to be, surely wasn't in her plans for that weekend.

I decided it was time to stop and have a talk before we got home to 1001 questions off the kids. I pulled off into the first services we came to, Sue didn't even realise we had stopped until I said,

"Coffee, toilet or both?"

A couple of blinks and she seemed back with us.

"Welcome back," I announced. "Where are we? Why have we stopped?" she asked.

"I thought it would be a good idea to have a brew and a debrief."

She rolled her eyes at me, she loved my military

speak, honest!

I went and got 2 cups of what could be loosely described as coffee and made my way to the table she was sat at, again staring into space. I asked her what was up.

"What do you think?" was the sharp reply. Ask a stupid question, you get a stupid answer!

"Ok, talk to me."

Sue looked me in the eye. "What the hell happened back there?"

"Well it was your idea to have an exciting/fun weekend, well that's how you sold it to me," I replied with a smug grin on my face.

"You're an arsehole sometimes, do you know that?"

"Yes I have been told once or twice, usually by yourself." I was doing my best to lighten the mood as I could see what had gone on was really troubling her. But maybe blaming her wasn't one of my best comebacks.

"Listen, what's happened has happened, I'm not sure what the hell is going on myself but we need to stick together on this, let's just tell the kids we had a fun time and leave it at that with them, me and you will be a different story. We need to talk this though and try and make sense of it all."

"Really, easy for you to say," was the reply.

"You think so, Sue?"

The rest of the journey home was in silence, I could tell Sue was running the weekend over and over in her mind, I was doing the same and I guess she was running into a brick wall like me. We arrived home to be met by the kids, welcome back to reality was my thought and I guess Sue was thinking the same as she looked at me and smiled which cheered me up no end I can tell you. Having got in, made a cuppa and sat down, the first job was to spin a yarn to satisfy the boys, which they took hook, line and sinker, thankfully. It had been a strange weekend to say the least but being back home brought back some kind of normality.

Monday brought the usual routine of getting the boys ready and off to school, Sue off to work and me? The morning to ponder the weekend's events before I left for my afternoon shift. As the week wore on life's routine seemed to blur the events of that weekend and 2 months down the road with life back to normal it was a distant memory, or so I thought!

My uncle had been ill for quite some time and things had taken a turn for the worst. He had been rushed into hospital with breathing difficulties, I was very close to my uncle, after my own father had buggered off with the local barmaid. Sid, my uncle, had come to be the closest thing I had to a father whilst growing up. I'd had a call at work from Sue to tell me Sid was in hospital and that she was there, our neighbour had kindly come over to look after the boys. Sue was very upset on the phone which told me things were not looking good, I arranged to pick her up from the hospital when I left work.

I left work at 22:00 having handed over to the oncoming supervisor and jumped in the car, it was only 10 minutes from the hospital so I would be there in no time. I left the factory and was naturally rushing even though it wasn't going to make the short journey any quicker, I stopped at the traffic lights, drumming my fingers on the steering wheel with impatience when from the rear of the car a voice said,

"No need to rush lad," my head snapped around to find Uncle Sid sat in the back of my car. All I can say is I'm glad I was stationary. I just stared at him, my mind was doing backflips and was unable to take in what I was seeing. He then said, "Lights have changed lad, best get going." I looked around and the lights were green, I drove off thinking here we go again, I looked in my rear view mirror and Uncle Sid had thankfully vanished.

I arrived at the hospital to find Sue and my mother outside, both in tears. As I walked towards them Sue just looked at me and shook her head, we wrapped our arms around each other and I held her as tight as I could as she sobbed into my chest. After a couple of minutes I asked her what had happened, she explained that Sid's carer had called an ambulance after she had arrived and found him on the living room floor struggling for breath, his carer had then called my mum, Sid's sister, she in turn had called Sue as she knew I was at work. Mum then explained to me that when they had arrived at the hospital Sid was in the resuscitation room. After about an hour the doctor allowed them to go and see him, they had only been with him about 15 minutes when all hell broke loose, the alarms on his monitoring machines started sounding and they were asked to leave, 30 minutes later the doctor came to see them in the relatives' room and told them Sid had suffered a massive heart attack and they had been unable to save him. I asked what time this was. Mum said it was about 10pm! A cold shiver ran down my spine, it was the same time that Sid had appeared in my car! I took them both home, now wasn't the time to mention Sid's 'appearance'.

A couple of days later we went to the funeral home so we could view his body. Mum had offered to take us but I declined, there had always been a bit of jealousy from Mum with regards to mine and Sid's relationship. He treated me like his son. Sid didn't have kids of his own and had never married. As such he was quite well off and a result, Sid would tell me that I would get everything after he died. This really pissed Mum off and she was not afraid to make her feelings known about it. Sue had confided in me that Sid had told her a couple of months ago how mum had been badgering him to change his will to leave it all to her! Nice woman, but it didn't come as any surprise to me. If she had her way we would never have married so she wasn't top of my Christmas card list either.

So we arrived at the funeral home, Kelvin the director met us and showed us into the chapel of rest, this really gave me the creeps. I had no intention of looking at Sid and I had told Sue this before we had left the house, it just wasn't my cup of tea. Anyway, this young lad met us and offered to take us up to the coffin. I told him I would be hanging back, so he escorted Sue up to the coffin, I was stood there feeling a bit of a spare part when this voice whispered in my ear, "She's a good lass, Gary." I almost wet myself and must have made some girly noise as the young lad looked in my direction. I looked around and surprise, surprise, Sid was stood there.

Having regained a little composure, I whispered, "Sid you have to stop doing that!"

"Lighten up, lad," was his reply, funny guy! Sid explained that he could remember travelling in the ambulance, the next thing he could remember was being above the bed, he could see the doctors and nurses around his bed, he said there was no fear or anything, he understood what was happening but felt at peace, the next thing he knew he was in my car, so I asked him why he was still here. He said there were still things to be sorted and that was where I came in. *Oh great*, I thought.

"Time for me to go, lad," said Sid. "We're being watched." I looked around and saw the young lad with Sue watching me with a frown on his face. Bugger, I thought. Sue came back down, doing her best to hide that she had been crying, I gave her a hug and a kiss and we left.

Two days later was the funeral, I was dreading this for more than one reason, I was hoping Sid wasn't planning on making a guest appearance but I had my doubts. Sid had requested a burial so we had the church service and we were asked to walk in front of the hearse to the grave side. Sid had been an old fashioned fella in life and this was no surprise to me.

As we were walking up, Mum had attached herself to Sue so I walked next to the hearse. The young lad from the funeral home joined me and introduced himself as Mitch, I shook his hand and told him I was Gary.

We carried on walking in silence which was broken by Sid's voice, "Nice day for it, lads." We both looked around, I'm not sure which surprised me the most Sid being there or Mitch hearing him. We both looked at each other, I said to Mitch, "Can you see him?"

He replied, "No but I can hear him. Who is he?"

I said, "This is Sid, the guy whose funeral it is!" Good of him to join us I thought! Not!

We both did our best to ignore Sid taking the piss out of us all the way up to the grave and through the service. Now Sid was a really funny guy and a couple of times almost had me and Mitch giggling like school kids. I copped the glare from the wife, only natural, we were at a funeral after all.

Once the service was over I told Mum and Sue I would meet them back at the car. Once they were out of earshot, I turned to Sid and told him he was an arse, he was still laughing at us. Mitch then asked me did I know who Henry Hope was. Naturally, I was a little surprised by his question, but I said yes, why? He proceeded to tell me that Henry had visited him on a number of occasions explaining to him that he would meet me and that it was important that we both knew each other and what was our purpose, as Henry liked to call it. I then told Mitch what had happened at Hope Hall. All this time Sid was still with us, a clearing of his throat reminded us he was still there.

"Sorry, Sid," I said.

"Don't worry, lad, it's time for me to go. If you need me I'll be there, you just have to call. Take care lad!" And with that he was gone. Mitch and I walked back down to the car where mum and Sue were waiting. I swapped numbers with Mitch and told him I would be in touch.

Mum and Sue were already waiting in the car which took us back to Mum's where our car was parked. The journey was made in silence but I could tell Mum was itching to speak to me about something. The car dropped us off, we said our goodbyes with Mum and left. On the short journey back to our house my wonderful wife gave me that oh so familiar look of, s*pill now*! So I told her about Sid at the funeral and what Mitch had told me about Henry.

"What's this all about, Gary?" asked Sue.

"I'm still not really sure, sweetheart," was my honest reply. I tried to explain what Henry had told Mitch and me and that I was not really sure how we were to go forward with it. In the next couple of days Mitch would provide the answers after another visit from Henry.

Mitch called me 2 days later to say Henry had visited and that we needed to talk, so after checking it was ok with Sue I invited Mitch to the house. We made sure the boys were asleep before we started talking, I explained to Mitch that Sue was already up to speed with things so far. So Mitch proceeded to explain what Henry had told him during his last visit, now this is where things got really interesting. so pay attention. Henry had explained that the battle between good and evil was very much still happening and not like you read in the bible etc. Henry explained that good souls needed to be shown the light and not taken into the darkness. This balance has an effect on human life on a daily basis, if the scales tipped to the good, more good things happened, if they tipped to evil then more bad things happened. People believe in all kinds of crap, from the TV, internet and mouth to mouth. Our task was to help with the mouth to mouth. False mediums had no ability to guide lost souls to the light and if they don't find the light then they go to the dark! As simple as that. We had to expose the frauds and promote the true mediums to allow the scales to keep tipping to the good. We would meet lost souls along the way. My job was to see them, let them know I can help them and then Mitch and I would guide them to the light! So no big deal then, I thought to myself. Bit of an understatement, I know. Mitch suggested we go to a local spiritualist church so I could see the good and the bad, as he put it. He explained that this first church was run by local wannabes, no real mediums, they all knew each other so it was quite easy to come up with things that were true, they liked to use 'guest' mediums, who were briefed beforehand about people in the audience. Mitch explained that he had been a couple of times and had been spoken to by spirits who wanted to know why the 'mediums' were ignoring them! So it was agreed that the following Tuesday we would be visiting Christie Road Spiritualist Church!

CHAPTER 4

The weekend passed quickly and Mitch arrived at the house at 6pm, this gave us a chance to have a chat about what we were going to do. Mitch suggested we keep a low profile and just watch what happened so I could understand what it was all about. So with my mum looking after the kids we set off for a night of fun, it turned out that this would be an accurate description of what was to come.

So we arrived at what was best described as a crumbling old village hall, it looked busy, we made our way to the entrance where we were met by Shirley, who introduced herself as the church chairperson and senior medium! The smirk meter was off the scale, senior medium! I kid you not. We sat down about halfway back from this little stage with a table and some chairs set up. The hall filled up quite quickly and Shirley kicked off proceedings with a short prayer, nice!

She then started her speech about the church, its

purpose and about donations at the end! Nice to see we didn't have to wait long for the mention of money. So Shirley introduced their guest medium for the evening, her name was Helen, she appeared to be in her 30s, long brown hair and milk bottle bottom glasses. Helen stood up and introduced herself as Helen Morgan, she explained that she had been able to communicate with spirits since she was a little girl, really! She took off her glasses, (now I liked this bit) as she wouldn't need them as the visiting spirits would guide her to who the message was for. 10 out of 10 for invention, I must say. Anyway, she stepped down from the stage and proceeded to pass messages to a couple of people at the front, much to their amazement. During this I noticed a woman who looked in her late 40s appear at the side of the stage, she was looking around the hall and her eyes met mine. I thought, shit! Too late, she appeared on the empty seat next to me.

"You can see me, can't you?" she asked. Mitch heard her also and looked around, I nodded and she said, "Good." Then she disappeared. Then a man in his early 50s stood up and asked the medium if she could contact his dead wife! I kid you not. Helen explained that it wasn't that simple, the guy started rambling on about how he needed to ask his dead wife why she had changed her will and left everything to her 2 children instead of him. This was like a soap opera, I had forgotten why we were there and was enjoying the show.

Mitch said, "Can you believe this guy?" Then his wife reappeared and proceeded to tell us he was a cheating bastard and that's why she had changed her will. Again I nodded, not wanting to draw attention to us. This guy was still ranting on about the will and money and Helen was still trying to explain that she wasn't able to contact his wife. I had to resist the urge to stand up and tell her I could. This guy was on a roll calling his wife all kinds of horrible names in front of complete strangers. Shirley decided enough was enough and tried to take control of the situation and asked the guy to leave, after a few more abusive comments this time directed at Helen and her 'skills' or lack of the guy made his way to the exit, as he approached the refreshments table near the exit his wife appeared. As he got level with the table the entire contents, for want of a better explanation, exploded off the table and all over him. He was covered in milk, sugar, coffee; there was a stunned silence as he staggered out.

We took that as our chance to leave, we walked back to the car and 'the wife' was waiting. I told Sue to wait in the car and that I would explain later. I introduced myself to her and she explained her name was Liz, she had died 3 months ago from cancer, her husband had been cheating on her with her best friend, she had found out and changed her will, leaving everything to her children. I asked if the table incident was her doing to which she replied,

"Yes."

"Well done," I said. Mitch then spoke and asked Liz if she could see the "light".

She said, "Yes."

Mitch explained that was where she had to go, she explained she couldn't, that her children needed her.

Mitch did what he did best and explained that the children would be fine and that she needed to go. She was not to be scared and that there would be people there to meet her. She smiled, thanked us and slowly disappeared from view.

"Well that was fun," I said. Mitch smiled and we got into the car. We explained to Sue what had happened on the way home, we dropped Mitch off at his place and he said he would be in touch, we then made our way home after another eventful night.

Over a coffee in the kitchen I explained to Sue that the medium was a fake, she had no idea that the guy's wife was in the room. I also explained that this was what myself and Mitch needed to do, expose the frauds and support the real mediums, to stop people getting ripped off and fed a load of bullshit in the process. I could tell Sue was a little worried where this was heading but to be honest what had happened at the hall had given me a real sense of satisfaction.

We decided an early night was in order. I had the early shift at work and Sue had the 'pleasure' of accompanying my mother to see Sid's solicitor. Rather her than me. But this was false hope as this visit turned out to be the start of all out war between myself and my mother. So with all the pre-sleep necessities carried out we slipped under the quilt, kissed each other goodnight and fell asleep.

The next thing I knew, I was woken up by someone calling my name, I looked at the clock, and it was 2am! I was not a happy boy. The voice persisted, and not wanting Sue to be woken up, I got out of bed. I made my way to the top of the stairs, the voice was coming from downstairs, the hairs on the back of my neck stood to attention. Now I know what you're thinking, after all I had been through why would I be scared? I was thinking the same thing but there was something about the voice that seemed familiar and scary at the same time. I got to the bottom of the stairs and could see a glow coming from the kitchen, I don't mind saying I was shitting myself. I pushed the door open and sat at my kitchen was Beth! Yes scary Beth from Hope Hall. I couldn't believe my eyes, it really was a twilight moment. I was thinking, what is she doing here, what does she want, where's that other shit Evan and more to the point how the hell did she get into my house?! My thought process was broken by her saying,

"Close your mouth, Gary it's not a good look." Cheeky cow, I thought. So with me back to my senses I asked the questions I had been thinking.

With a smug look on her face she proceeded to explain that she was, if you like, Henry's evil opposite. "That's how he likes to describe me," she pointed out.

"What do you want?" I asked.

You need to stop listening to Henry, he's putting you in grave danger, this is not your fight, and it could cost you your life."

I thought, fuck me, don't beat around the bush, love, don't hold back, say it how it is.

After my last encounter with Beth I decided to be a little defensive in my approach. So I asked her if she was a ghost. This didn't seem to go down very well and that evil, snarling face appeared again.

"A ghost? A fucking ghost? Do not insult me, you

worthless piece of shit, I have more power than you will ever know, I am an entity from a higher level of existence, with powers beyond your wildest dreams."

For some reason a sense of calm and confidence came over me and I replied, "Ok, love, keep your hair on I was only asking." She stood up and that horrible smell returned, the features of her face started to change and I was starting to regret my little show of bravado. At this moment Gwen and Albert from Hope Hall appeared either side of me, this seemed to stop Beth in her tracks. She looked at them, then at me and spat out that I had not seen the last of her and she just disappeared like a genie in a pantomime.

I looked around and Gwen was still at my side, she smiled at me and said, "Don't worry, her bark is worse than her bite, you will meet more of her kind along the way but don't worry you are never on your own. Myself and Albert are always watching over you, now back to bed and sleep." And off I went, just like that, I slept until 5am when my alarm went off and didn't give the incident a second thought.

Work was a typical morning shift, full of problems but no real dramas, that was until I finished. I left work and switched on my mobile, it went mental, there were 5 voicemail messages, 8 text messages and a number of missed calls, so I sat in the car and read the text messages first. One was from Mitch about what had happened at the spiritualist hall, 5 were from my mother asking me to call her and 2 were from Sue warning me that my mother was on the warpath and I needed to call her before I spoke with my mother. So I called Sue, she explained that she had been to the solicitor's with my mother and he explained that she was the executor of Sid's will. He had left his 2-bedroom flat to my mother and all his possessions which had put a smug grin on her face. The next statement would not just wipe it off, though, it would smack it off and start World War 3. Sid had never married, had worked hard all his life, had a modest home and a modest lifestyle, it turned out he had been a shrewd investor in the stock market, in total he had left me and Sue around £70,000. According to the solicitor this figure could be higher once all the stocks were sold, which Sid's stockbroker was in the process of doing.

Sue said she thought my mother was going to have a heart attack, she went white and started making these funny noises. Sue asked her if she was ok but she just waved her attention away. Having taken a couple of minutes to compose herself she proceeded to vent her fury on the solicitor, this went on for about 15 minutes and the solicitor had to threaten her with the police to convince her to shut up and leave. He explained to Sue that he would be in touch with me once all the stocks were sold and I would have to make an appointment to see him to finalise everything.

By the time Sue got outside my mother had vanished, she tried calling her but without any success, so she decided to warn me, good idea I told her. I said I would try and contact her and then head home. I ended the call with Sue and called my mother, she answered it on the first ring and I was met with a volley of abuse. I was gobsmacked. I had never heard my mother speak like this to anybody, I tried to get a word in edgeways without success so I ended the call. She called me back straight away and proceeded to continue her rant, again I tried to get her to listen, but again without success so again I ended the call.

This time I decided to drive home, my phone was constantly ringing all the way. When I arrived home I waited until I got inside the house and explained to Sue what had happened. My phone started ringing again and I answered it, my mother was still ranting so I explained that she needed to take a breath or I would end the call and switch my phone off. This seemed to have the desired effect. I explained that I only knew what had happened from what Sue had told me, I explained to my mother that she needed to think about what she was going to say before she said it as I was not impressed with her comments so far. So she explained what the solicitor had said which, of course, was the same as what Sue had told me, so I asked what she wasn't happy about. Naturally, it was about the money, no surprise there, I thought. So I asked her if she thought she should have had everything then? This was met with silence, now I knew that Sid had a lead soldier collection that was worth thousands along with some pretty rare military books; all this had been left to my mother along with his flat which had been well looked after. So I asked her if she thought everything should have been left to her. I was surprised by her answer which was, "yes." I asked her why she thought this?

"He's my brother, that's why."

I said that we could discuss the money once it had been sorted. She was having none of it, she called me a thief, a liar, that I had been secretly arranging this behind her back with Sid. I was devastated by her comments, it was like a knife through the heart, my own mother calling me these things, enough was enough I stopped her in midsentence and told her that the things she had said were lies and evil. I told her not to contact or visit my family anymore, I ended the call, looked at Sue and burst into tears, I sobbed like a child in her arms for about 10 minutes before I regained my composure, I decided if she wanted a war she could have one.

Later Mitch called and asked if he could pop over, it was the distraction I needed. Sue put the kids to bed and when Mitch arrived we sat down and discussed the events from the night before at the spiritualist church, naturally we were happy that Liz had passed into the light where she was meant to be and for me that was 1-0 to the good team. Mitch explained that he had set up a meeting with Shirley and the committee at the church on Thursday evening, his plan was to see who was fake and who was real, and this sounded like fun, I had to admit. I thought this would be a good time to explain to Mitch about my visit from Beth. Sue had gone for a bath and I didn't want her worrying that something had been in the house, it would freak her out, and I also made Mitch promise not to mention it to Sue. So I explained what had happened, described what Beth looked like just in case she paid him a visit also and how Gwen and Albert had come to my rescue, again. As it was getting late we called an end to our discussion and agreed to meet at the spiritualist hall at 18:45 on Thursday, I couldn't wait.

CHAPTER 5

I guess like me your wondering why now, why me? And to be honest I have no idea. I have always had some form of interaction with spirits, the paranormal. When I was a boy my parents' house gave me my first encounter. We lived in the middle of a terraced street. There was always something scary about upstairs, I was always scared of the dark and my earliest memory of this house was a recurring feeling that would terrify me. In our front room there was a stool where my father kept the newspapers, it was near the door. Not always but on many occasions my father would ask me to get him the paper. I would move towards the stool and be stopped in my tracks by an overwhelming fear that as soon as I got to the stool the door would fly open and I would be dragged out and up the stairs by an unseen force! The possibility would be so real that fear would freeze me to the spot and no amount of threats from my father would make me get that newspaper, bearing in mind I was scared of my father who was a very strict man.

There were other 'little' incidents in that house but the living room one was by far the worst. At the age of 10 we moved to another house because my father left my mother, my Uncle Sid lived round the corner from us and it was from then he took me under his wing and helped us out. Things were pretty quiet at this house, there was the odd occurrence but nothing major. At the age of 16 I joined the army as a junior soldier and spent a year training in Folkestone. I met a girl called Lily whose house would provide me with all the proof I needed that spirits existed.

I met Lily at an amusement park near the seafront, she captivated me from the very beginning, and she was reluctant to start a relationship at first as her mum told her, "no soldier boyfriends." But young love as it is, this was ignored. Eventually, she told her mum of our relationship. Pretty soon I had the invite to meet her mum, Lily's dad worked away so it would be just mum. My initial fears were soon calmed as we hit it off straightaway; she was motherly but straight talking. Soon I was staying at the weekends which was wonderful, all the home comforts without the military discipline.

Lily's mum took great delight in telling me that the house was haunted, naturally I thought she was joking but this soon proved not to be the case. The first incident occurred not long after. Lily, I and one of her friends were at the house being teenagers, the subject got onto the house ghost. Soon we were taking the piss out of Lily and generally winding her up. Bad move, there was a huge bang from upstairs and a loud noise from the kitchen, this stopped us dead in our tracks. We rushed into the kitchen to find both taps full on, we all looked at each other and Lily said,

"See this is what happens when you make fun of him." We all then went upstairs to find the sink and bath taps full on also, I was stood in the doorway and felt a strong chill as if someone had walked past me and I had a strong feeling of being watched. I couldn't wait to get back downstairs. This put a bit of a dampener on the evening, Lily's friend went home and I went back to camp.

At the weekend Lily's mum explained what had happened and why. She also explained that their ghost was a soldier from World War I who died in a hospital in Folkestone from severe burns. She explained that this was why he was always in the shadows, this sent a shiver down my spine and I let out a nervous laugh. The icing on the cake was Lily's mum saying, "He's sat next to you now." Naturally I looked around and saw no one, surprise surprise but what I did see was the indent of someone sat on the sofa next to me, I thought I was going to piss myself. I leapt up with a girly screech and ran out the front door, I know, brave soldier! I stood outside smoking with Lily, my hands were shaking and my brain was trying to compute what I had just seen, I knew what I had seen but my brain wasn't having it. 3 cigarettes later, I had plucked up enough courage to go back inside, Lily's mum explained that he wouldn't hurt me and that his name was Norman! Like that was going to make me feel better.

Things quietened down after that for a while until one night when I stayed there on my own, Lily's dad was home and wanted to take us all to a show in London. Unfortunately, I wasn't able to leave camp early enough to go so I was given a key and told to make myself at home, which I did. All thoughts of Norman were absent until about 21:30 when he decided to make his presence known. I was watching TV and could hear something jangling for want of a better description. I was unable to pinpoint where it was coming from so I turned the volume down on the TV and listened. The noise was coming from behind me, when I looked I saw a jacket hanging on the back of a chair, I walked over and checked the pockets. What I found was a set of keys, I shit myself. That was my cue to go to bed and wait for Lily to come home. I nervously made my way up to the spare room where I slept, turned on the portable TV and got into bed. Soon I had nodded off but was woken by footsteps outside the bedroom door, I had left the landing light on, I know, brave soldier. And I could see a shadow walking past the door. Now I thought this was Lily, her little sister and her parents. After a couple of minutes of watching the shadow walk back and forth I thought, ok, Gary, you have two choices, open the door and see who it is or look out the window and see if Lily's dad's car was there. Naturally, being a brave squaddie I looked out the window. NO CAR! Shit, I was back in bed like a whippet.

Morning came with a knock on the door from a concerned looking Lily.

"Ok, what happened last night?" she asked. I proceeded to tell her all that had happened. She explained that when they had arrived home she looked in on me and found the TV still on and me under the blankets, she knew straightaway something was wrong because I had told her I hated sleeping with my head under the blankets.

Later that day my encounter was confirmed by her mother that it was Norman, "keeping an eye on me." Thanks Norman, very kind!

I was to have one last encounter with Norman before I left for my posting to Germany. I had been to the toilet and as I left I had the overwhelming urge to look down the hall to Lily's sister's room. The door was always ajar, on this occasion Norman was stood in the gap looking at me. Scared was an understatement, I have never taken a set of stairs so quick in my life. I burst into the living room where Lily was sat, she took one look at me and said,

"You've seen him, haven't you?"

I replied, "Yes." I needed a smoke. What occurred in Lily's house terrified me and the memory is as fresh as if it happened yesterday, this opened my eyes to the world of the paranormal but I still wasn't ready.

I left Folkestone at 17 and joined my regiment in Germany, the barracks had been built before the Second World War, there were rumours about ghosts. I never saw anything but there were 2 locations that really gave me the creeps, very oppressive. The first was a small church at the back of the barracks, there was a gate that led to the married quarters and we had to guard it overnight. Whenever I did guard duty I dreaded my hour there, it was just one spot just in front of the church that used to make my flesh crawl, move a couple of metres either way and the feeling went, I spoke with some of my close friends in the regiment later and they confirmed the same feelings. We never found out what it was.

The other issue was in the middle of our accommodation. Each company had its own accommodation block, mine was on the ground floor, our floor was split into 2 parts, mine was on the far end and the other was in the middle, now there was something really scary about that part, one room in particular. It was a 4-man room and whoever slept in the first bed space on the right usually had some strange encounters.

One of the guys woke in the early hours to find a heavy weight pressing on his chest; it was so heavy that he was unable to move or call out, this happened to him 3 times before he decided to move. Another owner of this bed space was woken to the sound of something whispering German in his ear; again this happened a number of times. Having got a bit pissed off with this one night he told his mystery whisperer to "Fuck off". When he woke in the morning, he opened his locker to find a scene of devastation! All his clothes had been ripped off their hangers, folded clothes were at the bottom, everything was a mess. Naturally another tenant moved out.

Nobody stayed long there, some spoke about their experiences but many didn't. My only experience of this room was not long before I left the army, my regiment was in Northern Ireland and I was tasked with securing the vacant accommodation with one of the storemen. So we basically had to open every room, check that the windows were locked and no appliances were plugged in. We started at the far end, but the closer we got to that room the more oppressive the feeling. I could tell Will the storeman could feel it too. Nothing was said but the look on his face said it all, as we got to that room.

Will said, "You check that one and I'll do the room next to it." I thought, shit! So with a deep breath I unlocked the door, the room seemed much darker than the others but I strode in, looking straight ahead at the windows. I checked both sets were locked, checked the 3 bed spaces that were being used and tried to avoid the empty bed space. As I left it felt like I was being chased out of the room and to be honest I couldn't get out of there quick enough, the feeling was of pure evil I had goose bumps all over my body and my hair was stood on end.

We left the block and met up with the others outside who had been checking the other floors, we were stood there having a smoke and one of the boys said, "There's a window still open." Without looking I knew which room it was, I turned around and one of the top windows were open. Sergeant Hughes who was in charge asked who had checked it. I told him it was me and that I was sure they were all locked when I looked. Thankfully, he mumbled something about doing a job yourself and we watched him enter the block. I and the storeman just looked at each other and waited for him to return.

We saw him close the window and we waited for his return. Pretty soon he came charging out though the main doors as white as a ghost, he was shit scared. We asked what was wrong. At first we struggled to understand what he was saying, when he had calmed down enough to be understood, he told us that he had been unable to open the door at first, he had unlocked it but it was like someone was holding it shut. He locked and unlocked it again and entered the room without a problem, he said the room was freezing, he could see his own breath so he jumped up onto the counter, closed the window, jumped back down and headed for the door as fast as his feet would carry him. He pulled the door behind him and as he was locking the door there were 3 massive bangs from the inside causing him to drop his keys. He grabbed the keys and ran out. Having finished explaining what had happened and having regained his composure he made us all swear never to tell anyone or as he put it, he would hunt us down and kick the shit out of us! Enough said.

I left the army at 21 due to an injury and spent the next couple of years living with my mother and moving from job to job. Eventually I found a steady job in a local factory, nothing exciting but it put money in my pocket. Things were really quiet on the paranormal front which suited me fine.

A couple of years later I met Sue, she was working at a company who supplied us parts, I had to speak with her when we had any issues, for the first 6 months we only spoke by phone. I then got promoted which allowed me to visit the company. I got my first look at Sue, and for me it was instant attraction, she was stunning. I walked over and introduced myself, we shook hands and it was like an electric shook between us, she had felt it too, I could tell by the puzzled look on her face. I also noticed an engagement ring on her finger, Bugger, I thought.

For the next couple of months life ticked along, work was going well, I usually saw Sue once a week, any excuse but the engagement ring remained, bugger! Then one Friday afternoon I got a call from Sue regarding the following week's orders - this was a normal occurrence. We finalised the details and I wished her a nice weekend and out of the blue she asked if I would like to meet her for coffee after work? Would I? My heart skipped so many beats I thought I was going to have a heart attack. We agreed to meet at a local pub at 6pm, yes they served coffee and no it wasn't my idea.

I arrived early at the pub, looked around and found a quiet corner away from the bar and the route to the restaurant; I ordered coffee thinking Sue would be a little late! She wasn't, bang on 6pm she came through the door, she looked stunning. I had to check my mouth wasn't hanging open, she looked amazing. I stood up and waved, she blushed; well I think she did or she was embarrassed that I was waving at her like some schoolboy.

We sat down, I ordered Sue coffee also and we shared some small talk about work. I kept looking at the engagement ring and wondering why if she was engaged what she was doing here with me. Sue noticed me looking and saved me the embarrassment of asking. Sue explained that working for a company that employed only men and being the only woman she needed something to try and prevent any unwanted advances.

I asked, "Does it work?"

She replied, "Does it?"

I laughed, "Good answer."

So we spent the next couple of hours talking about our pasts, good and bad. We were very open with each other, I had this weird feeling that we already knew each other. We didn't, I can assure, you but the feeling never went away.

Before we knew it the landlord was shouting last orders, I asked Sue if I could give her a lift home as I knew she had been dropped off by her dad, she agreed. On the way home we continued talking, we arrived at Sue's parents and we spent another hour talking in the car. Finally, and to my disappointment, Sue said she had to go. I had noticed the curtains twitching a couple of times. So we said our goodnights and shared a brief kiss that made my evening.

As Sue got out she asked, "Do you believe in ghosts?" A strange question to end the evening on I know, but I told her I did. "Good" was her reply and with a blown kiss and a wave she was gone. I drove home to my mothers on cloud 9 feeling very happy, I didn't realise but I had just spent the evening with the love of my life and my future wife. So over the next couple of months we spent all our spare time together doing the things new couples do. I met Sue's parents who were wonderful people and thought the world of me.

Our first Christmas together was memorable but not for the reasons you would think. I had gone to Sue's for Christmas lunch, much to the disgust of my mother. Lunch was fantastic, Sue's brother, his wife and little daughter were there and Sue's younger sister, a real family affair, nice. So lunch was done and the drinking was starting, stories were swapped, Sue's dad was one funny guy, some of his stories had me in tears, I had not had such a happy Christmas. So early evening came and Chris, Sue's brother, and his family left. Mum and Dad were dozing on the sofa, Sue, myself and Emily, Sue's sister, were watching TV. The silence was shattered by a massive thud on the ceiling, I almost fell off the sofa, and Sue's parents woke with a start. Again there was a massive thud; we all looked at each other. I went to stand up but Sue pulled me down, I looked at her and she just shook her head.

It was weird everybody just sat there, then the sound of footsteps across the landing could be heard but everyone was ignoring it. Bizarre, I thought. Then it all went quiet and normal conversations started, "Are you hungry? Would you like another drink?"

I was sat there crapping myself and nobody else seemed bothered, well except Emily she kept looking at me and I could see from her eyes she was terrified. The rest of the evening passed without further incident and around midnight I left, I said my goodbyes and thanked Sue's parents for a wonderful Christmas day. Sue asked if she could stay at my place, which I knew wouldn't be a problem as mum usually went to Uncle Sid's after lunch and got so drunk she slept on the sofa.

So we got home and before I could ask Sue about what had happened she whispered in my ear, "Make love to me." What could I say? We made love twice before falling asleep in each other's arms.

Our sleep was broken at 8am by my mother arriving home from Sid's, slightly worse for wear, she went straight to bed. I and Sue showered, made love and showered again. We sat in the kitchen whilst I made some bacon butties, I couldn't hold the question in any longer, I had to ask Sue what had happened at her house.

Sue asked, "Do you remember I asked you if you believe in ghosts after our first date?" I did, she explained this was the reason why. This incident had been going on for some time along with others, I asked her to explain. She told me about 6 months ago, not long before our first date, things had started happening in their house, little things at first like lights being switched on, and things being moved. Nothing you could really explain but at the same time not really scary.

Then one evening all hell had broken loose, they were all sat in the living room watching TV when they heard footsteps running up the stairs followed by the slamming of a door. They thought it was Emily but soon realised she was in her room by the screams coming from her. Tim, Sue's dad, ran up the stairs and found Emily terrified in her room. She explained she had heard the running footsteps up the stairs and had opened her door to see what was happening. She could hear the footsteps coming towards her but could see nothing. As they reached her door it was ripped out of her grasp and slammed shut. By the time Tim got there Emily had opened the door and was running towards the stairs shouting, "He's in my room and he's laughing at me."

It took some time to calm Emily down but she was eventually able to explain that after the door had slammed shut she had heard more footsteps and what sounded like a child laughing. This gave me goose bumps.

I asked, "Does it happen often?" as I had been to Sue's a couple of times and not heard a thing. Sue explained it only happened when it was someone's birthday and now Christmas was added to the list. And it was the same occurrence every time, the running up the stairs followed by Emily's door being slammed. So on family birthdays Emily slept in Sue's room. What a conversation to have on Boxing Day. I explained to Sue about my encounter at Lily's house and she seemed happy that we had both had paranormal encounters and that I didn't think she was mad.

CHAPTER 6

So a year later we had married and 9 months later, having bought our first home, Charlie our first son was born. We had bought the 3-bedroom house from a couple who were moving away, it looked nice and the price was affordable. We set up the middle bedroom as a nursery as it was the smallest and next to our room. Right from the start Charlie wouldn't settle at night. Sue would get him off to sleep but no sooner had she left the room he would start to cry, so we decided to have his crib in our room for a couple of months, thinking it would help him settle. He slept soundly every night he was in our room. After 6 months we decided to try again; we had bought a cot and a set of monitors for when we were downstairs.

This time Charlie seemed to settle, no issues sleeping either day or night, it was bliss, especially as I was working shifts. After a couple of weeks Sue told me she had been hearing a woman singing nursery rhymes on the monitor, but when she went upstairs she could hear nothing. I told her it was probably someone else with a baby monitor on the same frequency as ours and that's what she could hear. Sounded plausible, I thought, but my theory was soon to be dashed big time.

A couple of nights later Charlie woke up screaming and crying, Sue could not calm him down, so, thinking he was teething, she popped him into bed with me whilst she went downstairs to get some gel. By the time she came back both of us were sleeping so she went back into Charlie's room to collect some things and noticed the bedding in the crib had been put tidy. Now Sue swore blind that it had been a mess when she had taken Charlie out and as she walked out of the room the door was shut behind her, she wasn't happy.

The following night about 30 minutes after putting Charlie to bed we could hear movement over the monitor, and then we could hear Charlie moaning in his sleep. Then to our shock we could hear a woman making soothing noises followed by her singing the same nursery rhyme that Sue had heard before, we just looked at each other in amazement, then she stopped. Neither of us wanted to go and check but Sue being brave went up. She found Charlie fast asleep and the room normal. And as quickly as things had started they stopped, well for a while anyway.

Life was good for us, my job was good, Sue went back to work part-time with both our parents helping to look after Charlie. Then one night I was alone in our living room watching a rather dull friendly between England and Mexico, watching paint dry was a phrase that sprung to mind, anyway I must have dozed off. The next thing I knew I woke up looking at the floor, there were a pair of child's feet, I looked up and there was a small boy of around 6 or 7 with blue shorts and a stripy tee-shirt on. He was just staring at me, naturally this frightened the crap out of me and I jumped up of the chair, then he was gone. I was struggling to believe what I had just seen, I knew what I had seen but it didn't make sense. That was my cue to rush up to bed. As soon as I burst through the bedroom door Sue took one look at me and asked what I had seen. So I explained about the little boy, Sue being Sue told me I had probably been dreaming, I wish I had, was my reply.

Charlie was 18 months by now and toddling around the place. During the day he had a habit of going to the cupboard under the stairs and blabbering away like toddlers do, plus he would take toys to the doorway, hold them out and say, "Ta." It used to send shivers up my spine I can tell you. By the time Charlie was 2, Sue was expecting our second son, Billy. The house had quietened down and Charlie had stopped delivering gifts to the cupboard under the stairs, thank god. By the time Billy was 2 things were wonderful, we had no dramas with Billy or the house, life was good.

With Sue back at work full-time and my promotion to production supervisor we decided to move to a bigger house, but first we had to sell ours!

From the time we had the sign put up things got weird. We would be woken on a Saturday morning at 7am, firstly by someone knocking at the front door; I would open it to find no one there. Then there would be a knock on the patio doors at the back of the house. When I got downstairs the lights would be on and the curtains open! This would happen every Saturday. During the day the phone would ring but with nobody on the other end, just static. We had to answer it as we had found a house we liked and were now in the dreaded chain.

By the time we moved I was glad to leave, it was like the house was pissed we were moving. So we moved into our new 4-bedroom house, it was just what we had been looking for, big enough for us and some more. We had a garage and a nice garden, the house was an ex-council house but the previous owner had done a really good job on it and being at the end of a 5-house terrace it was perfect.

We moved in on May the 15th. and by July the 15th we were thinking, what have we done? The house felt dark and gloomy all the time, there were cold spots everywhere. Things were being moved all the time, the boys were not happy either. We would be woken by something hammering on the bathroom door downstairs at night and we could hear running water constantly, but when we plucked up enough courage to investigate the taps would be off, nothing.

But the final straw came one night during the early hours, I was woken by the sound of running water again so I got up to go to the toilet as I opened the shower room door there was a dark figure stood in front of the toilet, with the light being off I could only see the outline. At first I thought it was one of the boys but when I thought about it the figure was too tall. I stepped out of the shower room with a fright and shut the door. Still needing to pee I took what I thought was the less scary option and went downstairs, again the lights were still off and the sound of water running was still there, although this time I could hear the cold water tank filling but at the time took no notice. As I stepped off the last step my feet landed into about 3 inches of water. Not thinking I switched on the hall lights and could see the whole area flooded. I went straight to the bathroom where I could hear the water running and found the bath and sink overflowing! Both had their plugs in! I was not a happy boy; I turned all the taps off and took both plugs out. I checked the living room and found the carpet floating. Bollocks, I thought. Next I checked the kitchen, same result. Double bollocks! By this time I was well fucked off, the whole of the downstairs was under 3-4 inches of water and it was 3am in the morning. I heard Sue coming down and warned her about the water, the look on her face was heart-breaking; she sat at the bottom of the stairs and cried.

"How did this happen?" she asked. I explained what had happened and she told me in no uncertain terms that we needed help. I knew what she meant and I had to agree with her. So we spent the morning mopping up the water and contacting the insurance company, when asked how I thought it had happened I blurted out that it must have been the boys! Sorry kids, needs must. I couldn't exactly tell them the truth, could I?

Meanwhile Sue had managed to contact a local paranormal investigating club called 'Spooks are Us'. Must have took them a while to come up with that one. NOT. So Mark, their 'Lead Investigator' as he liked to call himself agreed to come to the house later that week.

We arranged for Mark to come around 9pm, we made sure the boys were sleeping before he arrived. He arrived on time, good start, I thought. Sue showed him into the kitchen and introduced him to me; we shook hands and sat down. To be honest Mark seemed like a nice guy at first asking all the right questions and making the right noises at the right time. We explained everything that had been happening including the flood and then sat there in silence whilst Mark finished writing his notes.

He looked up from his notes and in a rather dramatic voice announced that our house was haunted! No shit Sherlock, was my first thought. Mark asked if he could bring his team in one weekend to investigate, naturally we said yes. Having agreed for him to come back the following weekend Mark left.

As Sue came back into the kitchen she looked at me and said, "Don't say a word, I know what you're thinking." I just looked and smiled, she knew me so well.

The rest of the week passed unusually quiet; there was the odd bump and bang but nothing that was to prepare us for what was to come. We arranged for the boys to stay with Sue's parents, they were well aware what was going on so were happy to have them, plus the boys loved being with their grandparents.

So Friday evening arrived and so did Mark and his 'Team', this included himself, his 'Tech' expert, another investigator and his 'sensitive'. Now excuse my ignorance but what the hell is a sensitive? Mark kindly explained after seeing the puzzled look on my face, I guess. So Mark explained that Gill was the team's sensitive or psychic, she would carry out a walk through the whole house and identify 'hot spots' for the team to set up their equipment. He had me convinced, no really he did. Mark introduced the rest of his team, Alex was another investigator and Alan was their tech man – Mark's words not mine.

We agreed that the kitchen would be the command centre, I started to smirk which was quickly removed by one of Sue's famous glares. So Mark and Gill set off on their walk round the house whilst Sue and I answered Alex's questions and Alan prepared the required equipment. After about 20 minutes Mark and Gill returned, Gill announced that she had 3 hot spots for Andrew to set up cameras, mine and Sue's room, Charlie's room and the living room. By 11pm they were ready to go; Sue and Gill would be one team, Mark and myself the other. Alex and Alan would monitor the cameras. And so the fun started, Gill and Sue went to the main bedroom and sat on the bed, Gill was using a small tape recorder for EVP (Electronic Voice Phenomena - as she explained to Sue). They sat there for an hour, nothing happened, not so much as a bump or a bang. It was the same for me and Mark in Charlie's room not a peep, much to Mark's disappointment.

So we swapped rooms and tried again. I was starting to get a little bored; I asked Mark why Gill thought these rooms were hot spots? Mark said she had sensed a presence in them. I asked if that's what made her a sensitive, Mark took this as me taking the piss! For a change I was being serious, I had never heard the term before, mediums yes but sensitives?!

Mark decided to change the teams after the second session ended without anything happening. Mark wanted to try a different approach and he though my negativity was having an effect on the investigation! Knob! So I was paired with Alan to watch the cameras and Alex went with Mark, they went to the living room for the next hour. Gill and Sue went back to Charlie's room as Gill explained she had sensed the presence of a small boy in there earlier.

After about 15 minutes of small talk, myself and Alan relaxed, I asked him about the group and how they had got together? He explained that he had been interested in the paranormal since he was a kid and had known Mark when they were in school. Having gone their separate ways after leaving school they had met each other again on a ghost tour and having kept in touch they decided to set up 'Spooks are Us'. Alan explained the name was Mark's idea, he saw himself as the founder so made most of the decisions which did make Alan's teeth itch on a regular basis. Alan also explained that he had little faith in Gill's abilities but Mark and Gill were an item and Mark would have nothing said against her. This did worry me a little but it was too late now we had already invited them here.

During our conversation I explained to Alan that I thought the area in the hall between the stairs and the utility room always seemed cold and when I was sat watching TV it seemed as if there was movement in that area. As the sofa faced the door it was always seen from the corner of my eye, but it would be constant some evenings. Alan suggested setting up a camera above the back door pointing back down the hall. So when the session came to an end without any evidence Alan explained to Mark why he wanted to set up a camera. Mark and Gill dismissed this as Gill claimed she had felt nothing in this area. After a heated discussion and a few shitty looks from Mark in my direction he agreed to allow Alan to set up the camera.

Mark decided himself and Gill would spend the next session in this area, my feeling it was to piss all over my suggestion, things were getting a little tense between Mark and myself which wasn't helped when I overheard him talking to Alex in the garden. Mark stated that he thought I was a bit of a crackpot and an attention seeker. I was helping Alan set up the back door camera at the time, Alan just looked at me and shook his head, he must have been reading my mind as I wanted to give Mark a piece of mine. But I bit my tongue and once everything was set Mark and Gill sat against the back door and the rest of us were in the kitchen. After about 20 minutes we started seeing what looked like orbs on the back door camera, Alex explained what orbs were, the spirits of the dead so it seems! Alex asked Mark if he could see anything. To which he replied, "no".

This carried on for about 10 minutes; orbs would appear in the middle of the hall by the stairs and then disappear through the utility room door. We then started to get interference on the camera but we could make out a black mass appearing where the orbs had been, we were all transfixed by what was happening before our eyes.

Alex kept asking, "Can you see it?" The mass kept getting bigger and bigger, eventually it stood around 6ft in the rough shape of a person, and our attention was disrupted by Gill screaming. We hadn't been able to see her or Mark as they were sat under where the camera was positioned, the black mass disappeared through the utility door just like the orbs. Mark and Gill burst through the kitchen door, she was white as a ghost, excuse the pun, she was shaking and crying and telling Mark she needed to get out. Mark took Gill to his car, he came back and announced that the investigation was over, he told Alex and Alan to pack up the equipment and he would meet them at his house later, then left.

We all just stood there looking at each other; the investigation had gone from 'yawn' to 'oh my fucking god' in a very short space of time. I helped Alex and Alan pack and store the kit on the van, they said their goodbyes and left. The only contact I had with the group after that was a text message from Alan saying the group had split up, this was Mark's decision but he never gave a reason and he never answered any of my calls or messages after that.

Sue and I discussed the events of that evening, she explained that all Gill talked about was Mark this and Mark that, she never asked a single question about the issues we were having at the house; Sue even doubted she switched the recorder on at any time. But we were both worried about the black mass we had seen on the camera, this worried us a lot and we weren't sure what to do next. We had our fingers burnt by Mark and his group and it wasn't an option we really wanted to try again.

Sue asked why Alan had set up the extra camera in the first place. I had forgotten that Sue wasn't part of the discussion and I had not told her about the hall, it was time to come clean. I explained what I had told Alan about the hall and explained that I had never seen the black mass before; this had become a big concern. We decided to sleep and think about it later. After a couple of hours of restless sleep we decided to visit my mum before going to see the boys and explain to Sue's parents what had happened. When we arrived at Mum's she was having coffee with an old friend called Jenny. I had known Jenny for as long as I could remember, she would babysit for me when I was little, and they had worked together as cleaners at the local hospital. Mum made coffee and we started chatting. Jenny asked how the boys were as we hadn't seen each other for a while.

Jenny kept smiling at me and Sue, I have to say it unsettled me a little but that's me. Then out of the blue Jenny asked, "How did last night go?"

I looked at Mum and she said, "Don't look at me I didn't say anything." I asked Jenny what she meant. Jenny explained that she was a medium and that she had been "visited" by an old couple who had passed over, they had explained that we would need her help. Even after all that had happened I was starting to hear the twilight zone music! Thinking back I believe it may have been Gwen and Albert. Jenny proceeded to explain that the area in our hallway was a portal of sorts, where spirits were exposed to our world, hence the reason I only ever saw fleeting glances of them. Jenny went on to explain that sometimes spirits may stop and look just like we do but generally they are just passing through. The problem with portals she explained is that sometimes spirits known as dark spirits get attracted to them and sometimes stick around.

"The black mass you saw last night was a dark

spirit," Jenny explained. At this time I was conscious that I was sat there with my mouth hanging open. How could this woman know all this? It had only happened a couple of hours ago and we hadn't had the chance to tell anyone.

Me being me I said to Jenny, "Let me guess, your spirit guide told you all this?" As soon as the words left my mouth I felt a fool, it was a stupid comment, a reaction to things that were way above my pay grade in terms of understanding. Jenny explained that spirit guides were nonsense; they didn't exist and were not even necessary.

I never knew that Jenny was into the paranormal and such, she'd never mentioned it in all the time I'd known her.

"You've been watching too much TV," stated Jenny. She continued to explain that she needed to get this dark spirit back through the portal and put something in place to stop it happening again, she explained that she couldn't close the portal, it was impossible, it was a natural occurrence and they could be found all over the world. I wanted to know what was the difference between a dark spirit and a normal spirit, I had heard the phrase before but I wasn't sure. Jenny explained they were spirits who were bad, evil in life and they took this dark emotion with them in death. It needs to be removed. I asked her how and she explained that she would need some time to prepare herself. This spirit would know she was coming so she had to be prepared. I asked Jenny if she had done this before.

"Once or twice," she stated with a smile.

We all chatted for a little while longer about this and that, then Jenny left. She told us she would be in touch to arrange when she would come to the house, we said our goodbyes and she left. I asked Mum if Jenny was serious about her 'gift'. Mum explained that when Jenny was teenager she liked to go to graveyards, Mum asked her why and Jenny explained that there were spirits everywhere but graveyards were the best place to see them. Mum explained that a group of her friends decided to play a trick on Jenny one night, they followed her to the local graveyard and watched Jenny walk into the middle. After a couple of minutes they could see white lights moving around Jenny. The friends were hiding behind a wall but they could all see the lights. Then a ghostly figure appeared on the far side of the cemetery and started moving towards Jenny, then stopped. A couple of seconds later Jenny turned around, looked directly at where her friends were hiding, Jenny walked to where they were and said, "You need to leave, she's not happy you're here." One of the girls said it looked like Jenny but didn't sound like her; they were so scared they ran all the way home. None of them mentioned the incident to Jenny and neither did Jenny. Mum had been told this by one of the girls that was there and worked at the hospital with them. So I asked Mum if we could trust her. Mum said she thought we could. So we said goodbye to Mum and went home.

Sue and I chatted about the conversation at Mum's. We were a little nervous about getting someone else involved and getting our fingers burnt again but Jenny seemed sincere and it was hard to explain but we trusted Jenny. As we discussed Jenny's visit there was a loud bang from the utility room, we just looked at each other and laughed, which didn't seem to go down too well as there was another loud bang. We decided to ignore it and change the subject; this seemed to have the desired effect as there were no more bangs.

A couple of days later Jenny rang and asked if it would be ok to come around Saturday evening, we agreed that would be fine. We would ask Sue's parents to have the boys for the night, the boys loved staying and Sue's parents loved having them so we knew it wouldn't be a problem.

The rest of the week passed without incident and Saturday arrived, the boys had left and we had about an hour before Jenny arrived. Me and Sue were sat in the kitchen discussing what we thought would happen when Jenny arrived. All of a sudden there were loud bangs and the sound of stomping feet coming from Billy's room which was above the kitchen, it sounded like a child throwing a tantrum.

We both looked at each other and Sue asked, "Are you going to see who's up there?"

I asked, "Do I look stupid?" This was met with a smirk and a raise of an eyebrow from Sue.

"I thought you were the man of the house," was her reply. So with a deep breath I stood up and walked to the bottom of the stairs and looked up. Sue followed me and put her hand on my shoulder which frightened the crap out of me, much to her amusement. So we climbed the stairs slowly, listening for any noises. We got outside Billy's bedroom door; all the noises had stopped since my arse had left the kitchen chair, thankfully. I looked at Sue and moved my hand towards the door knob, as it was inches away from it.

Sue whispered in my ear, "Boo." I thought I was going to die, I must have jumped a foot off the floor, I was not happy with her. I told her to pack it in and be serious; I opened the door and switched on the light. To my surprise there was nothing in there and nothing was out of place, I looked at Sue with a relieved look on my face.

Just then the doorbell rang which made both of us jump a little. We went downstairs and opened the door, Jenny was stood outside. We invited her in and we all sat down in the kitchen. Sue made coffee for us all as I explained to Jenny what had just happened. It came as no surprise to her as she explained that this dark spirit knew she was coming. I asked her how it knew, she said to wait for Sue to finish and she would explain. Sue finished making the coffee and took a seat next to me, Jenny first explained that whatever happened this evening we had to let her deal with it and not engage with it at any time. I was happy to agree with this believe me.

So I asked Jenny how she was going to deal with this dark spirit? She explained that all week she had been 'visiting' our house in her mind's eye. I must have had that look on my face as she responded quite quickly by saying that she understood it was a little difficult to believe everything but she asked us to be patient whilst she explained things as the evening wore on. She then took out a small wooden cross, it looked old and handmade. Jenny explained that she had been given it by an old man whilst on holiday in Jamaica. She told us that one night she'd had a very vivid dream about meeting an old man sat outside a tin shack. The following morning she got up, got dressed and left the hotel, the receptionist had offered to get her a taxi, which Jenny had declined, the lady explained that it was not a good idea to be leaving the hotel and walking alone, Jenny ignored this advice and left the hotel on foot. She explained it was like being on autopilot, she had no idea where she was going but felt she was being drawn somewhere for a purpose.

After about 10 minutes she turned off the main street into a side street, after another 10 minutes she turned off into a much smaller street, she realised that nobody really noticed her which surprised her as she had been warned by the holiday rep that some of the poorer areas were dangerous to tourists but she felt under no threat at all.

Eventually she stopped and noticed a tin shack that looked just like the one in her dream and not only that but the old man from her dream was sat outside. He looked at her, smiled and called her forward. He said "hello" and explained that he had been waiting for her. He then explained that he had a gift for her to assist her with dealing with bad spirits. Jenny just stood in front of him not knowing what to say, he gave her the cross and explained it would be her source of power and protection. Jenny took the cross and left. She explained she felt there was no need to respond to the old man, she said it felt like she was in the company of a family member or close friend. She walked back to the hotel with her mind in a whirl at what had just happened, her husband asked her where she had been, she told him he wouldn't believe her and he knew better than to press the issue.

Jenny explained that the cross was very important and that she had used it a number of times, not just for bad spirits but to help lost spirits also. She then explained that she would need to walk the house on her own to clear out the bad spirit, and with that she stood up and walked out the kitchen closing the door behind her. Me and Sue just sat there looking at each other waiting to see what would happen next.

After about 15 minutes Jenny walked back in and stated, "All done."

I said, "Is that it?" She explained that the spirit was drawn to the cross, it had no choice and once drawn it was cast into the light, never to return. I said, "That was easy then."

Jenny stated, "It is with the right knowledge and protection." She put on her coat and walked to the front door, as she opened it she turned and said, "You'll find out for yourself one day," said goodbye and left. "Well that was a little weird," said Sue. "It was a bit," I said. But to be fair we had no further issues in the house from that day on. Yes we still had movement in the hall but nothing bothered us or the boys which we were very happy about.

CHAPTER 7

So back to the present. Thursday came and we were ready to visit the spiritualist church again. I was looking forward to this after the last time, it hadn't been dull that's for sure. This was going to be the first time I was going into a situation prepared to use my new found ability in a controlled situation. Mitch had set up the meeting on the pretext that we were from a paranormal club and we wanted to do a small write-up in our newsletter. Mitch had explained to Shirley on the night who we were and had made arrangements for this meet. So off we went, the drive was only short and we had agreed how we would play it once we arrived. As we arrived in the car park we could see Shirley waiting for us. We parked the car and walked to the main entrance, Mitch shook hands with Shirley and introduced me, we shook hands and Shirley invited us in. As we entered the small hall we noticed that the table was still on the stage and sat around it were 4 other women. Shirley introduced the committee, they were, Ann, Mandy, Pat and Viv.

Shirley explained they were all psychic in some way that's why they were on the committee. She explained that she was the chair person and senior medium. I asked her if she could see and communicate with spirits. Her answer was a very serious "yes". Then each of the committee members introduced themselves and explained their ability.

First up was Ann, she stated she was a 38 year-old mum of 2, she was a sensitive. I asked what she thought that meant. She stated that she could sense when there were spirits around and who they wanted to speak to. Next was Mandy, she was 44 and claimed to have had the ability to communicate with the dead since she was a child. Pat was next, she was 63 and claimed to receive messages in dreams the night before the meetings and would pass them on to the relevant person at the next meeting. Last was Viv, she was 26 and claimed to have had a near-death experience after a car crash. During this she claimed to have met her 'spirit guide' who would guide her and keep her safe during her journeys into the spirit world. My thoughts went back to what Jenny had said about spirit guides but now wasn't the time to be opening my big mouth, patience was required for a change.

Mitch explained that we had been visiting local spiritualist churches to get some real accounts to put in our newsletter. He asked the committee what the main aim of their church was. They explained that they helped people communicate with their loved ones who had passed over. Mitch asked if they charged a fee. Shirley explained that just like a normal church at the end of the evening they would pass around a collection plate, so it was only donations.

I asked Pat if she had dreamt about our visit, she said, "no" and that she didn't know we were coming! I wasn't sure what difference that made but there you go. I then asked Viv who her spirit guide was; she explained that it was a young Red Indian man called White Cloud. I asked her if he was with us now, she said, "no"; there was no reason for him to be there at this time. Finally I asked Shirley if there were any spirits with us at this moment, she said "no". The reason I asked was because almost as soon as we had sat down I had noticed a young woman of about 20 hiding towards the back of the stage. After Viv had explained who she was the young woman had walked up to Viv and was staring at her. Quite quickly she realised that I could see her and she came and sat next to me, she explained that her name was Gemma and that she had been in the car that had crashed with Viv in it also, the car had been driven by Gemma's boyfriend who had escaped without a scratch.

Gemma wanted me to explain to Viv that she was sorry and wanted to say goodbye before she went into the light. So I asked all the women if there were any spirits present in the hall, to which they all replied "no". I looked at Mitch who had heard Gemma talking to me and he nodded at me.

I stood up and said, "Ladies, there is a spirit here, she is stood next to me and has already explained who she is and who she is connected to." I wish I'd had a camera as their faces were a picture; it was an image I would become familiar with over the coming months, that *oh shit I've been exposed as a liar* look.

I explained to the women what had happened at their last meeting and that I noticed no one had seen the female spirit who trashed the refreshment area. I explained that Mitch could hear spirits and that I could see and hear them. Shirley was a bit pissed at what was happening and tried to make out that she knew someone was here. So I asked her who it was, she tried the old double bluff on me by switching it around. I said that the spirit who was here was connected to Viv. I then told Shirley, "Your turn."

She came out with some old bullshit about it being an 'older' female relative, like a nan or an aunty! I couldn't help but laugh out loud which pissed Shirley off even more, I'm sure there was steam coming out of her ears. So I said to Viv, "Does that make any sense?"

"A little," she replied. So I warned Viv that what Shirley had said was crap but what I was about to tell her would be upsetting but I promised her it was the truth. I explained to Viv that her best friend Gemma was with me and that she had died in the car crash that she had been in. Viv was nodding with tears pouring down her face. I told her that Gemma was sorry because it was her who had distracted her boyfriend who was driving the car and caused him to crash. I also explained that, yes, Viv had nearly died and had gone to the light but it wasn't her time to go so her soul was sent back to her body. It was only Gemma's time. I also told Viv that Gemma was fine and she will go into the light as soon as she said goodbye to Viv.

Gemma smiled at me and thanked me for speaking to Viv for her, she asked me to say goodbye to Viv which I did and I stood and watched Gemma kiss Viv on the cheek and then she was gone. I looked around and all the others were in tears apart from Shirley, who still had a face like a smacked arse, but did I care? Did I fuck, she was a horrible woman. We stood up to leave and Mitch pointed out that lying to people about their loved ones who had died did more harm than good in the end and they needed to stop telling people lies.

As we got to the car Viv came running out and stopped us, she thanked us for what we did and explained that she felt Gemma saying goodbye which had helped her with not only her grief but her guilt also. I told her it was our pleasure and to stop being involved in the horseshit that Shirley was involved in. She promised us she would, she shook both our hands and left.

We jumped in the car and started the drive home, "I thought that went well," said Mitch.

I replied, "Me too, but I don't think Shirley will be applying to join our fan club too soon." Our first debunk if you like had been a great success and I felt really good about what we had done. When we got home we explained to Sue what had happened, she seemed as pleased as we did but I wanted Sue to be an active part of the team so I suggested that in future Sue join us and record what happened so we had an account of what had happened for future reference. So after Mitch left I went through what had happened at the spiritualist church so Sue could record the account. So after a cup of tea, a shower and some loving with Sue it was time to sleep, after all, the day job, so to speak still needed to be done but just one more shift before the weekend and a trip to Weymouth with Sue and the boys.

We left Friday late afternoon and arrived at the

hotel we were staying at for the weekend. Having booked in, found our room and dropped off our luggage we went off to get something to eat. We had agreed that over the weekend we would all pick one thing to do or see. So after food and armed with a handful of brochures we set about making our picks. Charlie picked the Sea Life Centre, Billy picked Monkey World, Sue picked a place called Durdle Door, looked really nice, and I picked the Tank Museum, no surprises there. So we agreed to do Monkey World and the Tank Museum on Saturday and Sea Life then Durdle door on Sunday. Thankfully the weather was fantastic and the trip passed without any dramas which suited me fine.

We drove home late Sunday evening, the traffic was fine until we got to the last stretch of motorway, traffic was slowing and eventually stopped. After a couple of minutes a police car passed us on the hard shoulder, followed soon after by a fire engine and an ambulance.

Sue looked at me and said, "I hope no one's hurt." After about 20 minutes the traffic started to move slowly. It took us about 10 minutes to reach the scene of the accident. A single car appeared to be the only one involved, the car was covered with a large sheet and as we passed the scene I saw a middle-aged man wandering around the emergency services personnel, trying to attract their attention. It was evident to me after everything that had happened that the man was a ghost. Reading about the accident a couple of days later confirmed this. The driver had a heart attack whilst driving and died instantly. The story showed a picture of the guy and it confirmed to me it was the guy I saw wandering around at the crash.

So back at work after my trip I was talking to one of the guys from despatch, Mark was telling me about his wife's obsession with trying to contact her dead father. They hadn't spoken for a number of years due to a family argument and he had passed away suddenly before they could patch things up, this left her very upset and ever since she had been visiting this medium trying to get some closure.

Mark explained that this guy, Clarke Richards, and been charging his wife, Ruth, £10 every time she visited him. Mark wasn't happy with this as he thought this guy, Clarke, was feeding Ruth bullshit just to keep her coming. I explained to Mark that myself and my friend, Mitch, exposed people like Clarke Richards but I needed more information first to prove he was a fake. I asked Mark if I could talk with his wife Ruth and get firsthand what Clarke had been telling her. I suggested to Mark we meet at a pub and I would bring Sue with me to help make the situation more comfortable for Ruth, Mark agreed and he would speak with Ruth and let me know.

The following day Mark called me and said we would meet at the Rose and Crown pub on Saturday at 7pm. I asked if Ruth was ok with this and Mark said she was a little pissed that he had been discussing it with someone at work but eventually she had agreed to the meet, but only because she felt that Clarke Richards was taking advantage of her. I explained to Sue what was happening Saturday and she was quite excited about it. I also explained to Mitch what was happening and asked him to do some digging on this Clarke Richards.

Saturday arrived and we met Mark and Ruth at the pub, they had already been there a little while and had picked a nice quiet corner where hopefully we could talk without being disturbed. We got some drinks and walked over to where they were sat, Mark carried out the introductions and we sat down. I had already explained to Sue that the plan was for her and Ruth to chat about the usual, kids, work, etc and myself and Mark would make small talk. This was designed to make Ruth feel relaxed before we got down to business, so to speak.

After about an hour of chatting I sensed that things were quite relaxed, Sue and Ruth were getting on like a house on fire so I thought now might be a good time to mention Clarke Richards. I explained to Ruth that Mark had told me about her visits to him. Ruth explained that she had got his name from a friend of hers and during the first meeting he had got so many things right it prompted her to go back. He had explained to her that the spirits don't always come through! Of course, sometimes they're busy shopping and such, man the crap some people come out with. Ruth explained that she had been really disappointed after her last visit 2 weeks ago. He had given her no new information and claimed her dad no longer wanted to communicate with her. Naturally Ruth had been very upset by this and had arrived home in tears. After explaining to Mark what had happened it had prompted him to talk with me. He knew I had an interest in the paranormal and we were good friends at work also.

I asked Ruth how many times she visited Clarke, she said 6 times. I asked her if he had ever told her anything helpful, to which she said no. At this time I was aware of an old gentleman sat at the table next to ours, he seemed to be taking an interest in us. I also noticed he had no drink and was dressed in a black suit. Mark went to the bar to get some more drinks and the women went to the toilet.

The old guy stood up and walked towards me, he asked, "Can you see me?" I nodded. "I'm Ruth's dad, I need you to tell her I'm sorry." Again I nodded; the last thing I needed was people looking at me talking to myself. I turned slightly and told him to sit in the chair to my right, Mark had been sitting there but I would put my coat on there so he would pick another, there was plenty there. I quickly asked the guy his name and told him to wait.

Mark and the women arrived back to the table at the same time, Mark went to move my coat but I shook my head and he moved to the next one. By this time the pub was quite noisy so there was no fear of us being overheard. I was thinking to myself how do I start this off? So I plunged in head first. I looked straight at Ruth and asked her if her dad's name was Bob. Naturally she was a little startled by not only the question but it coming out of the blue like it did. She confirmed it was and asked why. I told her that she was going to be a little shocked by what I was about to tell her but she needed to trust me. I then asked if he had been buried in a black suit with a white shirt and a Simpson's tie. She looked at me astonished, as did Mark, again she answered "yes". She explained that the tie had been a joke birthday present as he was always watching the show and the family had agreed it would make sense to bury him in his favourite tie.

I took a big breath and told them he was sitting in the chair next to me. Mark's mouth dropped open and Ruth started crying. I told them I was being very serious and they could ask me any question they liked to confirm it.

Ruth composed herself and said, "Where did we go for our first family holiday?"

I turned to look at Bob and he said, "Butlins at Minehead 1979."

I passed on the information and this caused Ruth to cry even more. Bob then told me that he had tried to get the guy Ruth had been seeing to pass on that he was sorry about the argument and that they had not been able to say goodbye. So I told Ruth this and explained that once he had made his peace with her he would go into the light. Ruth wanted to know why she couldn't see him, I explained that some can and some can't but he can see you and he is happy he has the chance to tell you he loves you, he is ok and he is happy. Ruth was smiling as tears rolled down her cheeks but I could see she believed me and that she was happy to have the chance to say goodbye.

She said to me, "Tell him I love him too, we miss him but we are glad he's happy."

I said, "You've just told him yourself. It's time for him to go." I looked at Bob and he thanked me for my help. "My pleasure," I told him and with that he stood up and disappeared.

After a couple of minutes of silence, Mark looked at me and said, "You kept that quiet." I explained that being able to see and talk to the dead was not something you broadcast, unless of course you were full of shit and a liar. I asked them both to keep to themselves what had happened this evening; they both agreed that they would.

So after another eventful evening we made our way home, on the way I called Mitch and explained what had happened, I told him I wanted to arrange a meeting with Clarke Richards. He agreed this would be a good idea, especially after some of the things he had found out about this guy. By all accounts he'd been living off the sadness of bereaved people for quite some time and was more than happy to take their money and exploit them. *Time for this to stop*, I thought.

After we arrived home Sue made a brew and we sat down, she looked at me and kissed me.

I said, "What's that for?"

She said, "Because I love you and what you did for Ruth at the pub was amazing." I told Sue that I was beginning to understand what was expected of me and believe me there was no greater feeling than seeing the look I had seen on Ruth's face when she realised she could and did say goodbye to her dad. Priceless.

The rest of the weekend passed quickly as all weekends seem to, Monday brought shitty wet weather and a letter from Sid's solicitor telling me that my wonderful mother was contesting the will. It stated that they would like to arrange a meeting to try and resolve the matter and both parties were invited. As it was only my mother and I named in the will it only required us to attend. It also stated that as my mother was contesting the will she was required to bring concrete proof to back up her claim. This wasn't the start to the week I wanted, I was working afternoons this week which wasn't my favourite shift and it meant we wouldn't be able to arrange our meeting with Mr Richards until the weekend or the following week. So I set my mind to deal with my mother, I phoned the solicitor and told them that any morning this week would be ok, they told me they would contact my mother and get back to me.

It came as no surprise that they called back in an hour to ask if I could attend a meeting Wednesday morning at 10am. I said that would be fine, I was looking forward to this, greedy woman. Sue called me from her lunch break just before I left for work and I told her about the solicitor. She couldn't understand why my mother was doing this, after all, it wasn't like she was getting nothing. In the grand scheme of things she was getting most of it, which was true, but my mother seemed to have got more and more resentful towards me and I had no idea why but I had decided that if she wanted a fight she could have one. I told Sue that I believed my mother blamed me in a way for my dad buggering off, but to be honest I think it was easier to blame someone else rather than herself. Such is life, as they say. During my conversation with Sue I noticed someone stood at the end of the drive looking at the house, I am one of those people who tend to wander around when I am on the phone. I wasn't too worried as we had a pretty good security system for the house which included a camera pointing at the drive. As I was wandering around talking to Sue I made my way to the front door, I opened it to see if the guy was still there and he was. He was dressed in a dark suit with a long overcoat. Our eyes met and instantly I turned away as they looked like black pools of water and really put the shits up me. I told Sue I had to go and placed the phone back in its holder, as I looked back out the door the guy had gone so I looked up and down the street but there was no sign of him which was fine by me. I'd never seen the guy before and to be honest I was in no rush to see him again so I got myself ready and left for work.

Being a Monday, work was frantic and I had no time to think about the guy until I got home. I explained to Sue what had happened when I got home and she suggested I check the recording for the camera. We made a drink and switched on the monitor for the cameras, I put in the time I had seen the guy outside the house and pressed play. When we looked the guy was nowhere to be seen, I couldn't understand it, the camera has no obstructions and I remembered seeing one of our neighbours driving passed which we could see on the recording but the man with the scary eyes was just not there. Sue asked if I was sure. Naturally, I got a little pissy.

"Of course I'm sure," was my sharp reply which I regretted as soon as I had said it. I apologised straight away but I couldn't explain why the guy I had seen as clear as day outside the house was not on the recording and it made my teeth itch. So I said, "Let's forget it and talk about something else."

"Good idea," was Sue's reply.

We discussed the meeting with Sid's solicitor a little more and Sue asked if I wanted her to come to the meeting. I told her it would be ok as I knew things were busy with Sue at work and didn't want to add to the stress it sometimes brought. I told her I would call her after the meeting had finished, which seemed to satisfy her.

Tuesday came and went and Wednesday morning arrived. I was a little nervous to be honest, after all she was still my mother, greedy, but still my mother. I arrived at the solicitor's 15 minutes early and the receptionist took me to a meeting room and asked if I would like a coffee, which I was thankful of as I needed it. The solicitor came in about 10 minutes later followed closely by my mother. She wouldn't even look at me, not that it bothered me to be honest. Mr Phillips explained the purpose of the meeting, that my mother contested the giving of Sid's stocks to me on the grounds of Undue Influence. Mr Phillips then went on to explain that this could only move forward if my mother had concrete evidence of this against me. He also went on to explain that it would be better for both parties to agree at an informal meeting like this. Mr Phillips then asked my mother if she wished to pursue this, she stated that she did. He then asked her if she had evidence to back up her claim, which she again stated "yes". Mr Phillips then informed my mother that he would record her request to contest Sid's will. Again that smug look appeared on my mother's face. I could feel my blood starting to boil and I was about to let rip when Mr Phillips held up his hand and stated that he was legally obliged to inform my mother that there was a clause in the will that penalised her if she contested the will. I thought her jaw was going to hit the floor; her face went pale then red with anger.

"Just what are you telling me?" she asked.

"In simple terms, Mrs Channing, as you have

contested the will you will forfeit parts of your inheritance, the more you persist the more you lose." The look on her face was a picture; I thought she was going to pass out. Mr Phillips informed her that so far she had lost the lead soldier collection and the military book collection. Now that did make me smile as I knew the first chance she'd got she would have sold them.

I was tempted to gloat at this moment but even though I was extremely tempted she was still my mother and that did stop me. I just sat there looking at Mr Phillips and listening.

Eventually Mum spoke. She looked at me, then at Mr Phillips and said, "Ok if that's what my brother wanted then so be it." Finally common sense prevailed. I would have been happy, extremely happy with the money from the shares but mum had been a bitch to me for no reason and plus I had no intention of selling any of Sid's collection so it would be safe with me that's for sure. So we signed the paperwork and Sid's estate was finalised. We both got up to leave but Mr Phillips asked me to stay. Mum just looked at me and walked out. I wasn't bothered by her reaction, after all, it was her loss as far as I was concerned. Parents, who'd have them?!

After Mum had left, Mr Phillips explained that Sid had foreseen this happening and made sure the will was bomb proof. Mr Phillips explained that the collections would be collected from my mother and delivered to myself, the expense was covered in the will, he explained! Sid knew his sister well that's for sure. So I left Mr Phillips and walked back to the car with a spring in my step, to be honest I was glad it was over. I got to the car and called Sue, she answered on the first ring. I explained what had happened and she asked what my plan with Mum was. I told her I would let the dust settle and go from there, she knew where we were.

Over the next couple of weeks things calmed a little. Sid's collection had been delivered and was now homed in our spare bedroom and the money had gone into our account, a total of £72,568 after the shares were sold. But little did I know that this was the calm before the storm. Two nights later we were woken in the early hours by Billy our youngest son screaming at the top of his lungs, I have to say it frightened the shit out of me.

I leapt out of bed and ran into his room. The first thing that struck me was the foul smell like rotten eggs. I looked at Billy who was sat up in bed, bathed in sweat, with a look of abject fear on his face. Sue was close behind me and overtook me to hug Billy like only a mother can. Having calmed him down, he explained that he had been woken by a woman's voice calling his name; he had thought it was his mother until he has switched on his lamp and saw this strange woman stood at the bottom of his bed. I asked him if he could remember what she looked like. I had an idea who it was but when Billy described Beth it made my blood run cold.

Again she had got into my house and now she was after my kids, I was not a happy boy. Having settled Billy back down I left Sue lying on his bed with him. I went downstairs to get a drink and try and make some sense of what had happened. I shut the kitchen door, poured myself a glass of juice and sat at the table. I closed my eyes for a second and as I opened them, there was Gwen and Albert. Their appearance didn't even shock me anymore. We spoke about what had happened and Gwen explained that the boys would get a "guardian" to keep Beth away. He would be with them at all times. Gwen continued to explain that his name was Gwyn; he had been 13 when he died so if by any chance one of the boys could see him then hopefully it wouldn't be an issue because of his age. I asked if him being so young would he be able to protect them from Beth.

"Oh he's more than capable," Gwen explained. And with that they were gone. Somehow they always managed to give me that sense of calm and wellbeing, if I could have bottled it I would be a very rich man.

So back to the job in hand, Mitch had arranged for us to go and see Clarke Richards, he was holding a 'Night of spirit visitors' - his words not mine - which suited me fine! It would give us a chance to see this guy at work first hand. His 'Night' was being held at a small theatre in town so I was hoping for a good turnout but with tickets at £15 I wasn't sure. On the night I was amazed how full the place was, this guy was going to make a tidy profit out of this.

Myself and Mitch picked seats at the back so we could get a good view of everyone. Mitch had a small video camera to gather some evidence, good idea I thought. As we were discussing our plan of attack, the lights dimmed and the theme music from *The Omen* started playing. Myself and Mitch just looked at each other. *Really?!*

The music faded out and Mr Richards himself was illuminated by a single spotlight. I had that itchy teeth feeling again. He announced himself as one of Wales's best known Spiritual Mediums who had done sessions with celebrities, not that he mentioned any! He went on to explain that he came from a long line of mediums and had first used his 'gift' as a child with his nan, who was a medium also.

So with his introduction out of the way he started his 'show'. He asked for people to think of the loved one they wanted to communicate with. This would help bring them from the spirit world, was his explanation; I could smell the bullshit already. He started off with the usual patter, "I have a gentleman here, and his name begins with R! He crossed over recently, Robert or Roy!" Eventually a middle-aged woman put her hand up. Another spot light illuminated the woman, much too her visual discomfort. Clarke asked what her name was.

She replied, "Wendy."

"Ok, Wendy. Blessings to you. I have a middle-aged man with me, Richard or Roy." Instantly myself and Mitch had noted that he had changed one of the names, nobody else appeared to have noticed. Wendy confirmed that she could take the name Roy. "He's your brother," stated Clarke.

"No, he was my best friend," was Wendy's reply.

"But he was like a brother to you," was Clarke's sharp comeback.

"Yes," Wendy stated as tears started to roll down her cheeks. Clarke asked if there was something she would like to say to him? Wendy replied she was sorry, she hadn't known how sad he was. Clarke jumped in with, "he hadn't meant to take his own life;

it had been a mistake, a cry for help." The lucky bastard had got it right, very perceptive. This trend carried on for most of the evening until he met Molly.

He had thrown the name Adam out and Molly had put her hand up, Clarke proceeded to chuck out vague bits of info at Molly and every time he got it wrong she just shook her head. This got him flustered; she was giving back no clues whatsoever. He asked her to give him a moment as the link to Adam was poor! Was he on his spirit mobile or what? At this moment a young man appeared next to Clarke, he was in his mid-20s at a guess. I could see him trying to get Clarke's attention. It was this that confirmed to me that he was a fake. Adam got frustrated very quickly with the fact that Clarke couldn't see or hear him. Adam looked around and instantly his eyes locked onto mine, the next thing I know he's stood next to me asking me why Clarke can't see or hear him? Luckily I was sat at the end of the row and most people's attention was on Clarke.

I explained in a whisper to Adam that Clarke was a fake. Adam told me that Molly was his cousin, they had fallen in love but he had been killed in a car crash 6 months ago. At the time he was having doubts about their relationship what with them being cousins. They had argued on the day of the car crash, the crash was caused by a truck driver who had fallen asleep at the wheel but Molly was convinced it was her fault because she had started the argument. Adam wanted her to know it wasn't her fault and that he loved her very much. I promised him I would pass the message on at the end of the show.

At the end Molly had been Clarke's only "failure"

and to almost everyone it had been fantastic! If only they knew. I asked Mitch to help me find Molly; thankfully Molly was a smoker so as most people disappeared she had stopped to have a cigarette. I walked over and introduced myself; I asked her what she had thought of the show.

"A crock of shit," was her blunt reply. I had to agree. I explained what had happened during the show and that Adam had spoken to me. Instantly she turned on me, "One fucking crackpot is enough for tonight so piss off." I understood her anger, I asked her to hear me out. I told her what Adam had told me, as I was speaking I could see the tears forming in her eyes.

At this point Adam reappeared. I explained to Molly that Adam really did love her and that he was with us now to say goodbye. Molly was looking around.

"Where is he? I can't see him." I explained to Molly that not everyone can. I told her to close her eyes and think of Adam, as she did I told him to hug and kiss her goodbye. I looked at Molly's face as Adam did this and I knew she could feel his presence. He thanked me for my help and vanished.

Molly was in tears but smiling also. "I felt him," she said. "I really felt him. Oh my god that was amazing, thank you so much, Gary." She then asked, "Why are you not holding shows instead of that fucking fraud?" I explained that it wasn't my purpose, I was here to expose people like Clarke Richards and if I could help people along the way then that was a bonus. Molly said, "I'd like to help."

I replied, "Ok, give me your number and we'll be

in touch."

As we drove home we both felt a great deal of satisfaction with the night's events and to be honest Mitch seemed a little smitten with Molly, which I took great delight in taking the piss out of him about it. A couple of days later we reviewed the video and it only confirmed what we had thought at the time, Clarke Richards was a clever man and had gleaned most of his information from the people themselves. I wanted to review the part with Molly, she had really got him flustered and I wanted to see if there was any indication at all that he had been aware of Adam's presence. Molly had done what everyone should do with mediums and that's to let them give you the information. If they truly are speaking to a spirit then the spirit will give them all the information they need, it's just like a normal conversation, simple as that. None of this "I have a Peter or Paul" bullshit.

So having reviewed the video we agreed that we didn't really have enough evidence to 'out' Clarke. So I suggested to Mitch that he arrange a private sitting with him at my house. I also told him to contact Molly and invite her around for dinner Saturday evening. Mitch started blushing much to my amusement.

"Stop teasing him," was the telling off from Sue, doing her best to try and keep a straight face.

So Mitch left, much to his relief and I explained to Sue that there was something about Molly that interested me. She hadn't cracked when Clarke had persisted in trying to get information from her and I think she had done her homework before going. So I told Sue that I was thinking about asking Molly to team up with us if she wanted to, Sue agreed but I wanted to know a little more about her first, hence the dinner invitation.

Saturday came and had Sue panicking about Molly and Mitch coming to dinner. Mitch had phoned me in the week to say that he had arranged for Clarke Richards to come to the house Saturday evening and that Molly had agreed to come to dinner. I resisted the urge to tease Mitch; I would leave that until Sunday.

I told Sue to relax, big mistake, I should have known better. She wasn't happy with this statement and told me so. I decided it would be a good time to get out from under her feet, so I told her I would take the boys to the park and get them lunch before dropping them off with Sue's parents. Good call, Sue agreed it was a good idea and with kisses and hugs all round she kicked us out.

So off we went to the local park. Having taken a football and had a kick about I left the boys to play whilst I found a bench to sit on and watch them play. They really enjoyed each other's company and very seldom fought or argued, we were very lucky. After about 10 minutes I had the feeling I was being watched and not a very nice feeling, the hairs on the back of my neck were stood on end. I looked around and after a couple of seconds I noticed the guy from outside my house a while back watching me from the other side of the park.

Against my better judgement I decided to confront him, so I started walking around the park keeping him in sight as I walked. As I rounded the corner I lost sight of him for a split second due to a large tree, then he was gone, vanished. There was no way he could have disappeared in the time it took me to go past the tree. This guy was starting to freak me out. I called the boys and much to their disappointment I told them it was time to go but with the suggestion of a visit to McDonald's this soon put the smile back on their faces.

Having finished our food we drove to Liz and Tim's house; as always they were glad to see the boys. Sue's sister, Emily, was also there and her and the boys disappeared into the garden. Liz offered me a coffee which I gladly accepted. I explained what had gone on with my mother, Sue's parents were wonderful people and I loved them for just being them. I explained about the guy at the park, he had really unnerved me but I wasn't sure why. Liz and Tim were fully aware of my 'gift' and gave myself and Sue all the support we needed, especially with the boys.

I described the guy to them and asked them to keep an eye out for him. Liz looked a little worried; I told her I didn't think he would turn up here but the more people looking out for him the better. So I finished my coffee, hugged and thanked them both and left for home.

When I got home calm was restored in the Channing household, Sue had done what she needed to do and was sat in the garden with a coffee.

"Is it safe?" I asked with a smirk. Sue smiled and told me not to be cheeky. She asked if the boys were ok. "Of course," I replied. As I sat down I could see that Sue seemed distracted, I asked her what was wrong, she replied that she'd had something strange happen whilst we me and the boys were out. She explained that she'd been cleaning the living room when the doorbell rang, she went to the door but nobody was there. This happened a couple of times which was just annoying, we'd had problems with the doorbell before, and ours went off when someone called to next door, so Sue took the batteries out. Then after a little while there was a knock at the door, again no one was there. This also happened a couple times until Sue got pissed off and ignored it. Then she started hearing a female voice calling her name but she couldn't make out where it was coming from. This spooked her, even after all we had been through; she said it had sounded like my mother's voice.

"Now that is spooky!" I blurted out.

"It's not funny, Gary, it really freaked me out." I got up, kissed and hugged Sue, and I apologised for being insensitive. So I told her about the guy at the park which freaked her out even more because the boys were with me. I explained that this guy was watching me; he took no notice of the boys at all. Sue asked if it was the same guy I'd seen outside the house, I told her it was. Naturally this didn't go down very well and generated questions I had no answers too, much to Sue's frustration.

Sunday arrived and so did Mitch and Molly, yes they arrived together. We all sat down in the kitchen after Sue and Molly were introduced. First off I explained about the guy in the park and Sue's experience on Saturday. I explained the importance of being observant and recording everything. With this in mind I asked Molly if she would like to be part of our little group. She said "yes" without any hesitation. I asked if she would deal with the admin side of things, keeping records of incidents etc. Her reply was a resounding "yes", which I was very pleased about and Mitch was too, he couldn't stop smiling. There was something about Molly that I couldn't quite put my finger on but she oozed positivity.

So we started to discuss the plan of attack for Clarke's visit. He would be here at 6pm and I wanted everything ready before he arrived. Our plan was to place false information throughout the downstairs. Things like pictures and some religious stuff, to see if Clarke would follow the trail and confirm what we all thought, that he was a fraud. Molly and Mitch would set up a webcam in the kitchen where we would allow Clarke to carry out his 'reading' and they could monitor and record it so we could review it after he had gone. This meant them sitting in my cluttered and cold garage, which the thought of didn't seem to bother them at all. I just hoped they would concentrate on what was happening rather than each other. It was clear to see that there was a very strong attraction between them.

So with their thermals and coats on I banished them to the garage. This gave me and Sue some time to go over what we would say and do. Bang on 6pm there was a knock at the door, he was prompt if nothing else. I answered the door and Clarke Richards was eager to introduce himself. I invited him in and was not surprised to see him scanning his surroundings. I took him to the kitchen and introduced him to Sue; he was very charming and polite. He should have been a doctor, I thought. Sue shook his hand and asked if he would like a drink.

"Just a glass of water," was his reply. Sue placed the glass in front of Clarke and he announced that it wasn't for drinking it was for the spirits. I managed to stifle a snigger which didn't go unnoticed by Clarke, that naughty schoolboy feeling was back. Fuck him, I thought. He sat there for a short while holding the glass of water and looking into it like a crystal ball. I thought, here we go. He then stood up and asked to use the toilet which took me a little by surprise.

Whilst he was gone Sue said, "I really don't like him, he made my skin crawl when he shook my hand."

I said, "Tell me about it, but he is following my predicted pattern, apart from the water thing, I didn't expect that."

We heard the toilet flush and Clarke returned to the kitchen. "Ok let's start," he announced. He closed his eyes and started breathing really deep. Then quite dramatically opened his eyes and announced that he had the spirit of a woman who has passed! We sat in silence waiting for him to expand. He stated it was a female, an elderly female. A Gwyn or Gwen. I liked his style; we had placed a photo and a cross on a unit near the toilet, with the name Gwen. He had taken the bait but had tried to be a little vague. He looked at Sue and asked if she could take the information he had given, she said, "yes."

He then stated the spirit was Sue's grandmother and she wanted to let Sue know that she was happy as she was with her husband. Bold move, I thought. As planned, Sue agreed to it all and started to cry. Clarke then announced that she had gone. He then looked at me, frowned and asked if I believed? This took me a little by surprise.

I said, "Yes, why?"

"I sense some negativity." I told him I just needed convincing that was all. This seemed to convince him and he went back to his eyes closed, heavy breathing routine.

"I sense the spirit of a small child," was his next statement, as predicted. We had placed a photo of Billy when he was 4 next to the photo of 'Gwen'. Again we had the same spiel about him being happy and with Gwen, no surprises so far. He then decided to strike up a conversation with Sue, asking about family, work etc. I thought the cheeky sod is trying to milk her for information.

I then noticed out of the corner of my eye a woman peeking around the door, I excused myself from the table and walked to the hall, the woman had disappeared. I asked her to show herself, not too be scared and that I could help her. I stood for a minute or so with no response. Worried that I would be missed I turned to go back into the kitchen.

I then heard a timid voice say, "Wait." I turned and saw a woman who appeared to be in her early forties stood next to the living room door.

I said, "Hello, my name is Gary." She ducked into the living room, so I followed. Thankfully she was still there. I asked her, "What's your name?"

She replied, "Sally."

"How can I help you, Sally?" I asked.

"I'm Clarke's wife; I died 4 years ago from breast cancer." She went on to explain that they had been childhood sweethearts and had been married young. They had never had children as she couldn't. She had been diagnosed with breast cancer after finding a lump under her arm, unfortunately by then the cancer was everywhere. She refused treatment, not wanting to prolong the suffering. Clarke had been devastated but rather than grieve he had convinced himself that he could communicate with the dead. Sally was devastated that he had been deceiving people this way. She believed he wasn't a bad person but needed to be told the truth. I asked if she wanted me to call him to the living room. She just nodded.

When I got back to the kitchen it looked as if Sue was losing the will to live, (excuse the pun). I asked Clarke if he was married, he replied he had been. I asked him if his wife's name was Sally. I thought his jaw was going to hit the floor. Time for a reality check for this fraud. I asked him to follow me to the living room, thankfully Sally was still there. I asked him if he could see or sense any spirits.

"Is this a trick question?" he asked.

"Not at all," I said, "for a man of your alleged talents it's a simple question."

I could see he was feeling backed into a corner and not wanting to commit himself. So being the nice guy that I am I put him out of his misery.

"Listen, Clarke, I know you're a fraud so let's cut the crap." I explained that he had been set up. I told him about the night at the concert with Molly and Adam. There was still a bit of defiance in the man so I played my trump card. I told him Sally was here, I explained to him what she had told me, the man crumbled. Sally stood up and hugged him, he felt her, I could tell by the look on his face and even though I thought he was an asshole, it still brought a lump to my throat.

I asked him, "Can you sense her?"

"I can, I really can." Tears were streaming down his face. I explained to Clarke that Sally wanted him to stop deceiving people and to get on with his life. It was time for her to go; she'd done what she needed to do. I told Clarke to say goodbye and we left him alone for a while.

After about 10 minutes Clarke came back into the kitchen and shook my hand, he thanked me for what I had done. I explained that he needed to stop, if not for Sally then for the people that he was lying to. He promised he would, I told him that I hoped so but I would be watching. To be honest watching him leave I was convinced that he would stop, he didn't look like the same guy that had knocked on our door an hour ago; I did feel pleased, for both of them.

Mitch and Molly came back in after Clarke had left.

"Nice work, Gary," stated Molly.

"Thanks, how was the garage?"

"Bloody cold," answered Mitch. So we had a debrief over a coffee and I asked Mitch who was next on the list.

He said that there was a lady called Val Davies who was advertising an evening of clairvoyance at one of the local halls. I asked Mitch what he knew about her.

"She's very popular, does all the spiritualist churches but doesn't do one to ones." I was a little surprised by that but each to their own.

I asked Mitch to get us 4 tickets, I wanted us all to go but this time Molly would be with me and Mitch with Sue, and I had a cunning plan. After Molly and Mitch had left, myself and Sue were sat on the sofa with a coffee. I was away with the fairies when Sue said, "You're a wonderful man, Gary and I love you."

I looked into her eyes, smiled and said, "I love you too, and you are my world, Sue."

Sue rested her head on my chest, quite soon I could hear her steady breathing that told me she was sleeping. I had to say at that moment I was a very happy man. It wasn't long before I had nodded off myself. As I was heading towards a deep sleep my journey was halted by the sound of someone calling my name, a female voice.

Feeling a little disappointed at being woken up I looked around thinking it was Sue who was calling me but she was still asleep on my chest. I looked towards the door and saw Gwen and Albert stood there, hand in hand. They both smiled at me and Gwen said,

"Keep up the good work, Gary," and they were gone, but I knew they were never far away.

Feeling extremely content I woke Sue and told her it was time for bed. That night I slept like a baby, no dreams, no visits and no voices. Happy days. The week passed with no dramas or incidents, Mitch had called to confirm that he had the tickets for Val's event and that he and Molly were planning to review the recording from Clarke's visit and would let me know if there was anything worth discussing.

Mitch and Molly called in on Saturday afternoon, they confirmed that nothing was picked up on the webcam but they had picked up something on a recorder they had left in the hall. I asked them what it was. So they played the recording, I could hear myself talking to Clarke in the living room, so this must have been around the time his wife was there to say goodbye. I could hear a low growling sound which kept getting louder until it was ended with someone or something screaming,

"Fuck, another one lost." The next thing we could hear was us leaving the living room.

We all just looked at each other. I knew that I had heard nothing at the time but it was so loud on the recorder, we couldn't explain it and it made the hairs on the back of your neck stand up, I didn't like it.

Having already spoken with Sue, I told Mitch and Molly that we needed some decent kit if we were going to continue this little club. I explained that the money had come through from Sid's estate and decided to use some of it for our investigations. I asked them to get a list together with prices etc and to give it to Sue. She was going to make sure I didn't spend it all on shit we didn't need, as she put it. Such a way with words my wife.

CHAPTER 8

Friday evening arrived and everything was in place for our next investigation. We met Molly and Mitch in the pub just around the corner from the venue. Mitch wanted to explain about some visitors he'd had on Wednesday. My heart missed a beat as I thought they were of the 'Beth' type. He explained that they claimed to be conducting a survey about people's lifestyles. He explained that something just didn't feel right about them so he played along. He invited them in and they sat down in his kitchen. At first the questions were standard but their eyes lit up when he told them he worked for a funeral company. One of them asked if they could use his toilet. Mitch being Mitch directed her to the bathroom upstairs even though he had a toilet downstairs. But he also had security cameras in every room upstairs. The other woman continued to ask Mitch questions, including what recent funerals he had done. He'd sussed them out very quickly.

During his research of Val Davies he had come

across some rumours about her gaining personal information about people who were attending her shows. All her tickets were sold online and delivered to a home address, hence the unannounced visitors today. So Mitch waited for an opportunity to plant some duff information. It didn't take long for the subject to get around to the paranormal and mediums etc. The other woman had reappeared from her expedition to Mitch's bathroom; Mitch knew she had been snooping as she had taken too long for just a number one but resisted. So Mitch stated he was a firm believer in the paranormal. One of the women asked if he had ever visited a medium. He stated that he went to a spiritualist church weekly and often had 'messages' from the other side, these girls were loving it, Mitch had them good and proper. He explained that he would be attending Val Davies' show with a father and daughter who had just lost their wife and mother, whom he had met at the church. He explained that the guy was a well-known local businessman. That was all they needed, they couldn't leave quick enough. Mitch explained that he had used the details from an article in one of the local papers and he knew that these two lowlifes would follow it up so he briefed myself and Molly on the details so we would be ready when the time came. So we finished our drinks and left for our evening's entertainment. There were plenty of people waiting to go in, it looked very busy.

Mitch being the eagle-eyed bastard that he was spotted one of the women who had called at his house. She had done her best to change her appearance but she hadn't fooled Mitch, he whispered to us where she was so we would know as well. Eventually we got inside and found our seats. But they were occupied by Mitch's visitor and 3 others. Making sure neither of them acknowledged each other the usual, "you're in our seats" conversation ensued.

Mitch asked, "Don't I know you from somewhere?" And took great delight in watching the woman squirm as she denied it. Out of nowhere this guy appeared making sickly apologies about there being some mistake and moving us to, unsurprisingly, seats at the front. Everything was being stage managed. It was easy to see - knowing what we knew - but to the unsuspecting things would be none the wiser. I was lucky enough to be sat next to the unhappiest looking woman on the planet. She had a handful of tissues and the show hadn't even started yet. After about another 15 minutes of people coming in the lights dimmed and I waited for the farce to begin. I have to say, after Clarke Richards's entrance, Val's was low key to say the least. The lights came up slightly, the curtain opened and there she was.

No grand announcements about past glories, no life history just this slightly glamorous middle-aged woman looking deep in thought. She walked to the edge of the stage and asked if there was a Gail in the audience? This woman in her mid to late 20s stood up and Val asked if she had recently lost a pet? Not the expected opener but I was curious where it was going.

The lady said, "Yes."

Val said, "Your cat has been meowing in my dressing room all evening, she's fine." Naturally this caused some laughter and was obviously designed to lighten the mood and settle everyone. Knowing this was one of Mitch's visitors, it was easy to see it was being stage managed from the start. Val started warming up with a couple of short interactions with members of the audience, the usual, "It's Bill, he's fine," etc. Then as predicted she made a beeline for me and Molly. Now the show would really begin.

Val spewed the information out in short bursts to allow us to confirm what she was saying was correct. To the unsuspecting she was fantastic, and coupled with mine and Molly's tears it was a success. The audience loved it, I was a little surprised that her researchers had not sussed out that we looked nothing like the businessman and his daughter in question but that didn't bother anybody at the time.

So after a few more successful 'hits' Val was on a roll and lapping it up. I then noticed a young man hanging about in the shadows behind Val; he seemed to be watching the woman sat next to me who was still in tears with even more tissue in her hands. He then tried to attract Val's attention by waving at her when she turned and took a glass of water. It came as no surprise to me that she didn't see him. I whispered to Mitch that we had a visitor; this was the cue for Molly to activate a hidden HD camcorder in her bag. Little did I know at the time but this would provide us with our most compelling and shocking evidence to date.

I looked at the woman next to me and was shocked by the look on her face; she could see him as well. Things were becoming interesting, my neighbour was getting very agitated by Val's lack of acknowledgement and decided to take matters into her own hands. She stood up and asked Val why she was ignoring her son! Val was completely taken aback by this; obviously this wasn't in the script. The guy saw what was going on and started to walk forward. Then all hell broke loose, the lights dimmed, a sulphurous smell filled the hall. Demonic screams and shrieks vibrated around the small hall and who should appear on stage but none other than Beth the She-Devil.

She shouted, "He's mine, fuckers." This took me by surprise as well. People were screaming and Val had done a runner. The guy tried to move towards his mother and she tried to move towards him but as he moved this black mass just appeared out of nowhere, enveloped him and he was gone, just like some kind of magic trick. I didn't have a clue what to do; all 4 of us were stood there whilst the rest of the audience escaped. The guy's mother was stood there calling his name over and over again. Beth strutted towards me, knelt down so our faces were level and with that horrible demonic grin that I had already seen too much of. announced, "He's mine. Taking the rotten ones are so much easier, they don't want to be saved." And with that she was gone.

I looked at Mitch and said, "What the fuck just happened then?" Even after all the things I had seen and experienced I was gobsmacked by what had just happened. When we looked around there was only the 4 of us and the guy's mother still in the hall, we all just looked at each other. Molly walked past me, put her arm around the lady and helped her outside. She was a good one that girl.

We got outside and most people had vanished, Val and her little gang were huddled in one corner. Eve, who was the guy's mother, was still with Molly but was obviously still very upset with what had gone on and she wanted answers, from Val. I told Molly to take her to the pub with Sue whilst myself and Mitch spoke with Val.

I approached Val and this rather large gentleman stepped in-between us, saying "Mrs Davies has nothing to say."

I looked him up and down and said, "You weren't this brave 10 minutes ago, were you?" I looked at Val and told her she needed to listen to what I had to say. She nodded at the hulk who stepped aside.

I explained to Val that I knew she was a fraud, she tried to deny it but after telling her what Mitch had done and who I really was she started to listen. I explained what had happened in the hall and that Eve's son had been trying to get her attention, believing she was a real medium and I added if she was she would have seen him.

I told her in no uncertain terms that if she didn't quit tonight I would put the story out on social media. I told her it was time for a change of career, she reluctantly agreed and thankfully she heeded my advice. I didn't want or need the publicity at the moment, in time it would serve a purpose but not yet.

We finally met up with the girls back at the pub and thankfully Eve was still there and much calmer than the last time I saw her. Myself and Mitch got a drink and joined the women at a table in the corner. The incident at the hall was the talk of the pub.

I asked Eve how she was feeling. She looked at me with eyes that were empty. "You saw him, didn't you?" was her opening statement. What could I say? She knew, there was no point lying to her.

"Yes, I did."

"Do you see spirits?" I asked.

"He was the first and hopefully the last," she replied. Eve went on to explain that Lee her son had committed suicide and she had gone to see Val hoping to get answers as to why he had done it. I explained why we were there and tried to make her as comfortable as possible in our company as I felt there was more to this story. Little by little Eve opened up about Lee, she explained that he had been abused as a young boy by a family member and had gone off the rails big time; Eve had been unaware of the abuse so was unable to understand the massive change in his behaviour. She had put it down to drugs. Eventually Lee had ended up in a young offenders' institute as a result of stealing a number of cars and crashing them. Eve had noticed that when Lee came out of prison he had become very withdrawn and secretive and being a single parent with 2 jobs she couldn't keep an eye on him.

Eventually Lee was arrested for molesting 2 young boys at a park and the police found more damning evidence on a laptop that belonged to Lee. At the time of his suicide he was on remand awaiting trial. He'd refused to see Eve whilst he was in prison. Naturally she had blamed herself until she had a letter delivered from Lee 2 days after his suicide. It explained the abuse he had suffered and that he had suffered more whilst at the young offenders' prison. Some of the details were too hard for Eve to recount and to be honest I think we had all heard enough anyway. Molly changed the direction of the conversation and ensured that Eve left us with some really good advice from her.

Sue said after Eve had left, "I don't know about you lot but I need a really stiff drink after all that." We all agreed. Whilst I was at the bar I noticed a guy asking a group of people on the other side of the bar about what had happened at the hall, they told him they hadn't been there.

As I paid for the drinks I could see him talking to a couple at a small table. After a short conversation he walked away, heading in our direction. I got back to the table just in time to warn everyone. The guy stopped at our table and asked if we had been at the hall this evening.

Mitch took the lead and asked, "Why, what happened?" The guy introduced himself as Simon Oliver a journalist with a local paper. He claimed he had picked up some information via social media and was following it up. Mitch told him we hadn't been there. He seemed satisfied and moved onto the next table. Unfortunately we had not seen the last of Simon Oliver. He would turn out to be a real pain in the ass. We finished our drinks in silence and I told Mitch to make sure Molly got home safe and we would meet at my house Sunday to discuss what had happened tonight.

We all agreed and left the pub. On the way home Sue asked, "What happened to her son?"

What could I say? "He's gone to the dark side, love," was all I could think of, my mind was buzzing. Lee was my first loss and he wouldn't be my last I'm afraid to say.

Sleep was difficult that night, my mind kept

replaying the events over and over again. Could I have done something to save Lee? Had I put the exposing of Val before everything else? I wasn't sure, I really wasn't. As sleep took me I heard Henry's voice telling me, "Some don't want to be saved, Gary, you can't save them all."

Saturday morning arrived with my mood still dark. Last night had been a big shock to the system. Watching Lee disappear in darkness really shook me up; I couldn't get the image out of my mind. I woke early Saturday morning; Sue was still sleeping so I wandered downstairs and made a coffee and some toast. Last night's events were still fresh in my mind and the disappointment of 'losing' Lee still hung heavy, but I had been warned this would happen. Last night had been my reality check and if I'm honest I probably needed it. It had certainly focused my mind but that was for another day. Today was going to be a family day. I took Sue breakfast in bed, which was met with the usual, *what have you done?* look from her, but being the male of the species I chose to ignore it.

I showered and phoned Liz to tell her we would be at her place in an hour to pick up the boys. Thankfully she didn't ask about last night, a conversation about it I didn't need right now.

Sue was one of those unique women who could get ready as quick as any man. I told her we would take the boys to a local pleasure park. They had crazy golf, some small rides, a little adventure park and a small sea life centre. The boys loved it, so our day was set. We picked up Charlie and Billy from Liz said our thanks and goodbyes and off we went. Thankfully the day was the distraction we needed. The boys had a ball (even myself and Sue enjoyed it) apart from Billy almost ending up in the crab tank thanks to a brotherly nudge from Charlie. Boys will be boys, I guess.

So after a fun day with the boys, a nice meal on the way home and a relaxing evening in front of the TV, Saturday had been a good old fashioned down to earth family day, which did wonders for my night's sleep. Thankfully that night I slept soundly and woke Sunday morning feeling refreshed and recharged. At midday Mitch and Molly arrived like two hyperactive kids.

"You have to see this," was Mitch's opening statement as he walked past me. Molly was trailing behind looking rather flushed and embarrassed.

We all sat down at the kitchen table, Mitch opened his laptop and after a couple of minutes an image of Val on stage appeared with a black mass to her right. I looked at Mitch and he explained that it was hardly visible on the video but he'd managed to capture it using video editing software. It was hard to dismiss, the mass was solid looking but with very little shape. Mitch explained that it only appeared on this one frame. I explained that when I saw it happen it was visible for longer than that. I asked if Beth was on the video.

Mitch said, "No, she's just out of shot."

"Can we hear what she said?" was my next question.

"Listen for yourself," was Mitch's response. All I could hear were voices in the background, like someone mumbling.

Mitch said, "Now listen to this." This time we

GARY DAVIES

could hear it much clearer, it was like a thousand voices screaming and moaning. I have to say it sent a shiver up my spine; I really didn't like the image it brought to my mind. Thankfully Sue and the boys were in the garden, this was something I didn't want them hearing.

"There's something else," said Mitch. The next image showed the guy I called 'black eyes'.

"Where was this?" I asked Mitch. It turned out we had walked right past him when we walked out, Molly had picked him up on the camcorder as it had still been running as we had left the building. As we had left the hall he had been stood to the left in the reception area. He appeared to be just watching what was happening, same expression on his face as always but nobody seemed to acknowledge his presence and I couldn't remember seeing him as I left. So this guy still remained a mystery to us, which did worry me as his appearances were becoming more frequent, he was a piece of the puzzle that I hadn't figured out where he fitted.

Molly and Mitch were writing up a digital report after every investigation and giving me a copy which after this latest one I really needed to get my head around what had happened. It included a written account of what had happened in the hall including the video footage and an account of our conversation with Eve in the pub, this also mentioned Simon Oliver which I was glad of as it jogged my memory about this guy.

Time to do a bit of research on him; I had a feeling our paths would cross again in the future. It turned out that Oliver wasn't a local he'd been born in

Manchester and had worked for the *Manchester Evening News* after leaving university and ended up as their leading investigative journalist. A little more digging, (good old Google) produced a story from a couple of years ago involving Oliver who'd been investigating a Satanic cult in the area and supposedly involved a number of high profile businessmen and councillors! The paper ran the story and almost immediately pulled it and ran a follow-up apologising to those named and publicly sacked Oliver. Interesting. But it didn't explain how he ended up working for the local paper in my town. It did make me worry a little that he was sniffing around. I sent a text message to Molly and Mitch warning them about Oliver and to let me know if anybody approached them regarding the incident with Val Davies.

It turned out that I wouldn't have to wait long to be introduced to Mr Oliver. I'd gone to town to get a few bits and pieces and decided to pop into one of the many coffee shops and enjoy a 'posh' coffee. It wasn't busy so I picked a window seat that would allow me to enjoy my favourite pastime of people watching. No sooner had I sat down that someone sat in the seat next to me, I looked across and there was Simon Oliver.

I tried to look cool, calm and collected but I think I failed as the first thing he said was, "Were you expecting me?" I thought, bugger do I look that guilty?!

I didn't see much point in bullshitting the guy so I just asked, "What do you want?"

Unlike me he decided to insult my intelligence by introducing himself formally and offering his hand, not a good start in my book. I ignored his offer to shake his hand and again asked him what he wanted. It turned out that he wasn't working for a local paper, he was in fact working freelance. I told him that I knew who he was and that I knew his background.

As soon as he smiled I knew I'd lost any chance of playing dumb, I reminded myself that I needed to engage my brain before my mouth going forward.

He came straight to the point and said, "You were at the hall Friday night." It was more of a statement than a question so I said nothing. "Quite a show, I thought," was his sarcastic comment. I just looked away and again made no reply. "Why were you there?" was his next question, again I just looked away and took a sip of my coffee.

Seeing he was getting nowhere he changed tact and proceeded to tell me what he knew about me, which was a lot more than I expected. He'd obviously done his homework and had found out almost everything to do with Clarke Richards and the spiritualist church. It turned out that he had family living locally and when the shit had hit the fan in Manchester he decided that this would be a good place to disappear for a while. But being the nosey fucker or investigative journalist (whichever you prefer) he'd gotten wind of the incident in the church and had initially investigated the crazy guy who had come to talk to his wife. Whilst following that he'd spoken to Shirley who'd told him about me! Sweet revenge for her I guess, we'd hardly parted on good terms so it came as no surprise. He'd then found out who were the popular 'Mediums' and visited them too. Again Mr Richards was happy to spill the beans about me plus it kept Simon from asking too many questions about him, or so he thought.

I sat there and listened to what he had to say but didn't respond, there wasn't much to add to be honest. He then played his trump card, the "we are after the same thing" statement. "I'm here to help; we could help each other out these fake mediums preying on the grief of those that have lost loved ones." I almost choked on my coffee as I burst out laughing. This guy made a living out of other people's misery, I wanted to tell him where to shove his offer but I could see he was waiting for it so I took a moment to calm myself and wipe the coffee off my chin and I told him I would think about it. I stood to leave and he offered me his business card, which I took, I knew our paths would cross again and I left.

As I drove home I knew I needed to think long and hard about the impact Simon Oliver was going to have on my plans, he was going to be like a dog with a bone regardless of what I did. My only option was to someway get him on my side and use him to our advantage, which turned out to be a lot easier than I thought it would be.

When I got home I told Sue about my little encounter with Simon and made sure she knew what he looked like, I didn't trust the guy. I also told Mitch and Molly as I was sure they would be on his list too. It turned out they were one step ahead of me and had encountered him outside Mitch's place that morning, they had just ignored him and left.

He was certainly a busy boy that's for sure, his involvement had raised the stakes for all of us and I wanted to make sure everybody understood where this was going and how it would affect us.

We decided to let the dust settle so to speak and got on with our 'normal' lives for a couple of weeks before deciding our next plan of attack. We agreed to meet at a local restaurant to figure out what to do next, this had given us a time to consider personally our situations and what had happened so far. Sue had said very little on the subject other than she would support me whatever I decided, I could always rely on Sue's support I was a lucky man.

We all met up one Saturday evening for some food and a catch up, which didn't take too long. Mitch and Molly were keen to point out that they were ready for our next assignment and had been the whole time but had understood the need to take a break and to take stock of things. We were nicely tucked away in a quiet corner at the far end of the restaurant which meant we would not be disturbed or overheard but also meant we could see who was coming and going, which turned out to be a big advantage when Simon Oliver walked in with a young woman. Thankfully he couldn't see us but I was able to just about see him. I told the guys who was here so they were aware when going to the toilet and such. We carried on our conversation but I was keeping one eye on Simon.

After a while I began to notice that there was no conversation between Simon and the woman and as the evening wore on I also noticed that she had not eaten or drank anything. My senses started to come alive and almost rocketed when she looked directly at me and smiled, I knew that look. I smiled back and as soon as I acknowledged her she was sat next to me, I quickly explained to everyone that we had a guest as I knew what would be coming next, I wasn't disappointed.

Having got over the usual, "you can see me" statement she calmed and relaxed a little. I told her who I was and that I was the only one who could see her but Mitch could hear her. Naturally my first question was, "Who are you?" She explained that she was Simon's sister and that she had died from cancer 2 years ago. I asked why she was still around and she explained that they hadn't said goodbye. She had been diagnosed with terminal cancer and within weeks had died. Simon had been undercover investigating the satanic story in Manchester and had not even known she had died until the investigation had all gone tits up, so to speak. Kim, Simon's sister, explained that they were very close as they had lost both parents in a car accident and Simon had virtually brought her up on his own. Kim explained that she knew she had died but needed the closure of saying goodbye before moving on. She explained that it was like a bond that kept her earth bound, for want of a better description.

She also explained that the attachment was to Simon and not as some people thought that you could just roam around where you liked but that wasn't the case. Where Simon went she went and she'd been waiting for someone like me to help her. I explained the current situation between myself and Simon and she wasn't surprised.

"He can be a bit of a dick sometimes." Her words not mine but I was inclined to agree. Whilst all this was going on Mitch was giving Molly a running commentary which meant we had taken our eyes off Simon and before I realised he was stood next to the table with a smug grin on his face.

"Well if it isn't Gary and his Ghostbusters," was his smartass opening. Kim was right he really was a dick.

"Do you mind if I have a seat?" he asked.

"It's taken," was my smug reply.

"One of your imaginary friends, is it?"

"Nope. just your sister." Now that wiped the grin off his face. "Sit down you're attracting unwanted attention." I told him to get a chair from another table, you could see the look of confusion on his face as there was a spare seat next to me. He didn't know yet that his sister was sat there, but he would.

"Listen to me, Simon, and listen good," was my blunt comment as he sat down. "You may not believe what I'm about to tell you but I guarantee you will by the time I've finished whether you like it or not."

He took a small recorder out of his pocket and placed it on the table. I picked it up and gave it to Mitch. "You won't be needing that" I told him. "This is for Kim's benefit not yours." I could see the look of surprise for a split second. Once a journalist always a journalist, I thought.

I looked him in the eye and told him his sister Kim was sat next to me; his response came as no surprise. A sarcastic, "really?" was all he could muster.

I explained in detail what Kim had told me about her death but he was having none of it, stating most of what I'd said you could find on the internet which was fair enough. Kim was disappointed by his reaction so I told her that she needed to give me something that only they would know. I looked at Simon who was rolling his eyes and tutting, a typical reaction of the non-believer. It didn't bother me so I pressed Kim for something that would make Simon change his mind.

Eventually that look spread across her face and I knew she had something. I smiled as she relayed the story to me, it was quite funny and it was hard not to giggle along with her, much to the confusion of Simon. I waited for her to finish and told Simon why Kim was here and what was needed to allow her to move on. I could see he was still sceptical but I was sure I sensed he was starting to come around. So I told Simon to listen and not interrupt.

Kim had explained that when she was 6 they had gone on a family holiday to Weymouth, their father had decided that camping would be fun. They had turned up at the camp site which resembled an image from the Somme. They had got stuck quite quickly and Simon and his dad had got out of the car to try and push it whilst their mother drove the car. After a couple of attempts they'd got the car moving. When they had stopped the car and looked back Simon and his dad were covered from head to foot in mud. Naturally Kim and her mother had found it extremely funny and it was a story that was recounted numerous times and always left them in tears.

I looked at Simon and I knew I had convinced him, tears were rolling down his cheeks. I looked at Mitch and Molly; they knew it was time to leave me alone. "Now do you believe me?" I asked. Simon just nodded his head, the arrogance had gone and I knew we could help Kim move on. I spent the next 10 minutes helping Kim and Simon say goodbye; it was going to be interesting to see the 'New Simon' after this encounter. I told Simon I wanted him to go home and think about what had happened this evening and how things would progress going forward. I could see he was still in shock so he just nodded, got up, held out his hand which I shook this time and he left.

I met up with Mitch and Molly outside and updated them on what had happed after they had left. I wasn't sure what Simon's reaction would be after the dust had settled but for some reason I was quietly optimistic. We went our separate ways with a plan to catch up and plan our next move as this meeting had been gate crashed, sort of.

CHAPTER 9

I left the restaurant and drove straight home, as usual Sue was waiting for me. I always made sure I updated her on what was happening, even though she was to keep her distance I wanted her to still feel included in what was happening and to be honest she was very interested in it all and always had good ideas for plans going forward.

She asked about my plans for Simon, did I trust him etc? I still wasn't sure but it wouldn't do any harm to see where things went regarding him. We decided to have an early night and catch up on some personal time; Sue had made it very clear that I had been neglecting her in that department. So after some intense lovemaking my head hit the pillow and I was gone. I was awoken a couple of hours later by someone calling my name, a female voice that, at first, I thought was Sue's but when I looked over she was sound asleep. As I awoke more I realised I didn't recognise the voice. I got out of bed and walked out to the landing. The voice was coming from downstairs so I walked down the stairs. As I got to the bottom all the hairs on my body stood on end, I thought, oh shit here we go! The atmosphere was completely different as my bare feet hit the hall floor and that was when things went twilight zone, an understatement to be sure.

It was like losing the picture on your TV, one second I was at the bottom of my stairs looking towards the front door the next I was in an open space with no features, just an intense brightness. At first all I could make out were shapes moving around in front of me, and then things started to clear and sharpen up. To my surprise Henry Hope was stood in front of me, behind him were Gwen and Albert and a number of other people who I had no idea who they were.

"Hello, Gary," was Henry's response to my obviously confused stare. "Relax, you're still asleep, we've hijacked your subconscious so to speak." Henry always had a way of making the off planet stuff seem like an everyday occurrence. I was eager to find out what this was all about.

Henry proceeded to explain how things were going to get a little more serious going forward and that I needed to prepare myself for some lifechanging incidents. I didn't get a warm fuzzy feeling from what Henry was telling me, he explained that he was unable to go into detail but I would be tested like never before and I would need all my strength and conviction to get me through it. I didn't like what I was hearing; Henry's 'gang' had the same sombre, serious look on their faces which just made matters worse.

Henry continued to explain that I had been picked for a reason and they had been monitoring everything that had happened since that first day at Hope Hall to confirm that I was who they needed. Naturally I asked how I was doing; it seemed like a sensible question at the time. Henry just looked at me and continued to explain that the work I was doing was vital and that I needed to keep progressing. I asked about the guy I had seen on a number of occasions who I referred to as 'black eyes'.

"Don't be concerned with him," was Henry's blunt reply and with that I was back in bed, the light was coming through the window and I could hear Sue downstairs. I felt energised, really boosted, difficult to explain but man I felt really good. The boys were already up too, watching TV, and Sue was making breakfast. The doom and gloom message from Henry was firmly at the back of my mind, which I was to regret very soon.

I had mistook the feeling of being energised the wrong way, I allowed myself to take my eye off the ball so to speak. I had never been one to answer my mobile to unknown numbers, relying on the idea that if it was important they would leave a message. By Wednesday I'd had a number of calls from the same number, every time there had been a voicemail left but no one was speaking. All I could hear was some background noise so I ignored them. But then on Friday I had a call off Mum's friend, Jenny, she asked if I had heard from Mum. I explained that I hadn't heard from Mum since the issue over Sid's will and that she'd made it perfectly clear that she didn't want to talk to me anymore. Jenny explained that she'd been away visiting relatives and last night she had heard my mum calling her. Straightaway my thoughts went back to the strange calls I'd been having. I told Jenny I would go and check on Mum.

I left work at the end of my shift and went straight to Mum's, she had moved into Sid's flat and sold the house, I had found that out via the grapevine. When I arrived at the flat, I rang the bell a number of times but there was no answer, I looked through the letterbox and could see a number of letters on the floor and I could hear the TV. I called Mum but there was no answer, panic was starting to set in something was telling me something was very wrong. I remembered that the neighbour opposite used to have a spare key when Sid was alive. I knocked on the door and thankfully Bert was in. I asked him if he had seen Mum lately, which he hadn't. I then asked if he still had the spare key which he did. I took the key and thankfully Mum hadn't changed the locks. I burst in through the door and went straight into the living room. Mum was lying on the floor, there was blood covering her head and face and on the rug where she was lying.

Everything after that was a blur. Bert had followed me in and thankfully he was an ex-policeman. He called the paramedics and the police, he'd also managed to get Sue's number from me and she'd come straightaway. I couldn't think straight, I was a mess. The police had spoken to Bert and taken a brief statement from myself and then told Sue to take me home. I couldn't process what had happened, even though we had fallen out she was still my mum. I was devastated my mum was dead.

Unfortunately this was just the start of my misery. After an autopsy and a police investigation I was told that Mum had taken a fall sometime late on Monday evening, she had broken her hip and knocked herself out. She'd suffered a bleed on the brain which had caused her to slip in and out of consciousness; the calls had come from her. She had changed her mobile number which I wasn't aware of, the more I was told the worse I felt. The time of death had been around 4am on Friday, which I later found out off Jenny was around the time she had heard Mum calling her.

Thankfully Sue was able to arrange the funeral and such as I was a complete mess, I kept blaming myself, why hadn't I answered the phone or at least tried to patch things up with Mum after the dust had settled? I'd simply been too busy playing Ghostbusters, to quote Simon Oliver.

The dreaded day of the funeral came; thankfully we didn't have a big family so the service was a standard crematorium one with the same number of mourners going back to the house. As we left the crematorium in the car I looked opposite the exit and to my surprise 'black eyes' was stood there, the same flat expression as usual but this time it was as if he was somehow mocking me. I had to bow my head I couldn't process this.

Back at the house the usual wake took place, kind words from family and friends of which most didn't stay long which I was happy about. Sue's parents took the boys for the night which I was extremely grateful for. Finally there was only myself, Sue, Jenny, Mitch and Molly left. There was an awkward silence between us all, all of us had questions but none of us seemed to have the courage to ask them, apart from Molly who came straight out with the question,

"Have you seen her, Gary?" I knew I could rely on Molly young in age but old in wisdom, it kickstarted the conversation that was needed.

"No," I replied.

"Neither have I," said Jenny, "not since Friday."

No sooner had the words left Jenny's lips when the kitchen went cold, the air was full of static and the lights started to flicker, we all looked at each other. I saw Jenny looking over my shoulder as I had my back to the kitchen door but I recognised the hairs standing on end feeling. I swivelled around on my chair and saw Mum stood in the doorway. I stood up and in an instant she was in front of me with a look of pure hate on her face,

"You left me to die," she spat into my face. I tried to respond but she cut me off with, "You ignored me and left me to die." I was shocked and stunned by the venom in her voice. I told her I was sorry and that I had never meant to let her die, I didn't know. I was so sorry. Her features started to change, she started looking like the mother I remembered and loved, then from nowhere the black mass I had seen at Val Davies's Performance appeared. Instantly I knew what was happening, this is what Henry had been on about. I grabbed Mum's hand, it was real, warm, it was a real hand but I could feel the pull from the black mass. I needed help.

I called Jenny and Mitch, they were the only ones who could help me or even understand what was happening. They both grabbed my other hand, I could feel a surge of energy going through my body, and the black mass felt it too. The scream from a hundred souls seemed to fill the room. For a split second I thought we had the advantage but the black mass seemed to increase in strength, we were losing, Mum was going to the dark side and there was nothing I could do.

In the blink of an eye it was over, she was gone and the black mass too. The 3 of us were sat on the floor completely drained. The black mass had beaten all 3 of us and took Mums spirit to the evil side, I was broken I couldn't even save my own mum. Jenny had to explain to Sue and Molly what had happened whilst Mitch took me outside. All I could think of was what Henry had told me. He'd known, the bastard had known what would happen hence the warning and lack of information from him.

I told Mitch all about it. What could he say, what could anyone say? I felt useless. What if they came for the boys or Sue what would happen then? I was terrified. I asked Mitch to leave me be, I needed time to taken in what happened. I couldn't process what was going on, we'd been pretty successful up until now and I believed that Lee had been taken because of his past and because he was the first, we didn't know what was going to happen, after all we were learning but that learning curve had just gone into orbit.

I felt someone sit down next to me, it was Jenny. She placed something into my hand, it was a crudely carved wooden cross, the one that had been given to her in Jamaica.

"I can't take that," I told her.

"Gary, listen to me, you're going to need this. What happened tonight happened for reasons you'll find out later." I couldn't understand what she was getting at. "Don't ask me for the answers, Gary, you need to find them yourself, stay on the path, carry on doing what you've been doing, we need you." And with that she up and left.

To my surprise Mum had left everything to me, which was ironic considering all the things that had caused her to stop speaking to me were now mine. I was in no rush to sort out the flat, my mind was still a train wreck after what had happened and I was for the first time in my life unable to cope. Even the simplest of tasks seemed beyond my capability. Sue was a rock which came as no surprise, giving me space when needed and a shoulder to cry on as well. Mitch and Molly stayed away, as did Simon which I was grateful for also, but deep down I knew I would have to 'get back on the horse' so to speak but until that time the 3 of them showed me what true friends are, even Simon, the reason for which will become clearer later.

Another thing that had slipped my mind was the cross Jenny had given me; it 'appeared' a couple of weeks after Mum's funeral. I'd come home from work and it was there on the counter in the kitchen, I asked Sue if she'd put it there but in fact she didn't know anything about it. I picked it up and felt a surge of energy course though my body. It was an immense feeling of love, happiness and positivity, really weird and my feelings of self doubt and weakness were completely washed away, it really was bizarre and whenever I felt myself slipping back into the gloom it would appear and have the same effect. I soon learnt to keep it on me like a teenager treats their mobile.

Soon after this I was able to go to Mum's flat. Sue had already been busy there with Molly's help. Everything was boxed and labelled to make it easy for me to decide what I wanted to keep etc. We had already decided to give all the furniture and clothes to charity which had already been collected. After that most of what was left was Sid's collections, I was really pleased Mum hadn't sold them. We moved everything back to the house and had arranged to sell the flat to Mitch and Molly, which I was very happy about for a number of reasons and made the whole selling process much easier to deal with, plus they got their first home at a price they could easily afford. I had offered to give it to them but they would have none of it and we eventually agreed on a price they were happy with. We addressed everything else with Mum's solicitor and that was that.

Sue had arranged for all the 'gang' to get together at the house, which was perfect timing as I had been considering it for some time. It had been 2 months since Mum's funeral and they had all been great with their support. So an evening of takeaway and booze was the perfect tonic to restart the reason we had all been brought together in the first place. It was to be an evening that would set and define our way forward for the future and set us on a road that would change all our lives, both good and bad.

I also learned a lot about Simon that night; he showed a completely different side to us all. He was open, honest and gave us an insight to what his investigation in Manchester was about; unbeknown to us this would very helpful in the future. The evening was a great success, not that my head agreed the following morning. Thankfully it was a Sunday, a good day to recover from a hangover.

I spent my hungover Sunday in the garage sorting through some of the boxes brought from Mum's. The first box I came across was marked as paperwork so I thought it would be a good place to start. Most of it was the usual, bank statements, bills etc. The kind of stuff you collect over time with no real purpose for it. So my pile for shredding was getting bigger and bigger.

I then came across some old certificates of Mum's, they related to nursing qualifications which came as a shock because I never knew mum was a nurse, I knew she had worked at a hospital but she'd said she was a cleaner not a nurse. I searched through the rest of the box and found other paperwork relating to nursing, I was intrigued why Mum would hide the fact she had been a nurse. I also found my birth certificate which started me thinking about my dad. Mum had always told me that he had run off with a local barmaid and wouldn't discuss him, in fact I was brought up to hate him because of this and never questioned it. Eventually the hangover won and I retreated to the sofa for the rest of the day.

Monday passed as Mondays usually do when I'm on mornings. Having got home to the usual empty house I made myself a coffee and worked my way through a pile of mail, most of which was junk. My peace was disturbed by the doorbell ringing, I answered it and stood there was a grey-haired man possibly in his 60s, my initial thought was he was a bloody Jehovah's Witness and I was about to give my usual, "sod off I'm not interested" response when the guy said, "Hello, Gary."

With a confused expression I returned the greeting after all I had no idea who he was but he knew my name so I held off with dismissing him. For a couple of seconds he just stood there looking at me which was a little creepy so I asked, "Can I help you?"

"More like the other way round," was his blunt reply. For some reason and against my usual response I suggested he come in. I offered him a coffee which he accepted and we sat down. Naturally my curiosity was getting the better of me so I asked,

"What's this all about then?" He proceeded to tell me that his name was Frank Channing and that he was my mum's ex-husband, this seemed a strange way to describe himself as this was the name I'd seen on my birth certificate. "You mean my father?" was my blunt reply.

"No, I'm not," was Frank's even blunter reply. So for the next hour Frank told me a story that would blow my mind and explain what had happened to Mum.

Frank had met Mum after he had been knocked off his bike on his way home from work. Mum had been going to work at the local hospital and had witnessed the accident. Apart from a few cuts and bruises he had been ok but Mum had made a big impression on him. Obviously this had been before the days of mobile phones so all he had to go on was that she worked in the local hospital. Eventually he had tracked her down and had met her outside the hospital with a bunch of flowers and their relationship developed from there. A year later they had been married and after 3 miscarriages mum had finally gone full term. She worked on the maternity ward so was in good company when she went into labour at work. Frank had been contacted at work and by the time he got to the hospital she had given birth.

The birth had been quite difficult but everything appeared ok and having seen Mum and his son he left. Remember this was in the 60s, so things were a little different. Fathers were seldom at the births and certainly weren't given time off work and such. Mum had stayed in hospital for a week and Frank had visited in the evening every day.

After coming home they settled into family life but never had any more children as Mum was dead against it. Frank had tried to persuade her but she would have none of it. At the age of 6 I had a serious kidney infection, the doctors thought I would need a kidney transplant and Frank explained that naturally he was tested for compatibility. It was then that he discovered that he wasn't my dad; naturally this was a hammer blow to him to find out his only child wasn't his and the fact that I eventually recovered from the infection and didn't need a transplant was what some people would call karma. To be honest I believed him, he had no reason to lie after all these years. He asked who the father was but mum wasn't telling. Over the next couple of weeks the anger grew, along with the accusations and arguments. Eventually one drunken evening the truth came out, Sid had offered to babysit for them as he was aware that something was wrong. Having got home the arguments had continued, Frank had demanded to know who my father was, Mum told him she didn't know which obviously didn't help but having backed her into a corner she couldn't see a way out other than to tell him the truth - which was to be mind blowing and would end their relationship.

Two days after Mum had given birth she had got bored with waiting for the nurses to bring her baby to her and knowing the score she had awoken early and made her way to the nursery where all the babies were sleeping. She'd gone to her baby's crib and found her son white and cold, he was dead! For reasons she could never explain to Frank she switched him with another baby, me! By this time I was sat there with my mouth hanging open.

"I know this has come as a bit of a shock," Frank said. No shit, Sherlock, smashed into my mind like a car crash, I couldn't believe what I was hearing, my whole life had just been turned upside down, and everything I thought I knew about myself had been blown completely out of the water.

Frank continued to explain that Mum had got away with it because she knew the procedures but was never able to explain her decision. Frank put it down to her almost obsession to have a child after her 3 miscarriages but it was something he couldn't live with. Within weeks he had moved out and eventually they had divorced and he moved away. I asked Frank why he hadn't said something, reported it to the police? His only answer was that he loved her, he explained that his own life had been blown apart and that he wasn't thinking straight either. By the time he had come to his senses and thought about it he decided there was nothing to gain from it and it would be his word against hers by then.

How the fuck was I going to explain all this to Sue? I couldn't take it all in myself. Frank explained that an old friend of his had heard about Mum's death and had told him, he'd got my address from the funeral home telling them I was his son. With that bombshell delivered, Frank stood up, shook my hand, apologised and left.

I was still sat at the table when Sue came home from work, she took one look at me and asked what was wrong, I broke down and sobbed my heart out. It took me some time to be able to compose myself and tell her what had happened, she couldn't believe it either.

"Do you believe him, Gary?" she asked. Good question but how could I know for sure, I couldn't but I knew a man who could probably find out.

Time for Simon to step up.

CHAPTER 10

The following week was a blur, I couldn't concentrate on anything. I wasn't at work which didn't help to be honest but as always it was Sue who picked me up off the floor, dusted me down, gave me a reality check and pointed me in the direction she knew I needed to go.

She told me that the past is the past, it's over your shoulder you can't change any of it but you can change the future. She said she would support me no matter what, if I wanted Simon to do some digging then she was with me but I had to be prepared to be even more shocked by what he might find. Sue was spot on and she knew it, she knew a little reverse psychology would do the trick and it did. I knew I needed answers and the only way to get them was to involve Simon, it would be right up his street.

I arranged via Mitch a meeting of the team, I knew this would be a little tough on me having to tell them what Frank had told me but I also knew it was my only option if I wanted to make sense of what was going on. I wasn't looking forward to it but needs must.

They all came to the house which under the circumstances suited me as I wasn't sure how I would react having to retell everything. To be fair it went better than expected even Simon was able to keep himself in check and as I was hoping he was more than happy to do some digging for me. I gave him my birth certificate and he promised me I would be the first to know when he had something. Strange how our opinion of someone can change. When I first met the guy I thought he was an idiot but I guess on reflection it was a front because having got to know him a little better he had proved me wrong, not that I was going to tell him.

I asked Mitch what our next move was going to be, I needed something to occupy my mind and focus on. I knew this would help me a lot as I really needed to understand this 'good versus evil' concept. Were we unable to save people who had done something bad? Was there some 'scale' that people were measured on or did the advantage just swing one way or another? I really didn't understand this but I felt this would give us the edge if I could get my head around it. Having seen the reality of this I knew it was probably the most important thing in my life at this moment. There had to be a way to save everyone but the answer was out of my grasp at the moment but I was determined to figure it out. By my nature I was a sore loser and these loses were really hard to accept so evil could kiss my ass. Mitch suggested advertising our 'services'.

"What, I see dead people service?" was my reply.

"If you listen, smart ass," was Mitch's excellent comeback, "I was thinking of something a little more low key, something along the lines of Paranormal Investigation Services." I liked the sound of that, it would give us a foot in the door so to speak and having put 'Spooks are Us' into retirement then perhaps there was a gap to fill. After all, with all the programmes on TV regarding the paranormal it would be easier to get people to respond, and plus the added fun of being able to 'debunk' the attention-seekers would just be a bonus and appeal to my warped sense of humour which you'll be glad to know was still intact.

So the next step was what equipment did we need, we both agreed that top of the range video cameras were a must. All the other crap that these 'Paranormal Investigators' used wasn't necessary for us, for example, 'spirit boxes'. Do they really allow spirits to communicate with us? No! They scan radio frequencies. Is it really beyond the realms of possibility that they pick up on broken up radio signals that shock, horror, sound like human voices and people spend £60 or more on these things? Another favourite is the EMF meter, if it spikes you've got a spirit. Have you?! Again think about it, what is it measuring or detecting? Is it again hard to believe that this varies from time to time in the same spot, considering how many different things generate electro-magnetic fields and how we ourselves are affected by it. Again it was something that wasn't going to be on our shopping list. Another favourite was the digital recorder; this was going to be added to our list but not for EVPs (or Electronic Voice Phenomena) again used to record spirit voices the human ear can't pick up. So the microphone on a digital recorder can pick up sounds the human ear can't! I can talk to you from the other side of the room and you'll hear me but a reporter for example needs to stuff a microphone in your face to pick up the same level of voice being used! Again are we expected to believe this? Virtually all EVPs I've heard have come with an explanation of what's being said and to be honest without the explanation I wouldn't have a clue what was being said. So for us the recorder would be used to collect information and for camera shy 'clients'. We would also use digital thermometers as we thought the instances of big drops in temperatures could be a result of spirits using the natural energy around us. Although I wasn't sure what the exact reason was I didn't think it would do any harm to have some. So with a few other bits and pieces added to the list that Molly had recorded it was agreed that we could add to it as and when necessary. There were so many things that these so-called paranormal sites recommended that we could have spent thousands but it wasn't because I couldn't afford it but from my own experiences so far most of it was unnecessary. Not wanting Sue and Molly to feel left out I asked them to come up with a name for us and to organise the advertising etc. We agreed to have a separate mobile and email only for this to stop any unnecessary interference in our daily lives. After all we all still had day jobs so to speak.

Molly asked if we would have uniforms and a special car like the 'Ghostbusters'. My look was enough to answer her question. Mitch wanted to organise a website for us as well which I agreed with, I knew deep down how big this was going to get, it was like a snowball rolling downhill. We needed to get ourselves out there investigating as much as possible and so *Paranormal and Haunting Investigations* were born.

Mitch and Molly left, Simon had already left having been given his mission as it were, leaving Sue and I sat in the kitchen reflecting on what had happened.

"This is all your fault, you know," I told Sue.

"Bullshit," was her blunt reply.

I smirked. "If you hadn't suggested going to Hope Hall none of this would have happened."

"For the record, smart ass, I might have suggested the event but you picked Hope Hall." As always Sue was spot on and she knew I was just taking the piss anyway. I knew deep down that this was what I needed. Of course for most people the paranormal was something that invoked nightmares and such but for me it brought a sense of calm, purpose and focus in my life. I knew it was going to be one fuck of a rollercoaster ride and for a man who in reality would never get on one; this was one ride that I was meant to be on.

Hold on tight boys and girls things are about to get really interesting, yes I know things haven't exactly been average, normal or quiet but believe me all your understanding of the paranormal is about to be tipped on its head.

After a couple of quiet weeks whilst we set up the website and advertised ourselves I tried to make sense of all that had happened without too much success. I was like a Jack Russell chasing his own tail so I tried to focus on our new venture. Molly had called to say a young couple had been in touch via the website claiming their flat was haunted, so we agreed to pay them a visit to see if it was worth investigating. Myself, Mitch and Molly turned up at the couple's flat one evening. They lived on the top floor of a block of flats owned by the local housing authority. The door was answered by a man in his mid-20s and introduced himself as Carl, he invited us in and escorted us to the living room where we were met by his girlfriend, whose name was Lauren, and who was about the same age as Carl. Having introduced ourselves and explained what we did, also that we didn't charge any money for our time Mitch asked them to explain what had been happening.

Carl explained that they had been living in the flat for 4 years but in the last 18 months they had been experiencing 'strange' occurrences. Mitch asked if it was ok for Molly to record the interview using a camcorder, explaining it would be used as part of the investigation and in case anything happened whilst we were there. Carl seemed happy with that and so did Lauren, a little too happy to be honest but I didn't think much of it at the time. Carl explained that they were being woken up at night by lights turning on by themselves, taps would turn on, and things would go missing and re-appear days later, the usual if I'm honest. But I let Carl go into detail regarding each occurrence, accompanied by lots of head nodding and encouragement from Lauren. Now call me a cynic but I'd seemed to have developed a sense for bullshit and this smelt of the brown stuff big time.

I asked Lauren to give me a guided tour of their hot spots. Carl jumped in and suggested it would be better if he did it rather than Lauren. I explained that as the Team 'Sensitive' - I hated that term but it was a necessary description on this occasion - I was getting stronger energy from Lauren so she was the best option. How I kept a straight face I will never know, so off we went. Lauren took me to all the rooms in the flat, which didn't take long as it was only a kitchen, bedroom and a bathroom and there was nothing there, absolutely nothing. We came back to the living room and I gave Mitch a quick glance and a shake of the head, he got what I meant. I asked them both if they were interested in the paranormal? Which was met with a resounding "yes". They explained that they had watched, read and visited anything and everything that was to do with the paranormal. I then asked if they had had any other paranormal investigators visit them, I almost choked on my coffee when they said that "Spooks are Us" had been there a year ago. I asked them what was their verdict was. Carl stated that they had told them the flat wasn't haunted which really surprised me considering my experience with them but wonders never cease as they say. I told them that I had to agree with them, the flat wasn't haunted. Before they had the chance to get pissed at me I explained that I believed it was their obsession with the paranormal that was causing them to think these things were happening and that if they gave themselves a break from obsessing then they would see a change. I was well impressed with my diplomatic skills. A year ago I would have told them they were "Fucking nuts and to get a grip"; again needs must.

We left the flat and when we got back to the car Molly said, "Well that went well for our first investigation." Within seconds Mitch and I had tears of laughter streaming down our faces, oh I hoped all our investigations weren't going to be like this. Thankfully our next one brought us back down to earth with a thump.

Our next investigation was to a single mum called Karen; she lived in an end terrace 3- bedroom house on a local housing estate with her 2 daughters. She was separated from her husband so working full-time and being a mum to 2 teenage daughters was stressful to say the least, so having been briefed by Molly we visited Karen. As agreed the girls were at a friend's house, I wanted to see if there was any difference with and without the girls. I needn't have bothered as when we pulled up outside her house I saw the face of an old man staring out the living room window. I asked Molly if there was anyone else living with them, as expected she said "no".

"Then I think I've already seen her problem." I explained to Molly and Mitch who or what I had seen in the window. "Ok let's still stick to the same format," I explained. "Mitch ask the same questions, let her explain. Molly make sure you ask for her consent to use the camcorder, you never know what we might catch."

We knocked on the door which was answered by Karen, and stood right behind her was the old guy I had seen in the window. I avoided eye contact as I didn't want him to know I could see him. I didn't want that confrontation now, all in good time. So with the formalities out of the way and coffee made we all sat down and Mitch got straight down to getting Karen to explain what was going on in her house. Karen explained that they had lived there 3 years and that the house had never felt comfortable, the girls had gone from well behaved to a nightmare in a very short space of time. The incidents were similar to Carl and Laurens but in this case I was sure the old man was responsible not the girls. Things had been fragile on the relationship front and that was one of the reasons why they had moved, her husband had lost his job and even though Karen earned enough to sustain them his male ego couldn't take it so he'd been offered a job 150 miles from where they had originally lived. Thankfully Karen had been able to transfer as she worked in a bank but having moved in things went arse up and the stress of moving, new jobs and things going bump in the night had taken its toll on their relationship and he'd moved out 2 months ago. Things had gone from bad to worse and when Karen had been pushed down the stairs and broke her wrist it was the last straw. She couldn't blame anyone as she had been home alone.

I asked her who had owned the house before her she said they had bought it from a family after their father had died; he'd lived there on his own after his wife had died. He'd been found dead in bed by his son. I asked Karen if she knew his name. She said his name was Charlie. I thanked Karen and explained that I would like to walk around the house with Molly to see if I could 'pick up on anything'. Man I loved all this paranormal speak. I'd already seen the culprit and I knew I would pick up on him, the grumpy old bugger had been giving me dirty looks ever since I'd walked through the door.

So Molly and I started upstairs first, when we got

there I explained why I had asked her to join me. "Whatever happens keep the camcorder running, ok?" Molly nodded and we walked to the door furthest away. As soon as I opened the door Charlie was waiting for me.

"Who the fuck are you?" was his opening statement.

"Gary Channing, pleased to meet you," I batted back which visibly took him by surprise.

"How can you see me? I've been trying to talk to these fuckers who stole my house for ages."

"What's your name, sir?" I asked.

"Charlie Blunt."

"Mr Blunt, these people haven't stolen your house, it's theirs." I explained to Charlie that he'd been found dead and that for some reason he hadn't moved on. Naturally this came as a shock to him, something was keeping him here and I needed to find out what it was so I could help him move on.

Charlie explained that his wife had died from breast cancer, he'd watched as she'd gone from a strong hardworking wife, mother and grandmother to just a shell. It had devastated him that he'd been unable to do nothing for her. He said he felt he had let her down and couldn't look her in the eye at the end; he thought his kids had felt the same that he'd let her die in pain.

I could understand why Charlie had been so aggressive to Karen and her family, this house was his last link to his wife, happy memories were all here. I asked Charlie if he was scared that she would be waiting for him on the other side. I already knew the answer but he confirmed it when he answered "yes" whilst looking at the floor and I knew then why he was still here. His sense of failing his wife was what was keeping him here. I needed to make him realise that this wasn't the case and that he needed to move on and allow Karen and her family to make their own happy memories here too. He looked up at me and asked me to apologise to Karen for his appalling behaviour.

"Of course I will, Mr Blunt."

"Please call me Charlie," he asked, I smiled at him and then from nowhere a bright light appeared. It was coming from everywhere and nowhere at the same time, I could hear a woman's voice calling "Charlie". He could hear it and so could Molly, I could tell by the look on her face.

"Can you hear her?" I asked Molly.

"Yes."

I looked back at Charlie and he was looking at me open mouthed. "That's my Mavis," he said.

"Go to her, Charlie."

"I'm scared, Gary."

"I know but you need to go, she needs you still." And then he was gone. I looked at Molly; she was stood there open mouthed as well.

"Close your mouth, Molly, it's not very ladylike." She blinked, closed her mouth and shot me the bird.

"What the fuck just happened?" she asked.

"Welcome to my world, sort of." We both smirked at each other and walked back downstairs.

"Did you find anything?" asked Karen. Molly and I looked at each other.

"I'll take that as a yes," Mitch said. I spent the next hour explaining to Karen what had happened making sure to pass on Charlie's apology, Karen was gobsmacked by what I had told her but I assured her that as far as the house was concerned her problem had been resolved.

I explained to Karen that our services were free, much to her surprise, to which I explained that the real ones never charge people money. All we needed was a review on our website, anonymous of course, I smiled, we all shook Karen's hand and left with that old sense of achievement and satisfaction, a job well done. A cliché maybe but there's no greater satisfaction of helping people with a gift you have somehow been given for free and using for the good of other people, FOR FREE.

I asked Molly and Mitch for a report as soon as possible as I wanted to find out what Molly had been able to capture with the camcorder and then add anything we had to the website, I had the bug back I wanted more successes and no more failures. They promised to have something ASAP, I asked Molly before she left how she felt after what had happened and with much blushing and embarrassment she said,

"Like I just had amazing sex." I winked at Mitch and it was his turn to shoot me the bird. We all hugged and went our separate ways. I was on a real buzz and couldn't wait to get home and tell Sue what had happened.

I let myself in and called Sue, she stepped out of

the kitchen with a serious look on her face, at first I thought something serious had happened, "Simon's here to see you, he has some news about your real mother." I took a deep breath and walked towards the kitchen, I needed to know what Simon had found out, I wanted to know what he had found out, it was a loose end that needed putting to bed, was I ready? Only one way to find out, Gary, and into the kitchen I went.

Simon was sat at the kitchen with a coffee waiting for me, we shook hands and I sat down.

Sue said, "I'll leave you to it."

"Don't go, I need you to hear this with me." Sue sat next to me and held my hand. I knew what he had to tell me was going to be heart wrenching but I needed to know the truth to help me understand what was going on in my life, somehow it was all linked but at the moment it was like an unfinished jigsaw puzzle with bits missing. I was hoping Simon had found the pieces, he didn't let me down.

Simon explained that he'd done some 'digging', as he called it, and had found some interesting coincidences from around the time I was born. Four children were born on the same day as me, three were boys and one was a girl.

"Well that narrows it down a little," I said.

"Well it was quite simple really," he said. He explained that the records had been easy to obtain from the hospital and having cross-referenced them with births, marriages and deaths; it had been easy to come up with a name. I was about to find out my real mother's name, my heart was pounding in my chest, I was scared and excited at the same time. Simon was sat there looking at me.

I said, "Come on then, it's not a fucking TV show, you don't need to pause for effect." Sue squeezed my hand and gave me that look. I apologised and waited for Simon to 'open the envelope' so to speak. When he told me her name I almost fell off the chair.

"Jenny Williams! Are you sure?"

"I'm positive, she was the only one whose baby died on the same day at the same hospital, I'm 100% sure she's your real mother." It was my turn to sit there with my mouth open. Jenny, my mum's friend for as long as I could remember was my real mum, I was gobsmacked. Simon stood up as he knew I needed time to process this, he left a folder with all the information on the table, shook our hands and left. Sue came back after letting Simon out, I just looked at her and kept saying Jenny's name over and over again. I was struggling to process what I had been told. Jenny had been Mum's best friend for years, and she was always at the house, visiting, babysitting, birthdays and Christmas.

I sat back down with Sue and said, "I need to talk this through with you, see if what I'm thinking makes sense and is pointing in the same direction for you as it is for me." We talked for over an hour, I explained all I could remember about Jenny as I was growing up. Thinking about it now she was always there, she didn't have any kids and wasn't married as far as I could remember, well I never saw or met a husband or a boyfriend come to think of it. Did she know I was really her son I kept thinking, I needed to ask her. I asked Sue if we had Jenny's number. It turned out that we didn't, we had gone through Mum every time. We needed to find a number for Jenny. So we got all Mum's stuff from the garage, thankfully she was old school and all her addresses and mobile numbers were in a book. I found Jenny's address and mobile number, we had a start. Sue rang the mobile number but it came back as no longer available. Fuck, bad start. I wanted to go to Jenny's home straightaway but Sue suggested first thing in the morning, it was late. As always Sue was my social handbrake, it made sense, and this was going to be a massive discussion between us with lots of questions from me.

Surprisingly I didn't get much sleep and was glad to get my arse out of bed; I was like a kid at Christmas. Sue told me to calm down as the boys would think something was going on. As always she was right, we agreed that I would go and visit Jenny on my own as this was going to be very personal and probably quite emotional, after all, it's not every day that you find out after 38 years that your mother is not your real mother. Whoever said that life gets easier as you get older needs to shut the fuck up. As I was driving to Jenny's the thought occurred to me that I had never been to her house, ever. It had always been at Mums or out and about. I pulled up outside the address and there was a 'To Let' sign in the garden. Something told me things were about to go tits up. I walked up to the front door and rang the doorbell, no answer, Again, fuck! I looked through the living room window and the room was empty, nothing, bare as a badger's ass. Fuck, fuck, fuck.

I called Sue and told her what I had found, I said I would call in on the estate agents who were letting it, they weren't too far away. None of this was making sense; it was feeling like a wild goose chase. Looking back I think I knew when I found the house empty I was wasting my time but at the time needs must and off I went to the estate agents. The guy I spoke to was really helpful, he explained that the landlord had been in touch a couple of days ago to put the house on the market, he was a bit perplexed as the previous tenant had been there for over ten years without any problems. She had called him out of the blue stating she needed to cancel her tenancy straightaway as she needed to move away due to a family issue. She'd paid the rent to cover the notice period and within 2 days she was gone, no forwarding address, nothing. The landlord was at a loss to explain what had gone on, the guy explained to me that this was the first time he had ever come across this from a landlord, it was usually the other way around when tenants left. I thanked the guy and took some contact details for the landlord, I didn't think there was anything else he would be able to tell me but just in case. I got back home and told Sue what had happened, neither of us could explain nor understand what was going on.

"This might explain where your ability to see ghosts came from," Sue stated. I'd never really thought about it, Jenny was always into the paranormal and I had told her about some of my experiences but she had never really given an opinion back but it never bothered me or made me wonder. Later that day I was sat in the kitchen on my own, Sue and the boys were out. Things were running through my mind and I was trying to make sense of it all without much success. In fact I was coming up with more questions than answers, like I needed more questions.

I thought about the only thing I had from Jenny, the wooden cross. I was wearing it around my neck as I was a nightmare for losing shit, putting it down and forgetting where I'd put it. I took it off and held it in my hand and I thought about Jenny and what she had said when she had given it to me. I could feel it getting hot in my hand and from nowhere Jenny appeared, no not in front of me or real, be serious. My eyes were still shut but she was there, as real as if they were open.

"Help me," I asked her.

"Not now, Gary, it's not time." Well I thought it was time, I had so many questions that only she could answer.

"When the time is right I will be there for you, but not until then, focus on the future." Well that helped, not. How the fuck was I supposed to focus on the future when my past had been blown out of the water?

"I need answers," I told her.

"All in good time, Gary." Not the answer I wanted or needed and then she was gone, the cross was cold and that was it. How the fuck had my life become so complicated in such a short space of time, another question with no answer, Fuck! I went for a walk and ended up at Sid's grave, there was a bench opposite that he had left in his will, they were all around the graveyard and to be honest up until then I didn't understand why people would want to sit in a graveyard, but it was a nice day and it was quiet, giving me time to think, well to try and think. I was miles away when I heard someone say, "Alright, lad?"

I nearly peed myself. Straightaway I knew it was Sid.

"Fuck, you nearly gave me a heart attack." He just sat there laughing, I composed myself, looked around to make sure no one was about, I apologised to Sid for swearing. He carried on laughing, typical Sid. I asked him what was so funny,

"Just the look on your face, lad, I didn't mean to frighten the crap out of you but it was funny."

"Yes, Sid, very funny ha ha. I thought I had to call you for you to turn up?"

"Usually, but as I'm always with you I thought you might need my help, under the circumstances." You're not wrong, I thought to myself.

"Ok, so you don't look like a crazy person talking to yourself I need you to listen and I will tell you all I know." Thank god for that the last thing I needed at the moment was to be reported as a crazy person in the cemetery talking to himself.

Sid explained that his sister Irene, the artist formally known as 'Mum', such a witty fucker me, had eventually told Sid everything after Frank had left. Sid threatened to confront Frank himself but they had agreed that it was best for me in the long term not to know the truth and he thought it would never come out. As far as he was concerned I was his nephew, simple as that. That reminded me why I loved Sid, he was a wonderful man.

"Don't get all soppy on me, lad," he told me. I asked about Jenny, what he knew about her, etc. He explained that Jenny and Irene had worked together at the hospital and had become good friends, Jenny had adored me and he put that down to her having no kids of her own. He'd asked her once why she didn't have kids of her own or wasn't married. She'd fobbed him off with some story about not wanting children and preferring her own company, which he could understand being a confirmed bachelor himself and never thought anymore of it.

"So you never knew she was really my mother then?" I asked him.

"I had no idea, never crossed my mind. She was never overbearing or possessive, yes she spoilt you but so did I."

"When did you know?" I asked.

"When I died, you'd be amazed what becomes clear, everything in a nutshell." Sid explained that he knew he had died, he was attached to his body for a short period and could see everything happening around him then he was at Hope Hall and everything was explained to him by Henry and things went from there. He then made his presence known at his funeral, as requested by Henry, and it has been a waiting game from there. I thought to myself, the twilight zone has fuck all on this. Sid carried on explaining that I can't know everything now as it would be impossible for me to understand at this time and would only complicate things. I needed to accept that everything would become clear eventually, I needed to trust him and go with it. If it had been anyone else but Sid I would have told them to fuck off but I trusted Sid. I asked about Sue and the boys, I was worried that they would be in danger in the future. He told me that each of them had a guardian protecting them but even so I still needed to be vigilant at all times. I noticed movement out of the corner of my eye, someone had entered the graveyard, and it was 'black eyes'.

"Who the fuck is he, Sid?" I asked.

"He's Henry's equivalent for the other side, he can't harm you, the same as Henry can't harm any of them."

"What does he want then, he gives me the creeps?"

"He likes to watch you but now he's seen me with you he'll know you know and you'll see less of him."

"Creepy fucker."

"If only you knew how creepy," Sid stated. I didn't want to know but at least Sid had solved the mystery of who he was.

"Ok, lad, time for me to go, if you need me, as always just call." And with that I was sat on the bench on my own again, even black eyes had buggered off, thankfully.

I made my way back home, Sue and the boys were home too so some family time was needed, we took them to the local park for a kick about with the football and some pizza on the way home, nothing like a bit of normality to bring me down, you really couldn't write this stuff, hang on a minute I am! Ah the old Gary is still there, thankfully.

The following day Molly and Mitch came over with their summary of the investigation at Karen Walters's house.

"Anything interesting?" I asked them.

"Have a look and see what you think," Mitch replied. He showed me a video clip from Karen's place of me talking to Charlie. What was interesting was you could hear me clearly talking to Charlie but his replies were like hundreds of voices together. Mitch explained that he'd tried to clean up the audio but the software did nothing to Charlie's voice. Also where he had been stood were orbs on the screen on the clear view that I had seen and sometimes there was interference on the picture.

I asked Molly what she had seen, she said that she'd seen nothing whilst I had been talking to him and could only hear very soft whispering that seemed to come from everywhere, oh, and that it was bloody freezing in the room. The only other thing she had seen was at the end, a flash of intense light and warmth but the flash hadn't been picked up on the camera.

"Is it on the website?" I asked.

"Not yet," Mitch replied. "We wanted to show you first."

"Put it up," I told him. "Don't wait for my approval." It wasn't what I expected but then again did I really expect to capture everything? It was something and hopefully it would spark people's interest in our 'services' and get our name out there.

The following week Mitch had arranged for another investigation, the son of an old lady had been in contact stating that he thought his mum's house was haunted. Mitch had agreed for us to call in for a chat first to see what was happening. Now I know what you're thinking, all the investigations on TV are much more in-depth and take much longer to investigate. Well that's because they are made for entertainment and need to last for a certain length of time. For us, even if we don't see anything we can usually tell if something is there, Mitch and I are like bloody magnets to spirits. I asked Mitch if he had any more information on the case. He explained that the stepson, Russ, had contacted him regarding his stepmom, claiming her house was haunted. Mitch explained that his father had passed away 6 months ago and he thought that it might be him.

We arrived at the house and were met at the door by Russ. Now I know it's not like me but I took an instant dislike to him, I couldn't explain why but as soon as I shook his hand it was like, "You're a wanker." We went through to the living room where stepmum, Gladys, was sitting, she looked terrified. Mitch and I looked at each other and frowned. Russ asked us if we wanted coffee, we both replied "yes" and I told Mitch to give him a hand, this would give me a chance to have a chat to Gladys.

I introduced myself to her and asked if it was ok to have a chat. I asked her if she was ok with us being there. Her answer was a little strange to say the least.

"I don't know where Alf's will or money is." Naturally I was confused with her reply and told her that wasn't the reason why we were there. I explained that Russ had told us the house was haunted and that we were paranormal investigators. It was her turn to look confused. She told me that Russ had said we were coming to find out where she had hidden Alf's money and new will. The original will had left everything to her and she didn't even know what Russ was on about. As far as she was concerned all the money they had had been in the bank and she didn't know anything about a different will.

Russ and Mitch came in with the coffees so I

asked Russ what he wanted from us and why he thought it was his dad haunting the house. Russ did his best to whip up some bullshit about Gladys being tormented at night by something, so I asked then why he thought it was his father. Russ claimed that his dad and Gladys had not been on speaking terms when he had died and that Alf had changed his will the week before he died.

"Ok," I said, "then why haven't you found it?" He claimed that Gladys was suffering from dementia and that she couldn't remember what she had done with the new will.

"That's why dad's kicking up a fuss," he stated. I asked if it would be ok to walk around the house. Russ was happy to allow it but he wanted to follow me, I tried to fob him off with the old, "It's better for the vibes if I'm alone" speech but he was having none of it, so I had no choice. He gave me the guided tour of the rest of the downstairs and we then headed upstairs. We got to the top of the stairs and out of the corner of my eye I saw some movement; I asked if we could go to the room where I thought the movement had gone into. With Russ leading we entered the room and a book came flying in our direction, Russ ducked and the book hit me just above my right eye. Not what I was expecting.

I thought I heard someone say "sorry" but I couldn't be sure as I was still shocked from what had happened. It had never happened before so it came as a big surprise. I asked whose room it was and he told me it had been his parents' room before his dad had died and that Gladys wouldn't use it as she had found him dead in the bed. We looked around the rest of the rooms without any further incidents but my focus kept coming back to that one room, as we passed it on the way back down I was sure I heard a male voice say "sorry" again.

We returned to the living room and I told Russ we would need to come back with some equipment and carry out a proper investigation, we shook hands with Gladys and left. We were stood in the garden explaining to Russ what would happen next and I glanced up at one of the bedroom windows and saw this man looking at us from around the curtains. I told Russ and Mitch that I had left my phone in the living room.

"I'll get it," Russ said.

"It's ok, I know where it is. Finalise the details with Mitch, I won't be a minute." Russ wasn't happy but he had no choice without making a fuss. I popped back in to the living room and told Gladys that I would be back to help her and Alf soon and I dashed back out. We said our goodbyes to Russ and left. I explained to Mitch about the book and told him we needed a plan that would allow me in that room on my own. I asked what had been agreed with Russ. Mitch stated that they had agreed to come back Saturday evening and carry out a full investigation. Russ told Mitch that he would make sure Gladys wouldn't be there, that worried me a little but it turned out for the best considering what happened.

So I decided we would all go this time, even Sue. She was a little unsure at first but once I had explained the details behind it she was up for it. Sue's mum had agreed to babysit for us and as always wasn't interested as to why. So Saturday came and with a plan in mind we set off for the next investigation. Mitch had phoned ahead and told Russ we would be there at 9pm and it came as no surprise to find him waiting for us. Sue took the part of being in charge, I had told her she was naturally bossy so would be great at it which was met with a swift punch to the shoulder. But it worked. Russ was like putty in her hands and whilst we pretended to set up equipment, which in fact were just cameras, Sue went through a whole made up schedule for the evening which allowed me, quicker than I thought, access to the bedroom where I'd been hit with the book. Mitch was with me with a camera and Molly was 'blocking' the stairs laying cables. We shut the door and straight away I called Alf, he appeared straight away smiling and apologising about the book. He told me it had been meant for Russ which didn't surprise me and made me chuckle. I asked Alf what was going on and he explained that Russ was an only child from a previous marriage who had failed in most things in life from work to two marriages. Alf had usually bailed him out but after Russ's second marriage had failed he had told him to "Man up and sort his life out".

Alf's first wife had left him for another man and Russ hadn't been happy when Alf had married Gladys and had basically ignored her ever since. None of that surprised me; it was typical second marriage troubles. So I asked Alf about the money and the will. He explained to me that there was no will apart from the one that had been executed and there was some money in a hidden safe behind some old books on a bookcase. I also asked if Gladys was suffering from dementia, again the answer was "no, it was a ploy by Russ to try and get her put into care etc so he could legally try and take control of the estate". *Little shit*, I thought.

"Ok, Alf, what do you want to do, how would you like this to go?" He explained that he wanted to teach Russ a lesson and make him understand that his behaviour was unacceptable. "Ok," I said. "Let's do it." My plan was to use the tried and trusted method and to get Russ into a conversation with Alf, using some information only Alf would know to convince him and then Alf wanted me to open the safe and give him the money inside.

So as planned we got Russ to come upstairs into the bedroom, Sue, Mitch and Molly all had cameras and I explained to Russ that whilst we had been setting up I had got in contact with his dad. I explained to Russ that his dad was here and he could speak to him through me and vice versa. Alf came and stood next to me. I could see Sue frowning at her camera but it was down to business. I asked Russ if there was anything he wanted to ask his dad, with a smirk on his face he asked how he could be sure his dad was really there. I told him that the book that was thrown the last time we were here was meant for him not me, Russ just scoffed at me. I then told him that there was no other will and that he knew there was no other will. That wiped the smile off his face and it was replaced with anger. I also told him that there was a safe in the room with money in it and that his dad had told me he could have it at the end. Russ just glared at me.

"This is bullshit, and how do I know you're telling the truth?" As I said earlier this was the tried and trusted method, I'd already asked Alf for something that only Russ and he would know about. This was a cracker to be honest, the best one yet. So I let Russ have it.

"Ok, Russ, you are 6 years old, it's your Christmas concert, only your dad is there as your mother was too busy with her fancy man. It comes to your part and you are so scared that you piss your pants."

"Do I need to go on?" I knew the answer, you always know, and all the anger and arrogance just falls away. Russ slumped onto the bed.

"I believe you, that's enough." I explained to Russ that his dad was very unhappy with the way he was treating Gladys and didn't he understand that everything would be left to him when Gladys went? I told him that Alf had left money in the safe for him, it was his, he would give me the combination to open it and what was in there was his but he needed to sort his act out now.

Russ was in tears, he knew his dad was there and that what he was saying was true. He made Russ give him his word that he would look after Gladys until she passed, which Russ did. I believed him too. He was still a little wanker but I believed him. So having got that all sorted I opened the safe with Alf's help and took out £2,000 and handed it to Russ. I asked Alf if there was anything else, He told me, "no". I asked if he wanted to say goodbye to Gladys but he asked me if he would see her again.

"I believe so but I can't be 100%."

"That's good enough for me," he said and with that he was gone. I looked at Molly and said "mouth". Again, I got the bird back. I looked at Sue and she was stood there with tears streaming down her face.

I'd forgotten this was really the first time she had seen this so I gave her a big hug and a kiss.

"Help the guys pack up the stuff, love." I grabbed Russ and took him to another room. I told him to look after Gladys the way she had looked after him. He knew what I meant and I told him I would be back to check up on him and finally that I knew she didn't have dementia. I couldn't be sure but I hoped Russ had got the message; I liked Alf he was old school, no nonsense and had worked hard for what he had, unlike his spoilt brat of a son.

So with another investigation done we parted company outside. Again I asked Mitch to upload anything we had to the website and to give me a summary of what we had, if anything, when they were ready. I got into the car and Sue got in the driver's seat.

"You are amazing, Gary," Sue told me.

"I know, love," I said with a cheeky grin.

"Wanker," she replied and drove us home.

Having got home we spent quite some time discussing what had happened at the house, naturally Sue had loads of questions and I tried my best to answer them all. I told her about my meeting with Sid at the cemetery and we giggled about how a year ago we had sat on the sofa watching this stuff on the TV trying to figure out if it was bullshit or not. The principle wasn't but the application was and I still maintained that all this was her fault; I prepared myself for another punch but it never came, a hug, a kiss and some lovemaking was a far better option.

CHAPTER 11

My Sunday morning lie-in was shattered by the phone ringing, it was Mitch, he'd put some video on the website first thing this morning and already he had had a call from a famous pub called the 'Hilltop Arms'. It had featured in a TV show on the paranormal and was a favourite on the ghost hunting circuit. Mitch explained that the landlord, Matthew Windsor, had called him 15 minutes ago and asked if we would like to help host a 'Ghost Hunting Night'. He'd told Mitch that he liked to do this for up and coming investigating teams and that he could promise us good publicity from the night. *Wow*, I thought, *this could be interesting.*

I told Mitch I would get sorted and we would come to the flat, make some plans. I explained to Sue what the call was about and that we needed to go to Mitch and Molly's. So having showered, had breakfast and called Sue's mum to say we would pick the boys up on the way home we set off. It was the first time we had been to the flat since they had moved in, it looked great. You could see the woman's touch that Molly had brought to it and it really looked great. So down to business, I asked Mitch to show me what we had captured last night. The footage was really good; it showed Alf in a kind of see through silhouette but no real detail which was a pity. Unfortunately my expectation was exceeding what we were getting but in reality it was much better than most of the crap that was being peddled on the internet. The audio was still the same though which still perplexed me. I asked Mitch what he thought and if he had any ideas in terms of capturing better audio. Mitch explained that at the time he could hear Alf the same as normal but having checked with Molly she could only hear what was on the camera audio. But having heard it for the second time she now knew what was happening, along with me having a full blown conversation that is. We decided the next time we would try the mini recorders, up until then we had used just the cameras which had given us all we needed, but Mitch thought it would be worth a try. Sue was off with Molly being given a guided tour of what had been done in the flat so I asked Mitch what he thought about the 'invite'. He explained that he had done some research on the place and it was very popular for ghost hunting events.

"What about when the TV show filmed there?" I asked.

"Interesting one that," Mitch stated. He explained that the TV show had covered the usual but nothing showstopping. There were rumours that the place was not all it seemed and some people believed that some of the things that happened were set up by the landlord. Before the TV show went there the brewery wanted to close it down as it was making a loss but being a listed building meant they would struggle to do much else with it. However, business was booming now with events most weekends. I liked the sound of this place, a chance to prove or disprove all the hype, right up my street. I told Mitch to call him back and make the relevant arrangements; I was looking forward to this.

After a couple of minutes Mitch was back, "You're gonna like this," he said. "In 2 weeks' time there is a paranormal weekend there. Us and 2 other teams have been invited. Each of us will get to spend the night there and there is a prize for the best investigation but it will cost us £100 to attend! Normally at this point I would have said, "tell him to go fuck himself" but there was something about it that had pricked my interest.

So I told Mitch, "Ok, let's go for it." I think Mitch was surprised by my answer as well because he asked if I was sure. I was. I had a good feeling about this one. We left Mitch's and went to Sue's parents to pick up the boys which turned into Sunday lunch, I wasn't complaining as I love a roast dinner and Liz made a cracking Sunday dinner. Sue's brother, Chris, was there with his wife and their 3 kids. I liked Chris and we had a good old chat about what was going on, Chris had a healthy interest in the paranormal as well which wasn't surprising considering his own experiences.

*

By late afternoon I was ready to go so we said our goodbyes and headed for home, the boys were sleeping 5 minutes after leaving. At 9 and 11 they still looked cute when they were asleep but I was also aware that as they were getting older they would notice more which would lead to lots of difficult questions.

It was the middle of the week and I decided we needed a new car sooner rather than later, we had talked about it but never made up our minds. The old one had been playing up so I said to Sue that we would have a look at the weekend for a new one, we had the money so why not. Sue had a friend at work whose husband worked in a dealership, she'd suggested we pay him a visit on Saturday and she would let him know her 'good friend' from work would call in.

Saturday came and we all headed off to Hills Motor Company which was only 10 minutes' drive. We parked up and had a wander around to look at what they had, after 5 minutes one of the salesmen came out and introduced himself as Nathan, this was the husband of Sue's friend. He was a nice guy to be honest, not too pushy and very informative regarding the model range they stocked. After about an hour the deal was signed on a brand new family SUV. Sue and the kids loved it and to be honest so did I, I'd never owned a new car so this was a first for me and it was great. We'd agreed a delivery date which would be in 2 weeks' time, it was going to be a long 2 weeks, and I was like a kid waiting for Christmas. Before leaving Nathan asked if he could have a quiet word with me, naturally I said ok so Sue and the boys went to wait in the car for me. Nathan was looking a little embarrassed so I asked what was up. He explained that his wife had told him about me and my paranormal team, so he'd had a look at our website whilst waiting for us to turn up. He explained that the company has a second hand car that customers kept bringing back due to various electrical problems but they were never able to find anything wrong with it, The last customer had brought it back claiming it was haunted. Not wanting negative publicity his boss had agreed to take the car back but as it had been Nathan's sale the boss had told him he needed to get rid of it. So as a last resort he was asking me if I could 'check it out'. Nothing like being put on the bloody spot.

I told Nathan I would take it for a drive and see if I could find anything. I was the one feeling embarrassed now but I thought taking it for a drive can't do any harm. So he brought me the keys and off I went, I'd explained to Sue what was happening so she wouldn't wonder what I was up to. I'd only been driving a couple of minutes when I noticed a small boy sat in one of the back seats, I jumped a mile when I noticed him and managed not to run into the car in front that had stopped at a set of traffic lights. I tried not to make it obvious that I had seen him but as usual it was too late. I looked in the rear view mirror and he was sat there smiling at me, so I said "hello". He carried on smiling and said "hello" back. I decided to find somewhere to stop, luckily there was a small car park just up ahead so I pulled in. I parked up, turned off the engine, turned around and asked him his name.

"I'm Sean," he replied.

"Nice to meet you, Sean, my name is Gary." He smiled back at me so I continued to ask him a number of questions, it was the first time I'd experienced anything like this in a car. He explained to me that he was 6 years old and this was his mum's car, he'd died of cancer and this was the car he used to travel in when they went for treatment. I asked him if he knew he was dead, he did. So I asked why he was still attached to the car, he explained that when they were travelling back and forth the hospital his mum would sing his favourite songs to him every time, which he loved. Even when the treatment had been bad and he'd been feeling really bad the trip home always made him feel better. He carried on telling me that when he had died he'd been glad in a way because the pain was unbearable at the end and his mum just cried and cried, so his mum had sold the car soon after he passed. He'd loved the times in the car that's why he didn't want to leave but he didn't want anyone else to have it either, plus he was scared. I explained to Sean that he needed to leave the car and move on; hard to explain to an adult never mind a 6 year-old but I needed to convince him. I asked him if he had seen the light, which he had. I told him to think about it and to concentrate. After a minute or two he told me he could see it, I told him he needed to go towards it but he wasn't convinced.

I told him he needed to trust me like he trusted his mum and that everything would be ok, he looked at me and smiled and inside the car brightened for a split second and he was gone. That warm fuzzy feeling came over me and I knew he was where he was supposed to be, I was well pleased. I drove back to the car dealers with a big smile on my face and was met on the forecourt by a nervous looking Nathan. I got out of the car and chucked to the keys to him.

"You'll have no problems selling it now," I told him. "Don't ask," I said as his mouth opened and I walked back to the car. "Let's go home, love," I told Sue.

After we got home and the boys disappeared upstairs I told Sue about what had happened in the car, it had both of us sat there with tears streaming down our faces but I knew he was in a happier place and that was all that mattered. Having this gift had its pluses sometimes and today was one of them but I knew there were still some testing times ahead. Then came the question I had been waiting for since I had made sense of what was going on, well since what happened to Irene. Sue asked if she and the boys were in any danger from all of this, understandable considering some of the things that had happened, good job she didn't know all of it. I wanted to tell her everything but I knew it would make her worry more, but she needed to understand. I went and checked on the boys, they were occupied with a game on their PS4, and they didn't even notice me sticking my head around the door. So I went back downstairs, got us both a drink and we sat down and I tried to explain to Sue as best as I could. I told her that even though finding out that Irene wasn't my real mum and Jenny was had been a massive shock, it explained why I had this gift; it had obviously come from Jenny.

Which posed the question did one of the boys have this gift too? By their ages I had already had some paranormal experiences but how do you go about bringing up the subject with kids that age? I also knew that we couldn't keep the paranormal stuff hidden from them much longer, especially with the website becoming more and more popular; we lived in a small town so I knew word would get out soon. Sue agreed, she had been thinking the same thing and she thought the sooner the better. The boys didn't have their own mobiles and the internet had parental controls on it, after all we are responsible parents, well Sue is!

I also explained that what was going on was sort of a battle between good and evil for souls or spirits that hadn't moved on. I tried to explain it the way Henry had explained it to me; if it made sense to me then I knew Sue would get it and she did. I told her the boys had a guardian called Gwyn who would ensure no harm came to them. I think it reassured her but mums are mums as they say, they are the protectors of their children no matter what. I think what happened with the little boy in the car helped, it showed her that it wasn't always about what had happened to Irene and my logic was that children were for the most part good, it seemed to be as we got older that people became bad. Now I know there are some people who think we are either born good or bad, kind of like our destiny but I wasn't so sure, I believe our lives are shaped by our experiences and the influences around us. Difficult to say, whether some people born to be rapists or serial killers! I'm no expert on this but I didn't want to believe it, I believe we had our own paths in life and made our own choices, some good some bad but one thing was for sure I was determined that mine was going to be good. We finished the conversation on that subject and I think Sue was ok with it all, well as ok as she was going to be under the circumstances. So the rest of the evening was spent watching a movie on TV with the boys and then bed, it had turned out to have been another eventful day.

We had arranged to meet Simon, Molly and Mitch for lunch at a local restaurant; it had a play area for kids so the boys were occupied whilst we chatted about the up and coming trip to the Hilltop Arms. I'd asked Simon to do a bit of digging around, find out who Matthew Windsor was and his background. Simon explained that Matthew had a connection to a guy called Charles Boyd, the name rang a bell. Simon told us that Charles was a 'TV Medium' who had his own show, a very popular one in fact, and he also owned the company that arranged ghost hunting weekends. It seemed that a couple of years ago Matthew Windsor had been caught up in a local news story in a small village called Stonebridge. He had been part of a paranormal investigation team that claimed the local pub was haunted, in fact it turned out that the pub had been run by his brother-in-law and was close to closing down. This was starting to sound familiar. The pub was then included in a paranormal TV show and became very popular, that is until it was debunked by a guy called Richard Brown who believed the paranormal was hogwash, a load of rubbish and had made it his life's crusade to go around debunking haunted houses, pubs etc and it appeared he was quite successful at it having also written a book about it and appeared on some TV shows exposing people. But after some success he was now avoided like the plague and his name/appearance was well-known in the paranormal world. At the time neither Matthew Windsor nor Charles Boyd were linked to the pub and the brother-in-law took the blame for it all, losing the pub soon after. I asked Simon if he thought Charles and

Matthew were involved again and if the Hilltop Arms was another scam.

"Only one way to find out, Gaz," was his reply. I hated being called fucking Gaz and he knew it, wanker.

Mitch had found some stuff online that was posted on the website of the company that organised the ghost hunting events. There were some EVPs that were actually quite clear and were easy to understand but following the usual script, "Get out... I can see you... Am I dead?" You could find these on any site that had EVPs on them, nothing unusual. Then there were some video clips, most were of orbs but there was one that showed a very blurry image of an old man sitting in a chair next to the fireplace in the main bar. It looked very interesting, the clip was only short but you could clearly see the figure come into shot and sit down in the chair. There was another clip of the glasses that were hung above the bar moving and rattling, again the clip was short and the quality wasn't the best but I asked Mitch to make sure we focused on both these areas when we went. I also asked Mitch what the prize was if we 'won'. He said the winners got to go on Charles Boyd's TV show called, *Paranormal Uncovered*, an all-expenses paid trip where you got to show your findings. There were usually 2 event winners per show and as the show was on for 30 minutes, each got a 15 minute slot with Charles but it wasn't put out live. I was a little disappointed by that but we did have to win first, after all, so maybe I was getting ahead of myself.

I asked Simon what he knew about Charles Boyd. Simon told us that Charles had been a medium for a number of years, making his name in Leeds but had then jumped on the paranormal bandwagon and had appeared on a number of TV shows, hosted popular clairvoyance shows around the country, with mixed reviews and then finally he had got his own show after becoming popular from doing celebrity 'readings'. He was a very well-known as a medium and claimed to be Clairvoyant, Clairaudient and Clairsentient! What the fuck did all that mean, I thought to myself?

"Let me guess, he has his own website," I said.

"Spot on," was Simon's reply. I made a mental note to have a look the first chance that I got, that was too many Clairs for my liking.

"What about Richard Brown?" was my next question to Simon.

"He's an interesting character. He used to be a detective in the Met in London and on the last case he worked on they brought in a medium to help as they had basically reached a dead-end in the investigation. It turned out to be a PR disaster and ended his career, a promising one at that. At the time there had been talk of him being a future commissioner but this one case made him a laughing stock and he quit soon after. Two years later he appears as a private investigator and soon becomes known for 'exposing mediums, paranormal investigators and anybody else claiming to be in touch with the dead' and especially those who claimed to have helped the police solve crimes. He seemed to be on a one man crusade and still is. It seems he's been after Mr Boyd for some time and anyone who appears on his show." Seems like our paths were going to cross at some stage. I asked Simon if he had any more for us.

"Not for now, Gaz." He was an excellent source of information but man he made my teeth itch. Thankfully he had to go so I walked him to the door, thanked him for his support and the information, I also asked him to stop calling me Gaz. His response came as no surprise which was, "Sure no problem, Gazza." He really was a dick, helpful, but still a dick.

I went back to the kitchen and told the others that Simon annoyed me. Molly's reply was,

"Why's that, Gaz?" I glared at her and she smiled back, payback was served, good job I liked her. So we agreed on a plan of attack for our visit to Hilltop Arms, what equipment we would take and who would be doing what. I was looking forward to this; we had plenty of background information and I was confident we would be able to win and get on Charles's show. If I'm honest, having heard about him I really wanted to meet him and find out if what my gut was saying about him was true. It was going to be a long two weeks until the event came around but I was excited all the same.

That night I was helping Charlie with a project that he needed to complete for school, it was fairly straightforward to be honest so I was a little surprised he had asked for my help. Charlie was quite independent for his age and seldom asked for help, in fact it was usually the other way around, especially when it came to technology around the house, and he was a whizz with all that stuff. Then out of the blue he asks, "Do you believe in ghosts, Dad?"

I almost fell off my bloody chair. What could I say; we never lied to the boys.

So I asked, "Why's that Charlie?"

"I think I've seen one," was his whispered reply.

I was shocked, even though I had discussed it with Sue the day before it still came as a surprise. My money would have been on Billy, maybe it would still be but still Charlie had surprised me. He explained that when we'd been at the garage on Saturday he'd seen a small boy sat in the back of the car that I had taken for a drive. I asked why he thought the boy was a ghost; it seemed a sensible response at the time, looking back it was a really stupid one considering my own experiences. So he explained that the boy had disappeared as soon as I had walked towards the car and still wasn't there when I drove off.

Naturally this put me in a difficult situation but I had no intention of lying to him so I called Sue up and got Charlie to tell her what he had told me. She didn't seem surprised which did surprise me but she looked at me and nodded so I took that as permission to explain to Charlie kind of what was going on. I told him that the little boy was a ghost, I explained they best way I could and also explained that I could also see ghosts and that my mum could as well. I wasn't going to explain there and then that I wasn't on about Nanny Irene, all in good time for that. He seemed to take it all in his stride and told us of a few incidents that we were unaware of but he seemed ok with it all thankfully. I did get him to promise that he would tell us of anything else that happened. I did ask him if Billy had told him anything but he hadn't, they were very close so I knew if Billy had seen anything his brother would have been the first person he would have told.

With the kids asleep it gave me and Sue time to talk a little more, I told her that Charlie had surprised me with his news but I was glad he had told us. From my own experiences as a child I understood how difficult it was to have this gift and not being able to share it with anyone. Sue went up to get ready for bed and I sat there contemplating how things had changed since our visit to Hope Hall, so much had happened it was hard to take it all in, having lost Sid and Irene and then finding out about Jenny. It was still hard to think of her as my mum, having all these unanswered questions in my mind and not being able to ask her. I was concerned that she had seemed to have disappeared off the face of the earth but I was still hopeful that Simon would track her down somehow. I had the feeling that she knew I was her son, don't ask me why or how, but thinking back to how she was with me growing up it made me think. Naturally at the time I didn't give it a thought, she was Irene's friend, a family friend and that was it but she was so kind, caring and loving with me even when I was a little shit when she looked after me, I could do nothing wrong but as a kid it doesn't register, Irene was my mum as far as I was concerned.

I went to bed that night and slept pretty well and the start of another week, the boys were up and ready for school by the time I'd showered and got downstairs. Sue left for work and the boys for school soon after. Having booked the day off work I decided to try and get some stuff done around the house, the wall outside certainly needed painting, the weather was good and I knew I had some paint in the garage so that was my plan. I had been painting for a while and was listening to some music on my iPod when I sensed someone stood by me, it was my neighbour John. I took out my headphones and said "hello".

John and his wife Jean had lived next door for years, certainly for as long as I'd lived here. They were retired and really nice, always said hello, took parcels, card at Christmas etc. They were never any trouble and were really nice to have as neighbours. John asked if I fancied a coffee which was a little bit of a surprise as I'd only ever been in their house to collect parcels and that was it. I fancied a break so I accepted and followed him into their kitchen. John made small talk but I could tell something was on his mind so I waited for him to come and sit down with the coffee and I asked if everything was ok.

I could tell that whatever John had to say was difficult so I didn't pressure him, He explained that his wife Jean had the early stages of dementia and was starting to struggle with her memory so their kids had bought her one of these Amazon Alexas to help with things. I'd seen some clips on social media of people swearing at them and that kind of stuff but my knowledge of them was limited. John told me that at first it had been wonderful, Jean was able to use it for all kinds of things and she loved it, then the kids had bought some bulbs that worked with it, they had fitted one in the utility room as the light switch was on the other side so they would be able to turn the light on before they entered the room. Again this had been a great help as they had both tripped over stuff in the dark a couple of times. I was wondering where this was going and tried to be patient, Then John explained that the light had started coming on on its own and that Alexa seemed to be acknowledging someone's request and it would also randomly speak out, again, as if it was being asked something. This started to worry them both and Jean was becoming reluctant to use it, which obviously defeated the object. I told John that he was asking the wrong man as I knew nothing about them and in fact I was a bit of a technophobe.

"Do you think we could be haunted?" was John's next comment. I just looked at him as first. I wasn't sure if he knew about what I was doing with regards to the paranormal but it turned out that he had seen the website so he was well aware. I asked him why he thought his house was haunted, so he explained that they had never seen anything but they had heard noises, things would go missing and such. I asked if there was any particular room or spot that these things occurred. His answer surprised me as it was in the same place in the hall way that I had experienced mine and that was where Alexa was positioned. I asked if I could have a look so we both walked into the hall, I couldn't see anything so I just looked around. Even though both our houses had been built the same over the years they had had different alterations, so where I had a downstairs bathroom and a door out to the back garden they had a conservatory. There wasn't a lot I could say, I couldn't see anything or feel anything so we went back to the kitchen to finish our coffees. I told John that I would ask my friend Mitch about it as I had no idea if it could be interference or something like this and I would get back to him. In the meantime my only suggestion was to maybe turn it off. We finished our coffees and I thanked John and promised that I would get back to him as soon as I could.

I finished painting the outside of the garden wall and packed away as I was keen to talk to Mitch about this. I got cleaned up and changed and gave Mitch a call, I told him about the conversation I had with my neighbour and that I'd seen nothing in the house. Mitch told me that he'd done some research on these type of devices and it appeared that there were a number of occurrences reported by other paranormal investigators regarding this, ranging from low level stuff to full blown takeovers where owners were forced to remove them from their houses. Mitch explained that in one case a guy was using them to control almost everything in his flat and would come home to the heating on full, lights on, music playing it was a nightmare. He would be sleeping at night and all of a sudden music would be blasting out around the house or they would be reacting to unheard questions and requests. In the end he had to get rid of them all but strangely after removing them all paranormal activity stopped. That was weird, I thought, but it made me think if John and Jean were having the same problems. I asked Mitch what he thought about this type of event and why had the activity stopped and not manifested itself in a different way. He believed that the entity was attracted not just to the energy but also to the way they had been able to control it as such but it was their only way to make themselves know and when the devices had been removed it had also taken away their ability to interact so had probably moved on.

I was really surprised by all of this, I'd never seen one of the devices let alone come across one being used as a tool by a spirit but it was certainly an interesting concept. I decided to visit John later but would wait for Jean to be there also. I had a feeling that it was more to do with her than John. Plus I wanted to talk to Sue about it too after all this really was on our doorstep and it was one thing having our neighbours know that we were paranormal investigators but it was another thing them knowing that I could see and speak to spirits.

I gave Sue a call at work and explained what had happened. She said, "I can't leave you on your own for 5 minutes, can I?" which did make me giggle. I explained it wasn't my fault I'd been painting outside and he'd come to me. I knew she was just poking fun at me so I asked if she would come with me after work to visit them. Of course she said "yes" so I popped around and asked John if it was ok for us to come over around 6pm so we could talk to both of them, he agreed so we went from there.

Having asked Molly to come and look after the boys we made our way to next door, John answered the door and invited us in. Straight away I noticed a difference in the house it was like the air was charged with static; the hairs on my arms and the back of my neck were on end. Jean was sat in the living room so we sat down and I asked Jean how she was, she smiled and said she was good. I asked about the Alexa and she said that it was like someone was asking the questions she was about to ask. It was strange, like someone was second guessing her and it would play old songs that she loved without being asked. I asked why she thought the house was haunted.

She looked at John who nodded to her. "I think it's my sister, please don't think I'm mad."

I smiled, "Far from it, Jean." She told us that her

sister had passed away a month ago from a heart attack, they had been very close but she had moved to Australia 30 years ago and hadn't seen each other for 10 years. They had promised each other that if there was a way to come back and say goodbye they would. All of a sudden the device started talking but I didn't catch what it said, then it started playing the song, *Down Under* by 'Men at Work' which made us all look at each other. I stood up and walked into the hall but couldn't see anyone. I heard a cough from behind me, I turned around and there was an old lady sat in the conservatory.

As always her first words were, "You can see me?"

"I can indeed, what's your name?"

She told me her name was Grace and that she was Jean's sister, she confirmed everything that Jean had told me, I asked her if she wanted to say goodbye to Jean, obviously she did so I told her I would get Jean. I walked back to the living room asking the device to stop as I passed. I explained to Jean that her sister was here; she smiled and said to John,

"I knew it." I told her that she wanted to say goodbye so Jean got up and we went to the conservatory. I explained to Jean where Grace was sat and Jean sat next to her. Jean's eyes went wide.

"Can you sense her?" I asked. Sometimes it happened, it was like a tingling on the skin and I could tell Jean was feeling it. I explained to Jean that Grace wanted to say goodbye and to thank you for being not only her sister but also her best friend. Jean started to cry. It was always very emotional and I always had a lump in my throat. Jean expressed the same and then Grace was gone. Even though Jean asked if she was gone she already knew, the sensation had gone. I helped Jean up and we walked back into the living room, she looked at Sue and said, "Your husband is an incredible man. Thank you both." Jean hugged us both and John shook my hand. I told them it had been my pleasure to have helped them, it always was.

Now I know what you're thinking, same routine as before, same explanation etc but think about it, how else would you try to get someone's attention when they can't see you? How do you let them know you're there without terrifying them? Put yourself in Grace's position for a moment and mine if you can. How else do you think it would pan out if you had the same gift, how do you think it would go? Remember they are there to say goodbye, that's why they are still there. It's like letting go of a helium balloon when they say goodbye, the act allows them to move on as they should and hopefully gives the living a little closure and as far as I'm concerned a darn sight better than charging someone £10 to make them think they are communicating to a loved one. Take a moment to let that sink in, I don't charge a penny for what I do and never would.

We sat in our house and Sue was just staring at me. "What?"

"You really are amazing, Gary."

"Stop it, love, you'll have me blushing." I think getting Sue involved was a good move, she felt more connected to what I was doing and understood more and more, plus it helped her keep my feet on the ground and it was changing me as a person. I seemed to gain strength each time I went through this with people and when I saw that look on their faces that told me they sensed their loved one it was amazing. Tell me how many times you've seen that at a medium show?

We explained to Molly what had happened after the boys had gone to bed and I asked her to write it up for the website, I was intrigued by the use of the device and wanted Mitch to explore this more. Maybe it was something we could use going forward for other investigations.

The thought had crossed my mind a couple of times over the past couple of months about the good/bad explanation Henry had given me. I understood the concept but I didn't understand why we weren't seeing the black mass at every occasion and, if you like, fighting for the spirit that was there at the time. I know some were still here for a reason, to say goodbye for example, or to try and relay a message to loved one but I wouldn't know who was good or bad at the time.

I was struggling to get my head around it, yes potentially all could be saved for the good because even the worst have some good in them I guess and likewise we as humans all have the ability to be bad, I just didn't understand how it was decided. Did they have a choice at the end? Was it about how good or bad they had been in life that decided? I didn't know. It was like having a hamster in a wheel in my head going round and around without an end in sight. My hamster was getting bloody tired I can tell you, the answers were out there somewhere but I just wasn't sure. My thoughts kept coming back to Irene, ok what she did when I was born was shocking and hard to forgive but she was a good mum to me growing up. Yes there were times when I wondered if she really loved me, especially with the issue around Sid's estate, that really did shock me. Of course if I had known then what I know now then that would have explained everything but at the time I couldn't understand the reaction from her.

So I wondered if it was a case of if you had done something horrible, evil, nasty, call it what you like, did it leave a stain on your soul or spirit? I really wasn't sure but it kind of made sense. Was it like a signal of sorts to the black mass or was it something you could erase over time by doing something good? I was coming up with more questions than answers; maybe I should get one of those devices and ask them, now that might be interesting. I spoke to Sue about my concerns before bed, I knew she didn't have the answers but if I couldn't get the 'hamster off his wheel' so to speak then it was going to be a long night. Thankfully getting it off my chest seemed to do the trick; I had a pretty good sleep and felt quite refreshed the following morning.

Mitch called later that day and asked if I fancied going out for a meal, all four of us. Before I could answer he told me it was already booked at the Hilltop Arms, he explained that Molly had suggested a 'reccy' of the place before investigating it. I wasn't sure to be honest as I didn't want any pre-conceived ideas of the place but Mitch explained that he thought it would help the investigation and if something was there we would know beforehand and be prepared. Mitch had won his argument and I agreed, it was booked for the Friday night. So with that agreed I text Sue and told her the plan for Friday night, she had similar reservations but I convinced her like I'd been convinced by Mitch, plus I'd told Mitch he had to pay as it was his idea. I knew Sue's parents would be happy to have the boys as Sue had already explained to them about our investigating and they'd told her they were happy to have them anytime.

CHAPTER 12

Friday came around quite quickly and it was time to drop off the boys at Sue's parents. Charlie was still upstairs so I went up to see what he was up to.

"You ready Charlie?" I asked.

"Dad, are you going out to find ghosts?" That took me back a little.

"Yes, son," I told him. I didn't want to start lying to him about this; I wanted him to feel that it was a subject he could talk openly to me about. But it turned out he was just being curious as to where we were going. So we dropped the boys off and picked up Molly and Mitch, then made our way to the Hilltop Arms. I'd never been there before so it was going to be something new to me; it was in quite a rural location and looked quite old. Mitch explained that it had been there for over 400 years and had started life as a coaching inn and had pretty much stayed an inn for most of its existence. I asked Mitch not to tell me about any of the alleged paranormal activity, I knew he had researched the place well so would have all the information on the place but I wanted a clear head going in and to see what happened.

We were taken to our reserved table by a young waiter called Robin, we ordered some drinks with him and he left promising to come back in a while to take our order. The position of the table was perfect; it was in one corner with a good view of most of the restaurant area. There was a bar next door where we planned to have a drink after the meal. I made sure I was sat with my back to the wall so I had a good view. Robin was back with our drinks and he took our order from what was a very good menu. The place was very busy and it was easy to see why it was popular, as I said the menu looked good and it was cosy and not too cramped which allowed you to have a conversation with each other and not be sharing it with everybody - which was helpful considering the reason we were there, the last thing we needed was an audience. I asked Mitch if he was picking up anything.

"Only the smell of good food," he answered. I explained that things seemed pretty quiet so far which was kind of a disappointment but it was early days yet. The food came and I have to say it was fantastic, I'd ordered veal and it was stunning, enough to leave you full but not too much that you had to waste any and Mitch was happy that no one wanted dessert. We were discussing how good each other's food was when I noticed an old man appear from nowhere, he walked to a spot near the open fire, went to sit down and disappeared - which was lucky as there was no chair there. I explained to the others what I'd seen and Mitch confirmed that he was a residual haunting. For those of you that are unsure what that means allow me to explain without the use of Google. This type of haunting is more like a playback of an event that has been captured in the fabric of the building, a bit like a video recording, that's pre-DVD for you younger ones.

Light is energy and sometimes that energy gets stored and releases that energy a bit at a time, hence the poor quality if you like and over time it usually gets worse until it just stops. The old man I had just seen certainly fell into that category as he was completely unaware of his surroundings and there was no interaction with the current environment at all. Molly jotted down the details and we carried on chatting. Robin arrived to collect our plates and Mitch asked for the bill which Robin supplied straightaway. I could tell by the look on Mitch's face that it was a bit steep; I asked him if he'd forgotten his wallet? I told him to put it on expenses, after all we were kind of working. With a nervous and embarrassed look on his face he declined and stated it was his treat. I asked Molly if he was always this nervous spending money. She replied that she didn't know as this was the first time she had seen his wallet which had us all in stitches, apart from Mitch, of course. We moved to the bar where I bought the drinks, giving Mitch a little wink in the process, which had us all giggling again at his expense. The bar was much quieter and with only one member of staff it gave us a chance to have a little nose about. There were a number of old photos on the wall of the inn and what I guessed were former owners or landlords. Sue and Molly went to the toilet together as women do, never understood that and was not going to ask. Myself and Mitch carried on looking at the photos and pictures that were on display. As we made our way around I noticed a woman walk in behind the bar, the guy there was completely unaware of her. I thought to myself that she looked familiar, which she did as I'd just been looking at her picture. Her name was Shelia Francis, a former landlady from 1972, according to the picture. Again it looked like a residual haunting as she appeared to be going about her job behind the bar and it looked as if the area hadn't changed much as she seemed to interact with what was there but nothing was moving. I watched her walk through the barman and saw him shiver, which made me smile. Mitch frowned at me and I explained what had happened.

"If only he knew what had made him shiver," I said.

Sue and Molly came back looking a little nervous, I asked what was up. Sue explained that they had been in the toilet when the main door had opened and they had heard footsteps coming in but when they had come out of the cubicles there was no one in there.

"Could they have been leaving?" I asked.

"No, we were in the only 2 cubicles that were there and it was definitely empty when we went in, plus it was freezing when we left."

"I didn't like it one bit," stated Molly.

"That's one for the investigation then," I replied. I explained to them about the landlady I had seen and showed them her picture on the wall. Just then someone behind us said, "She's still here some people say." We looked around and there was a man in his mid-40s I guess stood behind us. He introduced himself as Matthew Windsor, so we all introduced ourselves and he asked if we had enjoyed our food, which surprised me a little as I hadn't noticed him whilst we were eating so I just assumed that he had assumed we'd eaten. We all replied that we did and off he went, thankfully. He seemed quite pleasant and my first impression of him was he seemed like a nice guy. We chatted for about another hour and agreed it was time to leave. I went to the toilet before we left, they were right next to the ladies so I was interested to see if I would have anything happen. I was disappointed, my pee was uneventful and we walked back to the car. I was looking in my rear view mirror as I reversed out of my parking space and noticed a young woman stood in the doorway waving. I'm not sure if she was waving at us but I have to say it did give me a little chill for some reason. Once we had got going I explained what I had seen, allowing Molly to add it to her list from our visit.

"I think next week will be quite interesting," I said, which brought nervous laughter from the others. We chatted on the way home about how we would go about things on the investigation. I explained that we would need maybe a little more equipment to convince Matthew we were your usual paranormal investigators otherwise he might think we are not for real. I wasn't going to explain to him that we didn't need it and that me and Mitch could manage quite well on our own with just a camera. So Molly agreed to order some other bits and pieces ready for next week. We dropped off Mitch and Molly and went to Sue's parents for a drink and a chat before heading home.

Liz, Tim and Emily were watching TV when we arrived but were eager to find out what had gone on at the inn. They were aware of what had happened with Irene and Jenny and had been super supportive as always. I had told Sue on a number of occasions how lucky she was to have parents like hers but she already knew that, her relationship with them had always been good and so had mine. So we spent an hour chatting about what had gone on at the Hilltop Arms, with lots of questions that to be honest I couldn't really answer but they were like sponges for information especially given what they had gone through in their own home.

It was time to leave and as the boys were sleeping Tim had said he would drop them off in the morning. So we got home and opened a bottle of wine and chatted some more before heading to bed for another good night's sleep, I was getting to like this good sleeping.

Having got up a little later than usual thanks to the bottle of wine, which was nice, the boys arrived home and the peace and quiet was shattered. The boys were in a lively mood so we agreed a day out was needed and I asked the boys where they wanted to go. Surprisingly they asked to go to some Roman ruins that we had about 15 minutes' drive away, they had both been learning about the Romans in school and had been told by their teachers about the ruins. So it was agreed, much to the disgust of Sue, she was never one for history, but family time was important to her so off we went. It turned out to be quite interesting, I'd never been there before but it was quite good and the boys were battling to see who could impress us with the best knowledge of the Romans and this made it even more entertaining. Even Sue seemed to enjoy the trip until I suggested a trip to Stonehenge at some later date, which the boys thought was epic. The statement, "Well you can all go without me" seemed to let us know that it wasn't the best suggestion we had come up with.

"Don't worry, love, I'll book you a spa day instead," which was met with complete agreement by Sue, I knew my wife so well.

Back at home Billy disappeared upstairs to read his new book about the Romans and Sue was busy with sorting out some washing. Charlie was hanging about and I knew my son well enough to know that something was bothering him and he needed to talk. So I asked him if he wanted to help me with some stuff in the garage. He followed me out and once there I didn't waste any time asking him what was up. Charlie is quite an open boy who tells you what is on his mind rather than bottling it up inside. He told me that he had heard me talking to his grandparents the night before and I could tell he had a lot of questions that needed answering. I told him to give me a minute and I went and spoke to Sue. Ideally I would have preferred to have done it with Sue but with Billy here too we agreed he was too young to understand it all just yet. So she agreed to me answering all his questions on my own, as long as I told her later. I agreed, kissed her, and went back to the garage. I explained to Charlie where I had been and told him there would be no secrets and that I would tell his mum everything. He seemed happy with that so we got two old storage boxes to use as seats and I told him to fire away.

It came as no surprise to hear his first question was about Irene, as far as the boys were concerned she was their nan. So I did my best to give him a version of it that he would understand and that was truthful. Obviously there were lots of other questions but to be honest he seemed to grasp what had gone on and seemed satisfied with my explanation.

The next was about ghosts in general, he asked me who "Gwyn" was. I explained that he was their guardian, so to speak, to protect them from naughty ghosts. Gwyn was a 13-year-old boy who had died in a mining accident at the beginning of the 19th century and had been taken in by Henry. He had then been tasked with looking after Charlie and Billy after Henry's last conversation with me. I asked Charlie if he had spoken to him, which he obviously had, how else did he know his name? Dumb question I know. Charlie explained that he wanted to make sure it was ok to speak with him, I explained that he needed to be careful as not everyone can see spirits and it would only be sensible to speak to him or any other spirit for that fact when he was on his own. The last thing I needed was him being bullied by kids who didn't understand but I didn't need to worry, Charlie had seemed to have grasped the situation quite well by himself. Like I said he is a clever boy. I asked him to tell me if he saw anything going forward so I could help and support him, he was happy with that and I could see the weight being lifted off his shoulders. With that done I told him to go and annoy his brother as usual. He gave me a hug and thanked me which put a nice little lump in my throat and I needed a moment to compose myself before going back in to update Sue.

Another quiet week went by which didn't help the time go quick but by Friday I was quite excited about what was ahead of us. Emily was going to look after the boys at our house this time so when she arrived Charlie with a little guidance from me took Emily and Billy upstairs to look at the stuff they had got from the Roman visit at the weekend.

Molly and Mitch turned up not long after and we were pretty much set, we needed to be at Hilltop by 19:30 with our time to start at 20:00. So with everything we needed packed in the car we made our way there. We arrived just before 19:30 was met in the car park by Robin of all people. He didn't recognise us and introduced himself as the event co-ordinator and our 'Guide' for this evening. I asked what he meant by 'Guide'. He explained that he would accompany us throughout the night to ensure nothing was staged by us. I thought, you cheeky sod. I looked at Mitch and he just shook his head. I asked if that meant we had to stay together as a group. He explained that if we wanted to split into 2 groups that would be fine as there were other staff available. I was also curious about how they were able to afford to close the place down on a busy Friday night. Robin stated that there was a marquee at the rear of the building that was being used and a barbeque arranged for people that were attending another event that was running alongside this one.

"What's that?" I asked.

"When we run a ghost hunting weekend we have special guests here such as mediums, tarot card readers and ghost hunting workshops that people pay to attend and there are experts available with equipment for sale to allow them to put into practice the skill they have learnt from the workshops."

I was gobsmacked, this was one well planned money making weekend. No wonder they could afford to close the pub. So we followed Robin into the pub and he gave us a guided tour of the place, some of it we had seen already of course but he took us to the cellar and a small office which was in between the bar and the restaurant, the kitchen and a large store room at the back. He explained that there was one room upstairs that was the landlord's living area and was out of bounds during the investigation but there were 4 guest rooms on the same floor which we could investigate. I asked if anyone would be upstairs in the living area. Robin explained that no one would be there, Matthew Windsor, the landlord, would be around in the marquee but not in the main building until the investigation was completed at 4am. Happy days, I thought, so with the tour over we moved our equipment into the bar area. Mitch explained that we wanted 2 groups of 2; we would use this area as a start/return point after each mini investigation just to report any findings or activity and swap over personnel and equipment. Robin seemed happy with that and suggested we meet back up here at 20:00 to start the investigation. He also pointed out that there were refreshments on a table in the corner should we need anything. So with that we collected our stuff from the car, placed it on a table in the bar and agreed on a plan of attack. Sue and myself would spend the first hour in the cellar, Mitch and Molly would be in the kitchen. We would use the camcorders mainly just to record anything we found or missed for that matter. I took advantage of the 'free' refreshments and helped myself to a sandwich and a coffee. Bang on 20:00 Robin was back with a woman called Rachel who he introduced as his assistant and would assist myself and Sue for the first hour. So off we went, Rachel guided us down into the cellar and we found a spot roughly in the middle so we could turn off the lights and go from there.

To ensure there was no interference from the team upstairs I called Mitch on our walkie talkie and told him we were ready to start, he confirmed the same. We sat there for an hour listening to the usual old building noises but nothing else. We met up with the others in the bar who reported they had heard footsteps above them and the odd whisper but couldn't make out what had been said. So we swapped for the next hour and we pretty much heard the same things along with a door shutting, all above us which was interesting.

*

Next was the restaurant, it came as no surprise to me to see the old man taking his seat again but Sue saw nothing. Again we heard footsteps above and this whispering which seemed to come from all around us, I really couldn't pinpoint where it was coming from or what was being said which was a little frustrating. We met up with the others in the bar after an hour and again they had reported the same footsteps and whispering along with glasses clanking together. We had 15 minutes break which allowed Robin and Rachel to vanish and gave us time to have a little chat. I had noticed a number of security cameras that I hadn't noticed when we had come for the meal. The coverage seemed extensive to say the least, so I whispered to the others to be careful about what we said.

Something about the place was bugging me but I couldn't put my finger on it so when Robin and Rachel came back I asked them if there was anyone upstairs. Obviously they said "no" and I explained that we had heard footsteps and just wanted to be sure, they seemed happy with my explanation stating that this was one of the 'norms' on these investigations.

When we restarted I suggested we spend 30 minutes in each of the rooms upstairs which we all agreed on. Robin was in a deep discussion with Rachel so I cleared my throat loudly to show them we were ready to carry on. Robin reminded us that the left half of upstairs was out of bounds which we acknowledged and off we went.

As soon as we arrived upstairs the atmosphere changed, the temperature was much lower and with only emergency lighting on it seemed quite oppressive. Mitch and Molly went into room 1 and we started in room 4, the plan was to spend 30 minutes in each room until we had completed all 4. The first 30 minutes were pretty much uneventful and so was the next, then when Sue and I entered room 2 things changed. Straightaway the atmosphere seemed charged. I could tell Sue felt it and so did Rachel. We all sat down on the bed and I could feel it vibrating. I asked if the others could feel it and they could, the longer we sat there the stronger it got. So I got off the bed and used a torch to check underneath but couldn't see anything that would cause the vibrations,

I turned off the torch and straightaway I could see someone lying under the bed looking at me. I crapped myself, banged my head and squealed like a little girl before standing up. Sue asked what was up, not wanting to frighten her I said I'd seen a spider which I knew she would believe as I really didn't like them. The vibration had stopped on the bed but now the door to the en-suite was rattling like there was no tomorrow. There was no chance of hiding this, I got up and grabbed the door handle, instantly it was like I was under water. I couldn't breathe and the feeling of panic was overwhelming. I instantly let go of the handle and stepped back. I looked to my left and in the corner was the woman I had seen waving when we had left after the meal, she was dripping wet and just grinning at me. I didn't like it or her one bit, there was something oppressive about her and if I'm honest she scared the crap out of me. Again in an instant she was gone but there was a puddle of water where she had been stood, I asked Sue if she could see the water on the floor, which she could so I asked her to video it and then to keep the camera on me.

I stood there trying to regain my composure when I felt the hairs on the back of my neck stand up and I was frozen to the spot. I could feel a cold breath on my neck and knew whatever was in the room with us was stood behind me. I really was crapping myself now, I couldn't move a muscle, then I heard a woman's voice whisper in my ear, "Don't cross me, this is mine, you can't help me."

The smell was horrible and then I could move, I was gagging like a cat with a fur ball. The smell had been horrendous and was lingering in my nostrils which didn't help with my gagging. Soon I was able to compose myself and saw Sue and Rachel staring at me open mouthed.

All I could say was, "Don't ask." I left the room straightaway and was met outside the door by the others; they had been trying to get in without any success. I needed some fresh air and quick.

*

This hadn't been what I had expected, I had made the mistake of letting my guard down as I hadn't seen or sensed any of this during our previous visit. Our two guides had disappeared again and as we were outside I decided it would be safe to talk. I explained to them what had happened in room 2, Mitch had said he'd had a similar feeling on entering the room but it had soon disappeared. I told them I had no intention of going back upstairs but we needed to complete the investigation. Mitch and Molly looked at each other and Mitch nodded to her,

"Ok come on, spill."

I told them. Molly explained that when they had been in the bar she had noticed a tiny piece of mesh on the floor underneath one of the pictures; she then got Mitch to distract Robin whilst she checked behind the picture. There she had found a small speaker that was playing the whispering sound they had been hearing from the start, she had checked under a couple more and found others. She also said that the footsteps were only coming from the left hand side of the building, never the right. She believed that someone was upstairs walking around, I was well impressed.

"There's more," she said, there are twice as many cameras now than there was during the meal, she had noticed the brackets but thought they must have been old ones. Again she thought someone upstairs was watching them and making the noises to suit. I was stunned but I did know that whatever was in room 2 had nothing to do with the owners. So we agreed that from now on we would be looking for 'props' and I would look out for the scary woman and try to find out who she was, Mitch agreed. I looked at him and asked if he wanted to swap?

"Not a bloody chance," was his immediate reply. I couldn't blame him I was shitting myself and not looking forward to going back in. But needs must so off we went when our minders came back from wherever they went, I had an idea but kept it to myself.

So next up was the small office, there wasn't much in there to be honest. I did think that would be where the security system would be stored but there was just a PC and a few other bits and pieces. I asked Rachel where the security system was and to my surprise she said, "I have no idea, I'm Robin's girlfriend, I only help out at these events I don't work here."

I asked her what she thought of the place, if it was haunted. "Of course it's haunted," was her reply, "You've heard all the noises and stuff, what else could it be?" I realised there was no point in pursuing questioning her so we sat in silence for a time without any noises or incidents.

We met up with the others and I asked if they had anything, Mitch just looked at me and kind of grimaced. I thought, thanks Mitch. So we made our way to the storeroom which was at the back of the kitchen and it was really big for a storeroom. As soon as I stepped in the atmosphere changed again, just like upstairs, so I told Sue to give me the camera and for her and Rachel to wait outside. Sue handed the camera over and Rachel stated that she wasn't to leave any of us alone; I told her she was more that welcome to join me but I was advising her against it. She stepped into the room, her eyes opened wide, she looked at me and turned around and walked out. Great, I thought, on my bloody own, so I smiled at Sue and shut the door. I walked to the back of the room and sat down on a big bag of potatoes.

I knew I was being watched so I waited but she didn't appear, I knew it was her I could sense it but I couldn't understand why she was still hiding. Then in an instant she was in front of me, face to face, I almost fell off my seat in fright but this time there was no feeling of being paralysed which I was very happy about.

Trying to compose myself I asked her, "Who are you?"

"Angharad," was her reply. "Have you come for me?" she asked.

"What do you mean?"

"Have you come to take me from my home?"

"No, why would I?"

She looked at me as if trying to see if I was telling the truth. She stood up and walked away, then turned back. "I won't leave, this is my home." And then she was gone.

I left the storeroom, looked at Sue and smiled.

Rachel had vanished. "Where's she gone?" I asked.

"No idea, she heard the conversation and left."

"Could you hear both of us?" I asked.

"Yes, all of it." I was impressed. We walked back into the bar and were joined by the others almost straightaway. It was only 3am but Robin announced the investigation was complete.

"No shit," I replied.

"Mr Windsor would like to see you before you go," Robin stated. I was happy about that; I had a few home truths to tell him. Whilst we were waiting for him we packed away all our stuff and I explained to Molly and Mitch what had happened in the storeroom. "Make sure you switch all the SD cards from the cameras just in case.

It came as no surprise to see Matthew Windsor come out from the pub; he had been in there all the time. I told the others to wait in the car just in case things got a little tense. I could tell by his body language that he wasn't a happy man so before he could open his mouth I went on the attack.

"Mr Windsor, listen to me and listen well, your little scam is up. I know it was you upstairs walking around, we found the speakers for the whispering." He was stood there opening and closing his mouth like a goldfish but I had no intention of letting him speak until I had finished. "The best of it is your pub is really haunted, you don't need any of that. You have 2 residual hauntings and one scary woman who has told me she's going nowhere." I could tell by the look on his face that this had come as a shock to him.

Having put him on the back foot he realised the game was up, I had the advantage so he explained he knew about the 2 residual hauntings but not the other one. I told him her name was Angharad; again I could tell he knew the name. He told me that according to records she had been murdered by her husband in 1880 so he could take ownership of the pub which had been left to her by her father. But one night, drunk, he had told a prostitute what he had done and she had reported it. He was arrested, found guilty and hung but her body was never found. People believe she's buried on the property somewhere. That probably explains why she won't leave and still thinks it's her's I told him.

"So Mr Matthews, it looks like we won the event," I told him with a smile. For a second I think he considered saying no but realised I held the advantage. We agreed the event should continue as he planned but he needed to ensure we were announced as winners and would go on Charles Boyd's show. He agreed, we shook hands and I got into the car and we left.

"Well that was unexpected," I said, everyone agreed and we drove home in silence. I dropped off Molly and Mitch, telling them to review what we had as soon as possible but not to put it on the website until we all had the chance to look at it. Myself and Sue got home and just went straight to bed, I was exhausted. It had been an eventful night and one I wouldn't forget for some time.

CHAPTER 13

I struggled for sleep even though I was shattered, it was more mental than physical. Normally I found sleep quite easily having worked shifts for years but this morning it just wouldn't come to me. At 6am I gave up, Sue was sleeping like a baby which I was happy about but not wanting to disturb her with my moving around I got up and went down to the kitchen. I made a cup of tea and sat at the table, having looked at all the news on my mobile my mind went back to the night's events. The spirit, Angharad, was a new one on me, she was so full of anger and vengeance, it was almost overpowering. I knew in an instant that she was going nowhere and I'm pretty sure the 'other team' knew too. It was completely different to what I'd come across before and she had really scared me, her power, I'm not sure if that's the right word to describe it but it was so overwhelming I knew she wasn't to be messed with. More bloody questions and no answers. I went into the living room and switched the TV on hoping to find something boring to make me fall asleep.

It didn't take long for it to happen, although it wasn't the kind of sleep I was hoping for, It was what I called 'Henry Sleep'. Before I knew it he was sat next to me but I knew how this worked now so I wasn't worried if Sue woke up and came looking for me she would see me asleep on the sofa, nothing more.

"It's been a while, Henry," I greeted him. "What do you have for me?" I asked him. I knew he only appeared when he had something to share with me, he wasn't big on social visits our Henry.

"Time to answer some of your questions, Gary."

That's nice of him, I thought.

"No need for sarcasm."

Bugger, I forgot this was the twilight zone. So Henry proceeded to answer some of the questions that had been bugging me. He started with the one that had been bugging me the most, how we know which spirits are good/bad and how do we save the ones in between. Henry proceeded to explain that the good and bad were no issue and each side were drawn to them where necessary, how they lived their lives reflected in their souls. A good soul was like a bright star and gave off a positive aura; likewise bad or dark souls were negative and gave off that aura.

"But that doesn't explain the ones in between," I said.

"Patience, Gary. The ones in between are kind of in limbo, their souls are stained both good and bad which means both sides are attracted to them and whoever gets there first has the chance to help them decide as you've seen but when both sides are there then it becomes messy, whichever side has the strongest presence will draw that soul towards them. Let's use Irene for example as I'm sure you still want an explanation even after what you now know.

"With Irene the anger she showed towards you tipped the balance, she wasn't a bad person, yes she had made some bad decisions but her soul wasn't pure evil. She was as I said, in the middle but she attracted the dark side too and they weren't going to give up on this opportunity so once her anger had been released there was a small window where she could have been saved by us but they were waiting and took their chance. You were caught off guard, you had no idea what was about to happen and even if you did the outcome still may have been the same, I know it doesn't help but these are the harsh facts. In fact it did help because I had blamed myself for not saving her but I also remembered the venom in her voice at the time which had stunned me, after all, what had I done? As always Henry had helped me understand and that would help me and make me better prepared going forward.

The next thing I knew I was being woken up by Sue. "Wake up, Gary, why are you sleeping on the sofa? I need you in bed with me, everyone will be awake soon." And with that Sue took me upstairs and took my mind off everything which was fine by me.

It came as no surprise to me that I fell straight asleep after making love. Two hours later I could hear Emily and the boys downstairs so got up, showered and made my way downstairs to the kitchen. Emily was already cooking for us all, full English breakfast, she must have read my mind, and I was starving. Sue joined us soon after and with food ready we all sat at the table to eat. It didn't take long for Charlie to ask about last night.

"All in good time, Charlie," I told him. Naturally he was a little disappointed but I didn't want to discuss it in front of Billy. I was planning for us all to walk to Sue's parents which took us along the local canal which Billy loved and I knew he would be dragging Sue along at a thousand miles an hour, showing her everything like it was the first time he had seen it, he made me smile. So with everyone fed and Emily thanked for a wonderful breakfast, we left the house and headed for Sue's parents. It didn't take long for Charlie and me to lag behind the others, straightaway he had started a conversation about school and deliberately slowed the pace down to open a gap between us and the others, clever boy, I thought.

It didn't take long for him to change the subject and I could see that the others were far enough in front not to hear. So rather than delay I started talking about the investigation from last night. Charlie was captivated by what I was telling him, at one point he had almost fell into the canal so I made him swap sides. The last thing I needed was him taking a dip in the canal, I would laugh and Sue would kill me. It came as no surprise that he had loads of questions, I had left out the bit about Angharad, I thought that was a little too much at this stage, the last thing I wanted to give him was nightmares and again Sue would kill me.

We reached Sue's parents and Emily took the boys into the garden, over coffee I explained to Tim and

Liz what had happened, they were gobsmacked by what I was telling them, especially about Angharad at the end. They had been there a number of times for food and parties so it kind of gave them both a little shudder. Obviously with their own experiences they were very interested and I told them some more details about the other investigations.

Liz said, "Wow, you should write a book about all this," I smiled and said, "maybe one day Liz." Sue told them that everything was on the website if they want all the information on all our investigations so far. The next question came as no surprise and to be honest I'd been expecting it for some time.

Tim asked, "Is anybody in danger from all this?" obviously meaning are Sue and the boys in danger.

"Fair question," I said. "We all have guardians to protect us and it's more about me and the spirits I'm trying to help, I'm the only one in any danger." I don't think it reassured them much because they gave each other that, *I'm not convinced* look. Good job they didn't know about Charlie otherwise I think the conversation would end up getting a little out of hand but anyway Sue jumped in and made it very clear that her and the boys' safety was my number one priority and that we didn't discuss it in front of them at any time, well apart from the walk over but I wasn't about to divulge that information at that moment.

Sue's speech seemed to calm them a little and the mood seemed to relax. I went out into the garden and got involved in the kick about that was going on. We left Tim and Liz's after lunch and walked back home, Billy decided I needed to be shown all the things he had shown Sue earlier. Billy was a nature boy, he was showing me fish, birds, insects and knew all the names to everything, I was impressed and I learned a little too. It was quality family time that we all loved and to be honest it was times like this that I think stopped me from getting overwhelmed with everything else that was going on in my life, the boys had run on ahead and Sue's hand grabbing mine brought me back to reality.

"What you thinking, handsome?" Sue asked.

"Just how lucky I am to have you guys." And I really was. Sue smiled at me, kissed me and we walked the rest of the way home hand in hand.

*

We decided to make the evening a pizza and movie night, picked by the boys which was a bad idea. Their taste in pizza toppings were a little strange to say the least, thankfully it was the boys who were sharing and not all of us. Their choice of movie was much better, a cool family comedy that had us all snuggled up on the sofa and giggling our way through it from start to finish. When it was time for bed, Sue took the boys up as normal and I cleaned away the pizza rubbish. As usual I went up once the boys were in bed to say goodnight, Billy was already dozing and I think he was asleep before I closed his door, Charlie on the other hand was sat up in bed waiting for me.

"Dad, how old do I have to be before I can help you on the investigations?" was Charlie's opening line.

"Listen, Charlie, I don't really understand it all myself at the moment and there's no way I'm taking you somewhere that may put you in danger." I knew he wasn't happy with my answer but it was the truth.

I told him that I would speak to his mum and see if she would let him help Mitch and Molly with the website, he seemed happy with that and snuggled under his quilt, I kissed him on the forehead and said goodnight.

When I got downstairs Sue asked what had taken me so long, I explained to her the conversation I had had with Charlie.

"I'm not sure about that Gary, he's too young." I agreed but at the same time I understood what he was going through, I had been in the same situation at his age but I never had parents who would or could have understood. However, at the same time I understood where Sue's reluctance to allow him to get involved was coming from. I suggested that she get involved with the website as well then she could monitor what Charlie was seeing. I explained what I had gone through at his age, how lonely I felt and that I thought I was weird or something and that I didn't want Charlie feeling the same, after all it wasn't his fault he could see ghosts. Thankfully Sue agreed and I told her that I would let Mitch and Molly know tomorrow. Sunday was our usual get together day after investigations so it would be a good time to discuss it and it would allow me to get Mitch working with me closer on other stuff, plus it was Molly who did all the website stuff, Mitch usually did all the audio/visual stuff and I wanted to understand that side of it a little more, hopefully to our advantage.

So having slept well I woke up with a good feeling in my bones so to speak and couldn't wait to meet up with everyone later. I had text Simon before I went to bed last night and he had confirmed that he would be coming, hopefully not just to wind me up. Sue spoke to me whilst we prepared breakfast and said she had thought about what I had said regarding Charlie getting involved and she agreed which I was pleased about. I asked her to speak to Charlie after breakfast so he wouldn't sulk all day and especially when everybody turned up later. So later Sue took Charlie with her to town to grab a few things, much to his disgust, after all being seen out shopping with his mum at that age wasn't cool or so he told me but I told him it would be worthwhile on this occasion and to trust me.

It came as no surprise that he had a smile on his face when he came back and thanked me as he staggered past under the weight of his mother's shopping. I smiled and kissed Sue.

"Someone's happy," I said.

"He wasn't at first but I think I sold it to him and he understands the reasons why." Happy days, I thought.

We had arranged for everyone to come over at 8pm which allowed us to discuss everything and have the boys in bed on the pretext that there was school the following day and having spent the afternoon playing football in the local park they were tired enough not to argue.

*

Everyone arrived on time and we decided to review what we had captured from the investigation. Mitch decided to get the footsteps and the whispering out of the way first as we knew that it had been set up by Matthew. He had some orbs around the areas where the two residual hauntings were and I was a little disappointed that we hadn't caught what I had seen but we did have the noise of a chair being pulled out and the sound of an old till being used which I didn't remember hearing at the time so that was good but Mitch had kept the best bit for last. This was all to do with our encounter with Angharad; the first bit of video was from the bedroom where I had first encountered her. We had captured the bed vibrating and the door rattling, my hair was stood on end again just thinking about it. Unfortunately me banging my head and squealing was captured so to save myself I explained what I had seen. Simon commented that he was more inclined to believe the spider story; I just gave him the middle finger which just brought a smug grin to his face. We had the puddle of water that was on the floor but at the time Angharad had spoken to me the video was distorted with some kind of interference and the audio was just garbled so I filled in what had happened for the benefit of Simon. The next video clip was from the storeroom, it started from me entering the room, then Rachael walking out. At the point Angharad appeared in front of me the video showed a really dark shadow on one edge of the screen. Where she had startled me I had dropped the camera to one side so she was out of shot but what she had said we were just able to hear. Mitch explained that he had put it through some software and that was the best he could get, it wasn't the best but it was pretty good. At the point she walked away from me I had moved the camera back into position and you could see a very black shadow moving away from the camera, then it stopped but what she had said that time wasn't as clear then it moved off again and then disappeared. We all looked at each other, even I was surprised what we had captured and I had been there.

I looked at Simon and he just mouthed, "Fucking hell."

"Exactly," I replied. We all agreed that it needed to go on the website, what we had captured was awesome and this was the best evidence so far. Even though I had been shit scared at the time I was well happy with the evidence. We all also agreed that we would leave out the evidence that was faked for now but it might come in handy later, just in case Matthew Windsor decided to change his mind.

Having finished looking at what we had captured, I decided to tell everyone about Charlie so it would help them understand why I wanted him helping with the website. To be honest nobody seemed that surprised when I told them that Charlie was like me, Mitch said he had been wondering for some time if one of the boys would have my gift and Charlie had been his guess. Molly seemed happy with my plan to have Sue and Charlie helping with the website and I explained to Mitch that going forward I wanted him by my side at every investigation. After what Henry had told me I knew that we would need to combine our gifts if we were going to have the advantage with any further encounters with the black mass.

Mitch agreed that it was a good idea and having been witness to what had happened to Irene he knew full well what we were up against, I also believed that with him not being able to see them kind of gave him an advantage as far as he sensed them first and wasn't distracted normally by seeing what I sometime saw but we would need to fine tune our teamwork going forward if it was going to work.

Finally I asked Simon if he had anything new for us. He said he had some leads to follow up on finding Jenny and that he'd been in touch with Charles Boyd, mainly as a back- up to get him to know about me, just in case the investigation hadn't worked out. He told us that Charles wanted to meet up with me beforehand, I was happy with that as it would give me a chance to get to know him before hopefully appearing on his show.

So I told Simon to go ahead and arrange something for next weekend and with that we were done, everybody left reasonably happy, things were looking good for Paranormal & Haunting Investigations.

The following day, as an afterthought from our meeting the previous evening, I wanted to double check what Simon had told Charles about me and the team so I gave Simon a ring.

After what seemed like an age he answered, sounding like he was half asleep.

"Sorry, pal, did I wake you?" I asked with a hint of sarcasm, I knew I had as he had told us yesterday that he was working on a story about young homeless people vanishing off the streets and I knew most of his investigating took place late into the night.

"What's up, Gary, you missing me already?" was his annoying comeback.

"Not just yet, I was wondering what you have told Charles about us that's all."

"Ah right, don't worry he knows nothing about

your abilities, I told him you were an up and coming team on the scene and had done some good work, plus I mentioned that Mitch was able to hear spirits." To be honest I was happy with that. I wanted to try and find out just how good or not Charles Boyd was at being a medium, I had my doubts but obviously no proof yet. I thanked Simon and apologised for waking him and we said our goodbyes.

By the middle of the week our website's popularity had shot up, Mitch had put the evidence on from the Hilltop Arms on Monday and traffic had gone through the roof with plenty of comments, there were the usual doubter's comments which came as no surprise and some that were really encouraging. Either way we were getting known and that couldn't be a bad thing or so I thought. Mitch pointed out one comment that had been made by Richard Brown. We had pricked his interest quicker than I thought. He'd written a comment regarding the video clip from the storeroom. It said, 'Some people will do anything for publicity and it's amazing what you can find out about a place on Google.'

Nice guy, I thought, but he was right about Google as I'd found out all about him, granted with Simon's help and had confirmed Angharad's identity using it as well. But I wasn't bothered by his comments that was the joy of allowing comments to be posted in the first place. I asked Mitch to let me know if he had anything else to say on the website and I left it at that.

By Friday morning I was beginning to wonder if our visit to Charles was going to happen but my fears were put to bed when Simon called me just after lunch and confirmed that Charles would like the whole team to have lunch with him at his home on Sunday afternoon, naturally I agreed and having got his address and the timings I called Mitch and gave him the good news. We agreed to meet at my house before travelling to Charles's place; I wanted to make sure we all agreed on a plan of attack. Simon had explained that Charles had pumped him for information about all of us and naturally being his good friend he had gladly 'let slip' a few titbits and knowing what they were would help me know quite quickly if Charlie boy was a fraud or not. I was really looking forward to this little trip. Simon had also told me that he would be there and explained that as far as Charles was concerned we only knew each other from an article he had done regarding the big increase in paranormal investigating groups and that he had liked our approach to it compared to other groups he had interviewed.

So thankfully we were all well briefed by the time we left on Sunday, again thankfully Tim and Liz had arranged a little trip for the boys so Charlie wouldn't get too interested in what we were up to. As we drove the 45 minutes to Charles Boyd's place the conversation was focused on what we thought was going to happen, if I'm honest I was trying not to pre-empt what I thought would happen. I wanted a clear mind so I could focus on what he had in store for us, one thing I was sure of was that it was going to be interesting, I wasn't wrong.

*

So we arrived at Charles's 'place' which turned out to be a rather nice manor house in the middle of nowhere. Thankfully the new car had satnav so we didn't get lost too many times. We were met at the main door by Megan, who introduced herself as Charles's PA. After introducing her to the team she asked us to follow her into the drawing room, very posh, I thought. She asked us to wait and make ourselves comfortable whilst she went and informed Charles that we had arrived. No sooner had she left and Simon made his usual annoying entrance.

"Afternoon, Ghostbusters," he said with that irritating smirk on his face. We all just ignored him and thankfully not far behind him were Charles and Megan.

So I didn't really get what I was expecting, he shook hands with everyone and acknowledged all of us by name, which I was impressed with. He asked us all to take a seat and introduced himself with what was a very low key biography of himself, he really undersold himself. He then asked us to tell him a little bit about our group, how we met etc. I gave Molly a brief nod to let her know she was up. We had agreed earlier that Molly would be the group 'founder' so she explained that we had all met at a medium event, as couples of course. We wanted to try and keep as close to the truth as possible. Molly went on to explain that we had been sat next to each other during the show and then we had seen each other in the pub later. We had got talking about how disappointed we had been about the show and our previous experiences with the paranormal. We had then bumped into each other at a ghost hunting weekend and again had agreed that it hadn't been too good so Mitch had suggested maybe we could do better and it kind of went from there.

Charles had listened without interrupting but kept glancing in my direction which hadn't bothered me at all. I had an idea why he was doing this so I played along until he was ready. He then switched his attention to Mitch, asking him if he was the group's medium.

"Not really," Mitch replied. "I just seem to hear more than the others but I don't really see anything." Charles seemed happy with that and just smiled at Sue without saying anything to her. I knew he was coming to me next and I know you're thinking, surely he must have seen the stuff on the website, and you are correct.

He then asked me, "So Gary, what's your part in all this?" I tried to look a little embarrassed as I explained that I'd had a keen interest in the paranormal since I was a kid and that I'd seen some ghosts but that had all changed since we'd started the group and that things seemed to happen mainly around me. He asked if I thought I was a medium.

I laughed and said, "No not really."

His reply was straight to the point, "So how do you explain the encounter at the Hilltop Arms?" I knew this question was coming so I was already prepared.

"Listen Charles, the paranormal is big business and we want some of it so we enhanced some things a little."

He looked at me as if to say I knew it but he just smiled and asked, "So what do you hope to achieve from appearing on my show then?" I told him we wanted the publicity to help us get known nationally and hopefully get some TV work as well. I continued to explain that we were serious about investigating the paranormal but also very aware that we weren't the only ones. I also told him about what we had found at the Hilltop Arms investigation, the 'props' that were being used to enhance the experience. It came as no surprise that he skipped past that and assured us that he was the man to help us. So he explained that he would like us to appear on his show and the idea would be that we would have 15 minutes where he would show our evidence from the investigation and we would then discuss our findings with him.

Seemed easy enough, I thought. He then announced that there was some food arranged in the dining room for us all and that he would contact the producers whilst we ate, and off he went. Megan asked us to follow her to the dining room and having shown us where everything was she too disappeared. I have to say the food was excellent, not your average buffet. Some of it I had never even seen before but it was delicious and free, can't complain about that.

After around 30 minutes Charles and Megan returned.

"How was the food?" Charles asked, we all agreed it was fabulous of course. We all returned to the drawing room and Charles asked us to take a seat. He explained that the necessary arrangements were being made for our visit to his show; he told us it was pre-recorded before being aired which I had already guessed. He told us that Megan would be in touch with the details and travel arrangements as soon as possible. He then announced that with all the business details out of the way he would like to give us a demonstration of his gift.

"That's if the spirits want to play," he said with a

laugh. This was going to be interesting, I thought, because I hadn't seen anything and Mitch had confirmed that he hadn't heard or sensed anything either but we had a plan to play along and I had noticed that Simon had disappeared at this point. So Charles asked us all to close our eyes and try and empty our minds, which we all did. All I could hear was the ticking of a grandfather clock in the hall, then out of the blue he shouts,

"Adam's here." I jumped a mile. Molly looked at Charles and the show began, basically he told Molly exactly what we had told Simon about what had happened to Adam and what he had said to Molly through me. Thankfully Molly played her part well and interacted where necessary, Charles was sat there like the cat that got the cream. He then asked us to again close our eyes and clear our minds, I knew what was coming next, and it was my turn.

"Irene's here," he announced. No shit, I thought. Again he went through the whole story I had agreed with Simon. I knew he would check that the people he was mentioning had really died so that's why again we stuck to the facts as best as possible including the fact that Irene had died alone at home, only in Charles's version she forgave me for not knowing she had died and that she was in a better place. That really hit a nerve with me and it took all my strength not to knock him out. My tears were real and I think Sue knew what I was feeling as she grabbed my hand and consoled me as you would expect.

With his little performance over he thanked us for coming and hoped we were happy with what we had experienced, he was a bloody showman for sure and a fucking conman, my blood was boiling I couldn't wait to get out of his house. So with a quick thank you and a reluctant shake of his hand I had to stop myself from running to the car. As we drove away from the house Molly announced,

"Well he's a bit of a dick, isn't he?" We all roared with laughter and that improved my mood no end. We discussed what had happened on the way home and agreed with Molly that he was indeed a dick. I dropped them off at the flat with an agreement that Mitch would let us know as soon as he had the details from Charles.

Driving home Sue said, "It really wasn't your fault, you know." I looked at her and smiled.

"I know that, love, it's just still a bit raw that's all." She squeezed my hand and kissed my cheek, I knew she understood and I was happy about that, some things just don't need to be said between two people. The boys arrived home with Tim and Liz not long after we had got home and couldn't wait to tell us about what they had been doing.

"We've been treasure hunting," Billy announced. I looked at Tim and he explained that they had been doing something called geocaching.

"Me and Liz have been doing it for a couple of years," he said and he explained what the concept was, thus explaining why Billy had called it treasure hunting. The boys had loved it and had made me promise that we could do it together soon; I had no choice but to agree.

"It had better be good," I told Tim with a smile. We said our thanks and goodbyes to Tim and Liz and then spent another hour having the boys explain and show us the website and what geocaching was all about, to be fair it didn't look too bad and Sue and I agreed we would give it a try, much to the delight of the boys.

Sleep took its time to come that night; Charles had brought Irene back to the forefront of my mind. I didn't like it, the confusion and not being able to understand why she did it pecked at me like some crazy chicken and another thought started to run alongside it. Did Jenny know? The more I thought about it the more I believed she had, she must have known, how could she not? The hamster was back in his wheel and I think he was on steroids because this was just going around and around in my head, no answers just questions. Eventually sleep came but it was full of dreams that I really didn't like, Beth, Angharad and Irene were all there surrounding me, taunting me. Appearing and disappearing, shouting and pointing. Most of what was being said I couldn't make out, it was like a thousand voices all talking at once.

Then Beth had appeared in front of me and poked me in the chest telling me, "You'll never win, Gary, never." And with that I woke up bathed in sweat. I needed the bathroom, whilst I was peeing I could feel some pain and discomfort on my chest, once I finished peeing I looked in the mirror and could see a fist size bruise appearing where Beth had poked me in my dream, now that really did freak me out. How the bloody hell did that happen? It was a dream for Christ's sake, how was I going to explain this to Sue when she saw it, having already told her there was nothing to worry about and we wouldn't get harmed?

Shit, I thought to myself.

Morning came a little too quick and I felt like crap when I woke up, Sue was already in the shower so I jumped out of bed and looked at my chest, the bruise was still there, looking worse than earlier. So I chucked a t-shirt on and went to wake up the boys for school, thankfully I was able to get away with it for the time being but I knew it was a conversation that I would have to have with Sue at some stage and I wasn't looking forward to it. By the time I had showered and got the boys ready for school I was feeling like crap, my chest was killing me and I was burning up with a fever. I asked my neighbour if Billy could walk with her and her son to school which thankfully she was happy to.

"You look terrible, Gary, you should go to the doctors."

"I will, thanks." Charlie had already left so I phoned work and told them I wouldn't be in as I was ill and man I was ill. By mid-morning I thought I was going to die, I had vomited up the entire contents of my stomach and more from god knows where, I was so thirsty but everything I drank came straight back up. I called Sue at work but there was no answer so I left a message on her phone. I took a cold shower to try and cool my burning body down but that didn't last long so I took some of the ice packs for the cooler bags we had in the freezer and went back to bed.

I wasn't sure if I was dreaming or hallucinating but I could see Beth, Angharad and Irene at the bottom of the bed laughing at me. Bitches, I thought, this is all your doing. But they just laughed and vanished. I can't remember how long I had been asleep or out of it but I could hear someone calling my name, I thought it was Sue but it didn't sound like her. I tried to get out of bed but my chest hurt so bad that I couldn't raise my head off the pillow. Sometime later I could hear music coming from somewhere, I thought I was dead and the angels were coming to get me. Ok it sounded credible at the time but it was my mobile ringing, by the time I was able to reach the phone it stopped ringing. The next thing I knew Sue was bursting through the bedroom door, she was shouting at me but I had no idea what she was saying to me and then I was out again. The next time I woke up I had no idea where I was; again I thought I had died. I was in a room with all this medical equipment in the corner and it was dark. Bugger, I thought, then I looked to my right and I could see someone reading a book.

I told her, "You don't look like an angel."

She laughed and said, "Well I have been called one a couple of times, relax while I go and get the doctor," she said and was gone.

I was expecting Henry to pop out from somewhere as it had all the hallmarks of the twilight zone. A couple of minutes later and the nurse returned with a guy about my age who introduced himself as Dr Hughes. He explained to me that I had been unconscious for 36 hours and the only thing they could find wrong with me was a massive bruise on my chest, other than that there was no reason why I was unresponsive. They had carried out every blood test known to man and they had all come back ok, they had also x-rayed my chest which showed nothing, he asked how I had got the bruise and I told him I didn't know. I had woken up with it in the morning and that was all I knew. Not surprisingly they were looking at me as if I was nuts, I thought I was nuts so we were in agreement there. So the doctor carried out a few more checks and was satisfied I was ok, he asked the nurse to get Sue and let her know I was ok.

After the nurse had left the doctor said, "Listen, Gary, I'm going to be honest with you we thought we were going to lose you, we had no idea what was wrong with you but you were getting worse and worse. Then around 12 hours ago after the nurses' shift change, the oncoming nurse assigned to you saw a woman coming out of your room she called her but she just kept walking. The nurse came in and found this on your chest."

He showed me the cross Jenny had given me and a note saying, "I told you to keep this on you at all times." I was gobsmacked; I didn't know what to say. Dr Hughes then told me that from then on my condition had steadily improved until I had woken up earlier and the bruise has gone too. I had fucked up and I knew it but how could I tell him that so I played dumb. The nurse came back with Sue who was in tears and hugged and kissed me.

"I thought I'd lost you," she said. "No chance, love." She looked at me and laughed and cried at the same time.

In an hour I was given a clean bill of health by Dr Hughes who was still dumbfounded by what had happened to me, he wasn't the only one, so was Sue and I had to explain that it had all been my fault. I'd had a shower before bed Sunday night and had forgotten to put Jenny's cross back on, big mistake as I had found out to my cost. I told Sue what Dr Hughes had told me about the cross and the note.

"Do you really think it was Jenny?" she asked. "Who else could it have been and how the hell did she get the cross?" More damn questions but she had saved my life and I don't think I'm joking about that. That cross was never coming off again, I told myself and it never did.

Sue had told the boys I was away with work and Emily had stayed with them whilst Sue was at the hospital with me. By the time we had got home they were both sound asleep, thankfully. Sue took Emily home so I checked in on Billy first, gave him a kiss on the forehead and went to Charlie's room, I did the same to him and as I was walking away from his bed he said, "I'm glad you're ok now, Dad, that was scary."

I looked back and he was fast asleep. Another twilight zone moment in the life of Gary Channing. Sue was back in quick time, I said, "I hope you weren't speeding, love."

"Probably, you can't be trusted on your own, can you?" she said with a smile. I'd had a lucky escape and I knew it, shit I'd really been lucky.

CHAPTER 14

Mitch and Molly were the first to visit me the following day, I don't think Sue was too happy that I wanted visitors so soon. I was still weak from what had happened but I needed to make sure all the team knew what had happened, just in case. I told Sue I would keep the visit short but you know what it's like when you have something important to tell people. I told them both that I thought the attack was specific only to me, I was the threat and yes I had been lucky. If it hadn't been for Jenny it could have been much worse, Sue just gave me that look which told me time was up. So I told Mitch and Molly to be on their guard and to let me know if anything happened and that I would be in touch as soon as I was back fighting fit.

After they had left Sue made me go back to bed, I didn't mind to be honest, I'd only been up a couple of hours but I was shattered. I did make the mistake of asking Sue if she was going to 'tuck me in'. I knew it had been a bad move as soon as she turned around.

"Do you think all this is funny, we could have lost you, and you could have died. Do you understand how scared I was? Do you?" She sat down on the bed and broke down, I was devastated, I never liked seeing Sue cry and it was worse because I knew I had made her cry. I had always hidden behind humour; it was my kind of defence mechanism, only this time it had been poor timing. I pulled Sue towards me and hugged her as tight as I could, which wasn't as tight as I wanted to. I told her over and over that I was sorry until her sobbing stopped. I woke up a couple of hours later with Sue asleep on my chest; I was gutted because of what I had put her through. It was thoughtless of me and I think I had not really understood just how dangerous my life had become. I did now that's for sure, I had come close to leaving Sue and the boys alone. I needed to be a lot more serious about what was happening, this was no TV show, this was real life.

I fell asleep again and woke to hearing the boys downstairs, having come home from school. I got up and made my way down to the kitchen, Billy ran towards me and gave me a big hug, Charlie was still sat at the table watching me.

"You ok, Charlie?" I asked him.

"I am, Dad, are you?" He had a very worried look on his face and his eyes were filling up with tears. He then got up and ran past me and upstairs.

I looked at Sue and told her, "I'll go and check on him." She smiled at me, I walked over to her and kissed her. "Thank you," I told her, she kissed me back and told me to think about what I was going to say to Charlie. This was going to be an interesting conversation with Charlie, obviously he knew something was up and hadn't believed I had been on a business trip. I knocked on his bedroom door and after a short while I let myself in. Charlie was sat at his computer so I asked him what was up. He neither answered me nor looked at me, I knew he was crying. That hurt me; I needed to find out what he knew or what was upsetting him.

"Talk to me, Charlie," I told him.

"You nearly died, Dad, I felt it, you nearly died," and he started sobbing his heart out. I was devastated again; I didn't know what to say to him so I hugged him until he stopped crying.

"Tell me what you know, Charlie," I asked him. He told me that he had been in school during the morning and he thought he had fallen asleep because he could hear me calling him and asking for help. He could hear his teacher asking him if everything was ok and he 'woke up' as he called it and told his teacher that he needed to call his mum. Being a normally good pupil his teacher had realised something was wrong so had taken him out of the class. They went to the school counsellor and Charlie explained that he needed to contact his mum. He knew he couldn't tell her the truth so he told her that he had thought he had left the grill on at home when he had made toast for him and his brother. So she agreed to call Sue, the school had the main number for Sue's work and had set up an agreement with the receptionist that any calls from the school, she had to be told of straightaway. So she had been called out of the meeting she had been in and took the call.

The counsellor had explained what Charlie had

told her and Sue knew Charlie was no drama queen and had agreed to pop home to check. Once Charlie was told this he agreed to go back to class but had tried to call me and Sue during lunch without success as by then Sue had already come home and found me, calling an ambulance and we were already at hospital. I was gutted that Charlie had experienced all this because of me but on the flip side it looked like he had saved my life. Sue would normally not have been home until she had picked the boys up from school, who knows what state I would have been in by then.

"I'm so sorry, Charlie."

"I was so scared, Dad. I didn't know what else to do."

"You did ok, son," I told him. He then told me that the following evening he had been sat in the living room watching TV and had heard someone calling him and telling him to collect my wooden cross from upstairs. So without even thinking about it he went to my bedroom and collected it off the bedside table.

"I even knew where it was before I got there, Dad," he told me. I was amazed by what he was telling me.

"Go on," I told him. He explained that when he picked up the cross he could feel it vibrating in his hand and he knew that he had to take it downstairs, he opened the front door and he said, 'Nanny Jenny' was waiting to collect it from me. I was gobsmacked by what he was telling me.

He said, "She told me you would be ok and that I was a special boy. She kissed me on the forehead and she left. The next thing I knew I was sat back on the sofa and Emily was calling us for dinner. "I thought I was dreaming, Dad," he said.

"How did you know she was your Nan?" I asked him.

"She told me ages ago in a dream."

"What else did she tell you?" I asked him.

"She said she would see me soon, when everything was ok." I couldn't believe what I was hearing, after all that had happened to me this still felt like the twilight zone. I asked Charlie if he understood what it was all about. He said he had a good idea because Nanny Jenny had explained most of it to him but had asked him not to tell me yet what she had said. Wow, I thought to myself. So with that I got Charlie to come back downstairs with me. Sue asked if everything was ok and before I could respond Charlie said, "Of course, Mum," with a big smile on his face.

Sue looked at me and I just shrugged my shoulders and smiled.

Later when I had gone back to bed, having been told to by Sue, I explained to her as she lay beside me what Charlie had told me, she was as stunned as I had been.

"So Charlie knows Jenny is your real mum?"

"So it seems," I said. Within minutes I was sleeping again, I had an unexpected visitor this time. Jenny came to me; it was as if we were having a normal conversation is the best way to describe it. She gave me a bollocking that only a mum could give, I apologised of course and she also told me to stop 'wrapping Charlie in cotton wool'.

"He's a very clever boy," she told me. I knew that, well I did now. She explained that there was no time to explain what had happened in the past, it could wait. There were more pressing matters that needed my attention. "Be on your guard, son," she told me and she was gone and I was awake. I needed a pee so I went to the bathroom and done the business, I also decided to have a shower as I felt a little grubby. Whilst showering I noticed that the bruise on my chest had disappeared, happy days, I thought.

I went downstairs and joined Sue and the boys on the sofa for an hour before it was time for bed for them. It really struck me what I could have lost at that moment; it had been a sharp learning curve. Later on I told Sue what Charlie had told me and like me she sat open mouthed as I explained what he had told me and then the same expression when I told her about what Jenny had told me. I started to laugh and Sue told me, "None of this is funny, Gary."

I told her, "I know but that expression on your face was." With a slap across the arm and being called a 'knob' made me feel that things were back to normal! Whatever normal was now, I thought.

After a couple of more days rest I felt back to normal, I was eager to find out what I had missed so I contacted Simon first and explained what had happened and told him not to bother looking for Jenny as I had an idea that she would find us when the time was right. I then contacted Mitch to ask if he had heard anything back from Charles Boyd regarding the show. I was a little disappointed when he told me he'd heard nothing as yet but that we'd had a call regarding another investigation. He'd been contacted by a head teacher from a local school; she'd had a number of complaints from their caretaker about 'strange happenings' in one part of the school that was being renovated. Happy days, I thought, something to concentrate the mind on.

Mitch went on to explain that the school had been built in 1900 and had been taken over during the First World War to allow uniforms to be made for the army. The area that was giving them trouble was the old sewing room which was one large room with a couple of smaller rooms coming off it. Mitch had already arranged for us to go there Saturday evening which was fine by me as I was beginning to get cabin fever and needed to get out. I told Sue what was happening and it came as no surprise to hear that she had reservations about me being involved in an investigation so soon after my spell in hospital but I told her I needed this, a bit like getting back on the horse after falling off. So reluctantly she agreed and we were all set for another investigation.

We left home around 6pm Saturday evening and had agreed to meet Mitch, Molly and the head teacher there. When we arrived everyone else was already there so Mitch introduced us to Sarah Willis who was the head teacher at St Anne's Primary School and Ralph Walker who was the caretaker. Both had been there over 10 years so I shook both their hands and I asked Sarah if it would be ok to go straight inside and discuss what had been happening. She agreed and she took us to her office, which was just inside the main entrance. It looked like a typical school from that time, single storey and well built. We all sat down in

Sarah's office and once we all had a coffee I asked Sarah why she thought she needed our help. She explained that she had seen our website and was impressed with the approach we seemed to take to our investigations and our ability to keep certain people and places anonymous, well, as best as we could. Of course we would try our best and nothing would be put on the website without her permission we agreed. So she explained that 6 months ago they had been given funding to renovate what was called the, 'Old sewing room'. She confirmed what Mitch had told us about its use during WW1 and that it had stayed unchanged for many years. It was still used for art classes, mainly drama, as it was quite a large room. She also explained that the room had a bit of a reputation for being spooky; most teachers didn't like being there as they all complained of a feeling of being watched. Sometimes the room would be set up the night before and when they came back the following morning it would have been changed around. They'd had problems with toilets flushing on their own and taps coming on by themselves, in the beginning the children had been blamed but after a while it had been proven that it wasn't the children who had been responsible. But things had got worse since work had started, even the builders were complaining about tools going missing, along with mobile phones and keys, some had even refused to come back and carry on working.

Sarah then asked Ralph to explain what he had witnessed in that area, Ralph seemed a little embarrassed to start with which was understandable but once he got going and realised we were taking him seriously he opened up. He explained that he'd been in the sewing room one Saturday morning waiting for the painters to turn up. All the old fixtures and fittings had been removed; the walls had been replastered and were awaiting their first coat of paint. Ralph explained that he had arrived early to open all the doors and windows to 'air' the room before the painters turned up. He'd just opened the main doors at the back when he heard what he described as a sewing machine working.

He explained that he couldn't figure out where it was coming from, he had stood in the middle of the room and it had sounded like it was all around him. I explained that to me it sounded like a residual haunting and that I thought with all the building work that had been carried out must have released some stored energy from the sewing machines working back in the day. Ralph and Sarah looked at each other.

I said, "Let me guess, you've been told this before?" They both nodded and Sarah explained that one of the teachers had an interest in the paranormal and had came to the same conclusion. That is until the following weekend when the painters had finished, Ralph came in to again 'air' the room and the word, 'NO' had been painted in black on every wall in foot high letters. The painters had been back 3 times to cover it but they kept coming back. The new floor had been ruined by the toilets flooding, all the toilets had been blocked and the taps left on with the plugs in, flooding the entire area. At the time it was suspected that it may have been kids but the school had a pretty good security system covering outside but no one was seen entering or leaving the building during any of these incidents. For both of them the final straw had come when Ralph had been using one of the toilets, he heard footsteps coming towards the toilet and just assumed it was one of the builders that were due but the footsteps had stopped outside the toilet door and then without warning someone or something burst through the main door and started hammering on the cubicle door, followed by high pitched screaming. We all just looked at each other; Ralph's hands were shaking as he continued to explain that at first he couldn't open the door so he climbed into the next cubicle and ran out through the main door of the toilets into the sewing room. He told us that what he saw had stopped him entering that room again to this day. What he told us next chilled me to the bone, he explained that as he entered the main room the banging and screaming from the toilet stopped, the temperature seemed to drop so he could see his own breath. Then he could hear the sound of sewing machines working, gradually he could see rows and rows of sewing machines, each with a person sat behind it. He looked to the front and he saw what looked like the 'Grim Reaper' but without the scythe. It looked in his direction and pointed, the machines stopped and each 'thing as he described them looked towards him but none of them had a face, it was just black, no features, nothing he explained. He couldn't believe what he was seeing and he was terrified, almost frozen to the spot that was until he heard a van pull up outside which seemed to break what was holding him there and he just ran out of the building and straight past the builders who had just turned up. That had been 2 weeks ago and this was the first time he had been back to the school. He told us he had no intention of going back into that part of the school and just stood up and left. We were all stunned by what he had just told us; it wasn't that we didn't believe him, far from it but I could tell the man was so scared and I wasn't surprised. It was safe to say that my initial assessment of it being a residual haunting was a little premature and it wasn't going to be a simple investigation. So I asked Sarah if she believed what Ralph had told us.

"Without a doubt," she said. "I have known Ralph 15 years and he's never been like this, He's a very no nonsense person." I thought the same, this didn't look to me like someone seeking attention, it had scared the crap out of him. So I asked Sarah if we could have a look at the room in question. She agreed and I told Sue and Molly to grab some equipment out of the car, just in case something happened, that was to be the understatement of the year.

With the girls back with some cameras and other bit and pieces we followed Sarah to the double doors that led into the sewing room. She told us that she would wait outside, which was fine by me. I took one of the video cameras off Molly and asked Mitch if he was ready. He looked at me and nodded, we both looked at the girls and smiled but they didn't smile back. Could they sense it as well, I thought?

I looked at Mitch and said, "Let's see what's on the other side," and we entered the old sewing room. The girls stood in the doorway; I had asked them not to come in as I wasn't sure what was waiting for us. We walked to the area in front of the toilets so we could see all of the room. The first thing that struck me was how electric the atmosphere was, the hairs on my arms were stood to attention but I didn't sense any fear from it. I didn't trust myself this time; I'd made that mistake too often in the past. I looked at Mitch and he just showed me his arms. I nodded.

"It's like the room's alive," I said. Mitch nodded in agreement.

Mitch said, "Can you hear that?" I couldn't hear anything but that was the plus with having Mitch with me; he could hear things at a much lower level than I could.

"What can you hear?" I asked.

"Sewing machines," he said with a grin. After a couple of minutes I could hear the same sound and like Ralph had said it did seem like it was all around us, slowly building in volume. I was still confused because the feeling of fear I was expecting hadn't come but I was still on my guard. I then noticed the room starting to change, it was very strange, and what I could see looked like one of those videos where they overlap old footage onto new. It was a weird to say the least; there were rows of women sat at sewing machines with their backs to us. I asked Mitch if he could see it, he didn't answer me but I could tell by the look on his face that he could. Now this was unusual for him so I had a little giggle and said,

"Welcome to my world, mate."

I made sure my camera was recording and panned from left to right, the view never came solid or clear, just retained the same appearance which confused me. Then without warning it vanished. We both looked at each other and then to the girls in the doorway, again I knew they had seen the same without needing to ask, good start, I thought.

The atmosphere returned to normal as well so I called the girls in and we all checked our cameras to see if we had captured anything and we had, I was very happy, proof at last. Then without warning all our cameras shut off with dead batteries, I took out my mobile and that was dead too. The others checked theirs and they were all dead, something was draining the energy from our equipment. I told the girls to go back to the doorway and see if we had any fresh batteries. I could feel the atmosphere changing again; I looked at Mitch and said,

"Heads up, something's happening." You could sense it; it was like being in a room full of static electricity, like it was alive. This time I could feel a sense of fear which started to worry me. We moved back to our original position by the toilet, waiting to see what would happen. We didn't have to wait long, the view again changed in front of us, the same style but without the sewing machines but the figure Ralph had seen was there. I looked at it but there were no features to see, it raised its hands to its front and thrust them out towards us. Before I knew what was happening I'd been forced up against the wall behind me, it was like I'd been hit with a giant hand on my chest. It knocked all the breath from me and left me stunned. Within a couple of seconds I regained my senses and looked for Mitch, he was nowhere to be seen. I started to panic, the figure had vanished and the atmosphere had returned once again back to normal. I looked around calling Mitch, he was missing. I crapped myself and tried to calm myself and think logically, where he could have gone. Without much thought I pushed open the toilet door and saw Mitch sat on the floor with his mouth wide open. For some reason I started laughing and grabbed his hand and pulled him up.

"Are you ok?" I managed to say though my giggling.

"I'd be better if you stopped laughing at me." Again the girls joined us, naturally Molly was worried about Mitch but once she knew he was ok she saw the funny side of it which became contagious and we were all in tears within seconds, including Mitch. I asked Sue if she had captured it, she showed me the footage which was awesome; it even showed Mitch flying through the toilet door which started us off again.

Once we all calmed down, the girls explained that they had changed the batteries on the cameras just in time to catch what had happened. I was curious to see if the same thing would happen again with the batteries. I asked Sue if we had any more and she confirmed that there were two left. I suggested that Sue go back to the doorway and wait with her camera and myself, Mitch and Molly would stay in the room. Mitch and I changed our batteries on the cameras and waited. After 10 minutes things were still quiet, I looked at Mitch and he shook his head. I decided to take a break and we went back to Sarah's office, thankfully she was still here. She explained that she had come straight back to her office so she was unaware of what had happened, so over coffee we explained what had gone on so far. She told us that since renovations had begun the school's electricity consumption had tripled. The council had got their energy supplier to investigate and they had got contractors in to check inside. Neither of them could find any faults with the supply or system.

"Seems a coincidence that all this has started since the renovations have started," I said. It was obvious to me that whatever was going on was using any energy available to help generate all these happenings. I asked Sarah if it was ok for us to carry on as I didn't want to leave without an answer. She agreed on the condition that she could stay in her office, I was happy to agree with that. So we made our way back to the doorway and discussed what to do next, Mitch believed that whoever was causing these incidents would eventually show itself.

"I think these are its party tricks if you like to frighten people off, eventually it will have to confront us."

"You ok with that?" I asked.

"No," was his honest answer. I could understand where he was coming from, I had learnt not to presume anymore, expect the unexpected was the way I now looked at these investigations. We agreed to use the same approach as before with Sue and Molly in the doorway and myself and Mitch in the room. We agreed that this time we would change position this time and stand at the opposite end of the room, facing the toilets this time.

We both grabbed a chair and sat down, the atmosphere was normal but I knew it could change in an instant. After a couple of minutes I could hear footsteps, I looked at Mitch and he nodded to acknowledge that he could hear them also. They got louder and louder, like they were coming towards us and then they stopped. Shit, I thought, instantly the static was back and I knew it was game on. I looked down at my camera which was dead again and Mitch's was the same. I looked back and stood in front of me was a little old lady, she looked to be in her 70s at least but I wasn't letting my guard down. She took another step towards me and I glanced across at Mitch who appeared to be sleeping. I looked back at the old lady who was even closer.

"Hello," I said. Well it seemed like the right response at the time. There was no response from her but I noticed her appearance changing, she became taller and her features began to change, still female but younger. I had a bad feeling about this so I grabbed the cross that Jenny had given me and instantly the changes stopped. I could see a look of confusion on the woman's face. I took advantage of this and said," Stop wasting energy trying to scare me, it's not going to work use it to tell me what you want." I could tell this took her by surprise. I kept hold of the cross and also noticed that Mitch had woken up. "Welcome back," I said but he just blinked and shook his head. The old lady's appearance was fully back to what I had seen in the beginning. I asked her again to talk to me but it was like she didn't understand me. I waited awhile and asked her again; this time I noted some signs that she understood me.

"I want you to leave," she told me.

"Talk to me, we're not leaving, what's your name?" I asked her. No response, this is going to be difficult, I thought. Again she told me to leave, with a lot more venom this time. And my response was the same, firm but not too confrontational. I didn't want a fight I wanted to help her. She vanished and I thought, bugger she's gone, but within seconds she was back but sat next to me this time. I sensed a change in the atmosphere, calmer.

"What's your name?" I asked her again, this time she answered me.

"Ms Williams," she replied. Good start, I thought. I needed to keep it going.

"Tell me about yourself," I asked, and she looked at me suspiciously. "Ok how about I tell you about myself first?" She agreed with a nod of the head. I noticed that she was very formally dressed and sat very upright. So I explained all about myself and why we were here, she nodded and acknowledged but said nothing more. Once I finished I merely nodded and she proceeded to explain who she was.

It turned out that her name was Lillian Williams, she was the headmistress of this school and she had been in charge when it was being used to make uniforms and a teacher after it was turned back to a school, her school, she pointed out. She continued to explain that she had never been married and that the school had been her life's work. That explained a lot, I thought, she said that she wasn't happy with the changes that were being made, no one had asked her. I asked her if she knew she was dead. Her response was blunt and to the point.

"Of course, young man, do I look stupid?" She made me feel like I was one of her pupils. "I've made my presence known enough for someone to ask me my opinion," she told me. So I asked her what her objections were and she told me that she wanted something to stay to allow her to stay grounded with the school, if they took everything away then she wouldn't be able to stay. I asked her why she didn't want to move on; again her answer was to the point. "Move on to where? This is my life I told you, yes I know I can't teach and such but you'd be surprised how many children can see me," which brought a smile to her face. So we agreed that I would talk with Sarah and agree with her to ensure something was kept in the room to keep Lillian happy. I told her I would come back before I left to which she nodded. I went back with the others and explained to Sarah what had happened.

"I had a feeling it was her," Sarah told me. Sarah explained that Lillian had passed away in the school doing what she loved, teaching, and that one or two teachers over the years had claimed to have seen her. So after a discussion over another coffee we agreed a plan to hopefully satisfy Lillian. I made my way back to the sewing room and called her, she appeared in front of me which made me jump a little which seemed to give her some satisfaction. I explained to her that the current head teacher had suggested that they renovate one of the old sewing machines they still had to allow the children to see it working, which she agreed with. Also a small plaque acknowledging the work carried out when uniforms were made here, again she agreed and finally I told her that the school had already agreed to name the room the 'Lillian Williams Room'. This brought a smile to her face.

"Thank you, Mr Channing," she said. "Can you apologise to Mr Walker also; I taught his father here you know?"

I smiled, "Of course Ms Williams." In return she agreed to allow the rest of the renovations to be completed without any interference from her and that she would be on her best behaviour as long as the school kept their side of the deal. I promised her that would be the case, I thanked her and told her it had been a pleasure to meet her.

"Eventually," she added. "Likewise, Mr Channing" and she was gone, like they always do only this time she would remain a permanent fixture here at her beloved school.

I made my way back to Sarah's office and explained that Lillian had been in agreement with the plans and that she would have no more problems with her but she would be staying around.

"I can live with that," she said. "Oh and she asked if you could say sorry to Ralph for her and that she taught his dad." And with that another investigation was over. We were getting good at this, I thought, and each one was different. After all everyone loves a happy ending don't they? We left the school and as usual parted with an agreement not to put anything on the website without checking with Sarah first.

CHAPTER 15

Having dropped off Molly and Mitch after agreeing to come to their flat after lunch to review what we had hopefully caught on camera, we made our way home. Thankfully everyone was asleep so I suggested some herbal tea to try and counteract all the coffee we had drunk. We sat at the table and Sue looked me in the eye.

"What?" I asked.

"If I died before you would you find someone else?" Strange question I thought, so I said that I didn't know and asked her the same. "I don't know either," she replied.

"Let me help with that," I said. "Imagine you are in bed with your new partner, making passionate love, I'm going to whisper in your ear, 'I'm watching you'."

"You're serious, aren't you?"

"Yep, I'm going to haunt you," I said with a giggle which started Sue off as well.

"You crazy man," she said through her laughter. I wasn't joking but she didn't need to know that, well not yet anyway. We both showered and got into bed; Sue was asleep as soon as her head hit the pillow. I took a little longer, I was thinking about Jenny and the cross she had given me, it certainly had worked and I could feel its power and almost Jenny's presence next to me. It had been a strange feeling, a good one and extremely empowering. Sleep came and what seemed like a short time later our alarm was going off, well actually it was Charlie asking us to wake up. I was surprised to see the time was 10am; I had slept really heavy and felt extremely refreshed. I looked across at Sue, we smiled at each other, I kissed her and said, "Good morning, beautiful. Ready for some breakfast?"

"Please, I'm starving." So was I. It was time for another of Emily's fabulous English breakfasts. She must have read my mind as I could already hear her in the kitchen so I made my way down and helped her prepare breakfast.

"Everything ok, Em?" I asked.

"Of course, how did it go?" I explained what had happened at the school.

"Wow, were you scared?" she asked.

"A little but she was a nice lady to be honest," I told her.

I could hear the boys coming down the stairs so I just put my finger to my lips and smiled, Emily smiled as she knew what I meant. Breakfast was wonderful as always and we all agreed that a walk was necessary to help digest it and Billy always enjoyed the walk to his grandparent's house, plus I knew Charlie was itching to quiz me about last night but Billy put a spanner in the works as he'd found a new geocache on the way and as I had the app on my phone it was up to me to help him find it. Charlie wasn't happy so I told him, "All in good time, Charlie, we will visit Mitch and Molly later so relax."

That news brought a smile to his face and he then decided that he too wanted to help find the cache. After going round in circles for 10 minutes we found it, much to Billy's excitement. So we filled in the log and the app, Billy decided I had served my purpose and ran after Sue to tell her the good news.

It didn't take Charlie long to bring up the subject of last night's investigation but we weren't far from Liz and Tim's so I told him to be patient and that he could look at all the stuff from it when we got to Mitch's later. He wasn't happy, patience wasn't something that Charlie was good at which I understood very well, after all he got that from me as well.

Having stopped for coffee at Liz and Tim's we made our way back home and had lunch, I spoke with Mitch who confirmed that they had looked at the footage from last night and it was pretty impressive but he'd already spoken to Sarah who didn't want the evidence put on the website, which to be honest I could understand. I'm sure it wouldn't be difficult for people to work out where it was and unfortunately this subject did bring out the kind of people you wouldn't want hanging around a school frightening the crap out of everyone and we had agreed with Sarah that her word would be final, so we had to honour that and that was my plan.

We drove over to Mitch's flat, I hadn't had a chance to discuss with Sue what we would do with Billy whilst we were there but it turned out that Molly had already organised something. She'd already reviewed the evidence with Mitch so she had arranged to take Billy to a local park where there were a number of geocaches, Billy was over the moon.

"You're a legend," I told Molly.

"I know," she replied and off they went. Mitch had already edited most of the video which he'd pointed out didn't need any work; it had all been good quality. We all sat and watched open mouthed, we had captured everything which pissed me off a little as I would have loved to have put it on the website. But we'd agreed so that was that, I looked at Mitch and said, "Gutted."

He knew what I meant. Meanwhile Charlie was still looking at the computer screen.

"What's up, Charlie?" I asked. He asked Mitch if he could look at the footage from when Lillian appeared in front of me. I again asked Charlie what was he looking for, Mitch had got the video back to where Charlie had wanted and Charlie said, "What's that in the background?"

Mitch paused it and because the video was from Molly's camera we could see to the left of us, it was the black mass, I couldn't believe what I was seeing, I hadn't seen it at the time. I asked Mitch to carry on playing it. We could see it forming like before but at the point I grabbed the cross around my neck it vanished. I was shocked.

"Well spotted, son," I told Charlie.

Mitch said, "I don't remember seeing that."

"That's because you were kipping," I said with a nervous laugh. We watched it a couple more times and for sure it vanished when I grabbed the cross but I was confused why it was there and I didn't have an answer to that question. Mitch put all the evidence on my flash drive so we had more than one copy and I wanted to have another look at the black mass footage later, without Charlie.

Billy and Molly came back 15 minutes later. "Find any treasure?" I asked.

"No but Molly fell in the river," Billy told us.

I laughed and looked at Molly. "You ok?"

"My knickers are wet and I'm hungry. Any more stupid questions?" she asked with a smirk.

I raised my hand to my forehead and made the shape of an 'L'.

"Is that Loser or Legend? Think very carefully before answering, Gary," Molly told me.

"Legend of course," was my immediate reply.

"Good answer," and off she went to get changed. Billy was happy because they had found all 4 caches and wanted to tell Charlie all about it.

"Humour your brother," I told Charlie and off they went into the living room. Molly came back and I told everyone that I was a little worried about the appearance of the black mass and that we'd all missed it. After some discussion we still couldn't figure out why it had been there so we left it at that for the time being. I thanked Molly for entertaining Billy; of course she was happy too she loved the boys, even if she had got wet in the process.

Again the weekend had flown by and by the time we got home it was time to start preparing for another Monday, school for the boys and work for myself and Sue. I was actually looking forward to getting back to work after all that had gone on. I wasn't looking forward to my return to work interview as there wasn't much detail I could tell. The fit for work note stated an unknown viral infection but my manager was a nosy sod who would want to know the ins and outs of a camel's ass but there you go, he would have to be satisfied with that.

So work had decided to allow me back on 'light duties' which meant 'dogsbody' in the production office. My return to work interview started as expected with my manager asking numerous questions to which I had no answers and just kept referring back to the doctor's note. He didn't seem happy with this and decided to try a different approach. He started asking about our website and if my 'illness' had anything to do with my activities outside work. I had to laugh because there was no logic to his line of questioning, did he really think I would tell him the truth and actually expect him to believe me! I told him I wasn't happy with his questions and that I had given him more than enough information to complete the relevant paperwork. He wasn't happy with this and stated he would be arranging an appointment with Occupational Health, fine by me I thought, signed the form and left.

Just after lunch Claire from HR came and found me sorting through a mountain of paperwork, she asked if I would follow her to HR. Of course I agreed and she actually took me to the Occ Health nurse. It turned out that Barry my manager had arranged for me to have a drugs test. The cheeky fucker, I thought, but I wasn't worried as I knew I'd pass, so I pissed in the cup and it came as no surprise that I passed. She then asked me why I had been in hospital, I didn't want to seem defensive so I went through it all again and she asked if it would be ok for the company to ask for a copy of the doctor's report. Of course I wasn't bothered, I had seen the report, and it stated that I had been treated for an aggressive viral infection of the lungs and not much else. Not that there was much else he could write, I asked what the purpose of all this was as my sickness record was spotless prior to this and this kind of treatment was usually reserved for those with bad sickness records. She would only tell me that it had been requested by Barry as he was concerned about my ability to do my job. I wasn't happy with this but I knew there was no mileage in his investigation so I decided to let it take its course. I managed to stay out of his way for most of the day until it was time to leave and it was like he was waiting for me, I didn't want any hassle with him so I said goodbye as I walked past him.

"I've got my eye on you, Channing," I stopped just before I opened the door.

"I'd be more worried about who's haunting you, Barry," was my blunt reply and I walked out the door to the car. I told Sue about it when I got home, I wasn't happy with what had happened, Barry was a bit of a knob but we'd always got on quite well in work.

Unbeknown to me he'd been trying to chat up Sue over the last couple of months; this had come as a bit of a surprise to me as she'd not said anything before. She told me that Barry had split up with wife 6 months ago, she had left him for another woman which had dented his male pride to say the least and he'd decided to take a shine to Sue. Naturally I wasn't happy with this but she explained that he'd asked her for a date about a month ago, obviously she had told him no which he hadn't been happy about and she hadn't seen or spoken to him since. The sly little fucker, I thought, but it didn't surprise me as there had been a number of women at work who described him as sleazy but there you go I guess. At least I had sort of a reason why he was being a dick with me but it was just work and he had nothing on me so I wasn't too bothered with that but I did want to smack him for trying to chat up Sue. We let the matter drop as I didn't usually bring work home and I wasn't planning on starting now so I occupied my time with helping to cook tea and the boys with homework later.

Around 7pm I had a call on my mobile from another mobile number I didn't recognise, I didn't usually answer them and would let the answerphone kick in, after all if it was important they would leave a message right? But after what had happened to Irene I felt compelled to answer it, bad move. The male voice on the other end asked if he was speaking to Gary Channing.

"Who's asking?" was my defensive reply.

"Richard Brown, Mr Channing, I was wondering if you had a couple of minutes spare," he asked.

"For what?" I replied.

"I've been looking at your website, Mr Channing,

very inventive, all your own work."

"I'm not sure what you're getting at, Mr Brown, who are you anyway?" I asked, trying to play dumb.

"I'm sure you've heard of me, Mr Channing, a man in the business of conning people with stories of the supposed paranormal."

Wow he's not beating about the bush, I thought. "I'm not sure what you're getting at, Mr Brown."

He decided to get straight to the point and called me out as a fraud and that I was misleading people for my own gain. I pointed out that I didn't charge people any money for what I did, nor did I accept donations of any kind.

"Am I right in saying then that you persuaded Matthew Windsor to let you win his alleged ghost hunting weekend?" The little shit, I thought, I knew he couldn't be trusted but he could wait I had already got what I'd wanted via Simon anyway.

I was having a day of it that's for sure, work, now this. "Ok, Mr Brown, what do you want? I'm sure there's a purpose to this unexpected call."

"Of course, I just wanted to let you know that I'll be seeing you on Boyd's show, be prepared." And with that he hung up. Sue asked who it was, so I explained the conversation I'd just had. I wasn't too surprised as I'd guessed that I'd hear from him direct at some time after his comment on the website but still the information that we'd be on the same show came as a bit of a surprise, not what I expected.

I decided to give Simon a ring, which turned out to be a good move. Simon explained that he had given

Richard my mobile number and had convinced Charles Boyd to let him on the show on the assurance that I would make him look a complete fool. I'm glad Simon had that kind of faith in me and having explained that if I could convince him then I could convince anyone, including Richard Brown. He had a point; I wasn't a fraud after all so I had nothing to be worried about.

"Cheers, Simon, a bit of warning next time would be nice," I told him. "And where would be the fun in that, Gaz?" he told me and hung up.

Man he knew how to press my buttons. I told Sue about my chat with Simon then called Mitch and told him and Molly what had gone on.

"I want us to take the school footage when we go on the show, just in case," I told them both. I didn't want to use it but at the same time I wanted it as a backup. After all it was the most compelling evidence we had captured so far.

Work dragged on the rest of the week; it was a constant battle with Barry and stopping myself from knocking him on his arse. Friday morning I was called back to Occ health, this time I wanted Claire from HR involved. It was time to give Barry a taste of his own medicine. The nurse confirmed what I had told her was correct, the doctor was unable to confirm the origin of the infection but could confirm that at one stage it had been life threatening. I looked at Claire and told her that I had said all of this during my return to work meeting with Barry and as he had instigated all this I wanted to raise a grievance against him on the basis of unnecessary harassment. I left with Claire and she took a statement from me, I also included the drugs test, which was supposed to be random. I also included what had gone on with Barry and Sue. Claire didn't want to include it as she claimed it had nothing to do with work. I pointed out that wasn't Barry my manager and Sue my wife?

"Yes," was Claire's answer.

"So it's relevant then." She conceded it was and when the statement was completed I asked what was going to happen next. She explained that her manager would have to take a statement off Barry and then all the evidence would be reviewed by the Factory Manager. I told Claire that I wanted the rest of the day off as I didn't want to be working with Barry whilst the grievance was being investigated. She asked me to wait whilst she spoke with the HR manager. Ten minutes later Dawn Harris the HR Manager turned up. She asked if I was sure I wanted to go ahead with this. I confirmed I did and she said that she agreed that it would be best to take the rest of the day off and that she would be in touch Monday.

I left work straightaway, I called in on Sue to warn her what had happened, she agreed that this was the best decision and that one of the other women in the office had overheard Barry asking Sue out and that she would be happy to help if necessary. I was hoping that wouldn't be necessary but I knew Barry was a stubborn fucker so we would have to wait and see.

I was sat at home pondering over what had gone on at work when Mitch called, he told me that Charles's PA had been in touch to say that all the arrangements were sorted for the filming of the show. An email would be sent with all the timings etc, and that we just needed to confirm our attendance. Mitch confirmed it would be the following Friday so I ended the call and rang Sue to get her to book the day off work, I also called Dawn at work stating that I needed that day off on the pretext of a follow up hospital appointment, thankfully she agreed.

The big day was in sight, I was very excited and with good reason, it was time to make myself know to a bigger audience.

So over the weekend we all got together to discuss the appearance on Charles's TV show. I was concerned about Richard Brown, it was obvious that his opinion of me was already made but this wasn't my main concern it was the audience who would see the show. What did concern me about Mr Brown was why he was appearing on the show in the first place. Was Mr Boyd on a death wish or something? After all Simon claimed that Richard's sole purpose in life now was to expose all mediums etc as frauds. Something didn't feel right about it and I needed to make sure we were all on our guard.

I turned up at work on Monday to be told that Barry had been suspended pending further investigations and that I wasn't to talk to anyone about it, which was fine by me; my only focus was the show on Friday. The week went very slow, work was hard to concentrate on and the only blip was bumping into Barry on his way to HR to give another statement, he went to say something to me but thought better of it and just barged past me.

Thursday night came but sleep didn't, I had so many thoughts going through my mind about the following day. I knew it was pointless as thinking about it wouldn't help but I did it just the same.

Eventually I dropped off around 2am, well that was the last time I remember looking at the clock. I woke up with a start and sat up in bed but the room confused me, it wasn't mine, everything was different. I got out of bed and looked out of the window but I could only see blackness, nothing else. It was like the windows had been blacked out, which only added to the sense of confusion. I could hear voices coming from one of the bedrooms; it was a man's voice, not so loud that I could hear what was being said. I walked towards the room and the door was open slightly, I could see a small girl stood in the middle of a pentagram that had been drawn on the floor. There were candles everywhere and chanting but very quiet. Someone was talking to the little girl but I couldn't see them, he was saying,

"Don't be scared Elizabeth, Daddy will take care of you." All of a sudden the girl looked in my direction and she vanished, the room was empty and the chanting had stopped. I pushed open the door and walked into the room but there was nothing to see, again there was just blackness all around me. Then I could hear a baby crying from further down the hallway. I stepped back into the hall and the door disappeared so I walked towards the sound of the baby crying. Again there was a door slightly open, the chanting was back and the pentagram but this time there was an older girl stood in the middle of it, possibly 13 or 14. I couldn't be sure as the only light was from the candles, the girl was crying as well with a pleading look on her face.

The same man's voice spoke, "Elizabeth, calm yourself, your child has to be sacrificed we discussed this, don't make Daddy angry." Again she looked in my direction and she vanished. This was freaking me out, I was sure I was still sleeping and this was another of those crazy dreams but something was keeping me there for a reason, I was sure of it. I backed away from the door and as before it disappeared, I could then hear sobbing from further down the hallway; I was getting the hang of this now. I walked towards the sobbing and surprise surprise I came to another door only this time it was closed. I could hear the sobbing and a girl saying,

"Please, Daddy no, please don't do it I'm your daughter, you said you loved me, please." The pleading was heart-breaking so I grabbed the door handle but the door seemed to be locked. The pleading from the other side of the door became more urgent as did my need to get inside but he door wouldn't budge. My other hand grabbed the cross around my neck and the door flew open. The scene was familiar only this time there was a man in a black robe holding a knife stood in front of a teenage girl, she was tied to the floor on the pentagram. At once they both looked in my direction; it was Beth and black eyes. The last image I saw was him plunging the knife into Beth's chest, then everything went black and I could hear Sue calling my name.

I was bathed in sweat and it took me a little while to gain my senses as it was still dark in the bedroom, I fumbled for the switch for the lamp and felt a little calmer when the light confirmed I was awake and back in my bedroom. Sue asked what the hell I was dreaming about as she had been trying to wake me for about 5 minutes so I explained what I had dreamt to her. Like me she could hardly believe what I was telling her, it was hard enough for me to believe and I was there, so to speak. I needed to write everything down so I would remember it, as I took a pen and notebook from the bedside table I noticed that the time was 3am, I had only been asleep for a short period of time which really did surprise me. Somehow I managed to go back to sleep after writing down everything I could remember and felt shattered at 7am when the alarm went off but what had happened was still fresh in my mind.

After a shower and some breakfast I called Mitch and explained to him what had happened.

"It was fucking Beth, I can't believe it, it really was her," I told Mitch.

"You really think she was part of some kind of devil worship sacrifice?" he asked me. I wasn't sure myself but what other explanation did I have for what I had seen. Obviously neither of us had the answer to that question so I told Mitch I would pick them up at midday as the trip to the studio would take 2 hours by car and filming was due to start at 4pm and I didn't want to be late.

Sue had already taken the boys to school and we had arranged for Liz to collect them and stay the night at hers. With Sue back from the school discussed what I had dreamt over coffee, it was hard not to think it had some relevance. Why had I seen it all of a sudden? I no longer ignored anything and we both agreed it had happened for a reason.

CHAPTER 16

B efore we knew it, it was time to leave and pick up Mitch and Molly, naturally my dream was the topic of conversation for most of the trip to the TV studio. We ended up with more questions than answers by the time we arrived. Having been let through the security gate we were met by Charles's PA and taken to a hospitality room that had all we needed food and drink wise. She told us to make ourselves comfortable and that Charles would be along soon to explain what would happen next. We were all a little hungry after the trip so we helped ourselves to the food and drinks that were available. A short while later there was a knock on the door and a man entered and introduced himself as Paul Lockhart the producer of the show. We all shook hands and he explained what would happen during our "15 minutes of fame," as he put it. I just looked at him, I think he was waiting for some kind of reaction but I was going to disappoint him.

Once he realised that I wasn't biting he proceeded

to explain that they would show some video clips from our website and then Charles would introduce us to the audience and proceed to ask a number of questions. He handed us all an A4 sheet of paper with the questions he would ask, they were the standard ones. 'How did you all meet? Who did what in the investigations? Do you really believe in ghosts?' That one made me laugh, why else were we on the show? As he moved to leave I asked him about Richard Brown.

"Ah yes, Mr Brown, he's the sceptic, well we do need one from each side to have a debate, don't we?"

"Are we having a debate with Mr Brown?" I asked.

"So it seems," was his sarcastic reply. "Someone will be with you in 10 minutes for makeup and mics," and out the door he went.

"Well he's a prick," was Molly's response to the door closing. We all laughed at that but she was right and we had been right to be on our guard. I told them that I didn't think Charles would stick to the list of questions and we all dumped them in the bin.

As expected there was a knock on the door and a young man called Anton entered and explained he was here for makeup, we all looked at each other and he said, "What, don't I look like a makeup artist?"

We all smiled at him and shook his hand. As soon as our hands touched a man of a similar age appeared next to him, he held out his hand to me as well and without thinking I shook it. I knew straightaway that everyone was looking at me so I asked the guy what his name was.

"Marvin," was his reply, "and yes I know I'm dead before you ask." Straight to the point, I thought.

"Would you like to help me during the show?" I asked him.

"Of course, see you later," and he vanished. Anton was looking at me open mouthed.

"Makeup, Anton, all will be revealed later," I told him. After he had finished and left I explained to Sue and Molly what had happened.

"Who is he?" Sue asked.

"I'm not sure yet but he'll be back that I'm sure of."

The sound guy followed soon after and took us out onto the set, got us to sit on the sofa in the order laid out by Charles so he could fit our mics and check sound levels etc. Over to my left in the shadows I could make out Richard Brown watching us, the guy gave me the creeps. I couldn't put my finger on it but there was something about the guy that bothered me. I also noticed a young woman sat on her own in the audience seats.

"Can you see the young woman sat in front of us?" I asked Sue.

"No, there's nobody there, well not that I can see." That was confirmed when I looked back up and she was gone. I looked across to where Richard Brown was standing and she was stood next to him, Interesting, I thought to myself. So we had at least 2 spirits who had made themselves know to me already, good start, I thought. With the sound man finished he switched off the mics as in his words, "he didn't want to hear us peeing" and with a giggle off he went.

Charles Boyd then appeared with Paul Lockhart, shaking everyone's hand again with a little too much enthusiasm he explained that there had been a change to the schedule as the other investigation winning team had been unable to make it, so in their place Richard Brown would be joining us on the sofa for a lively debate as Charles put it.

Paul piped up with, "Looks like your 15 minutes of fame just got doubled you lucky people." Molly was right he was a prick. So Paul announced that they would start in 15 minutes and we were taken back to the hospitality room with instructions from Paul to use the loo and no fizzy drinks. As soon as we got back I told everyone about the woman I had seen and having had Sue confirm that she couldn't see her it was fair to say she was a ghost.

"I think she has something to do with Richard Brown." I asked Mitch to quickly Google him to see what's available. Top of the list was a story about his last case, a serial killer had abducted 4 young women and had raped and murdered them but they had been unable to find the body of his fourth victim. Her name was Megan Harris; she had been 22 when she went missing after leaving work. Looking at her photo it came as no surprise that it was the woman I had seen earlier, Mr Brown was in for a shock, a big shock.

There was a knock at the door with someone on the other side explaining that it was 5 minutes until the show started, unbeknown to us they were planning to air the show live via the internet on Charles's website, now that wasn't in the contract that's for sure but it was going to make spectacular viewing for those lucky enough to be watching, maybe you were lucky enough to have seen it, if not then you won't find it on YouTube or anywhere else for that matter but read on and I will explain.

So we made our way back to the sofa on the little platform, Charles was already there waiting for us. There was an audience of about 200 people which for some reason I hadn't thought about, I'm not sure why but for some reason I felt a little nervous. We sat down and he explained that he planned to "go with the flow" in terms of direction which was fine by me.

The show started with some video clips from our website followed by a lengthy introduction from Charles. He proceeded to ask some of the questions that he had given us on the paper but then seemed to get bored with them. He then asked if any of our videos were, 'digitally enhanced'.

I told him, "There's no value in conning people as they would soon find out when they agreed to allow us to investigate their specific problem."

"Do you charge for your services, Gary?"

"Never, the only real cost to us is our time and we agreed from the start that it would always be free."

"And what about people's privacy, do you always honour that or are you tempted to show things regardless?" These were all questions we expected to be asked so answering them was simple and truthful.

"Yes we always honour the agreement, if our client says no then we stick to that regardless of what we capture."

"Has this happened, where the evidence you have is so compelling that sharing it would prove that ghosts really do exist?"

"Possibly, Charles, but like I said we honour our

agreements."

"So for example, say a major newspaper or TV company came along with their cheque book open, what would it take?"

"You mean how much money would it take to break that agreement and sell?" I asked.

"Yes of course, everyone has their price, don't they?" he asked with a smirk.

"Maybe you do, Charles, but we don't, some things don't have a price," the team all nodded in agreement and the audience applauded which helped me relax a little.

Charles decided to change direction a little and asked us about the investigation at Hilltop Arms. I decided to let Mitch take the lead on this one; we had decided to expose Matthew Windsor after his little stunt with Richard Brown. Mitch had arranged to have the video evidence of the speakers in the pub shown. So Mitch went through the evidence we had from the pub and at the end explained about the speakers and the additional cameras. It was obvious from the look on Charles's face that he hadn't expected that and he didn't look too happy about it to be honest. His reaction was to put me on the spot and ask if my supposed talents were real and if they were then did we have any 'guests' with us.

I wanted the audience to understand that supposed mediums who started their 'performance' with, "I have a man whose name begins with B, (pause) Brian or Barry" rubbish true mediums can hear and sometimes see them like we see each other and they can communicate just like we do, by talking. For example I have already met a man before the show started; I know his name, how he died, who he is related to here and why he's still here. A gasp came from the audience, just the reaction I wanted.

"Is he here with us now?" asked Charles.

"Of course," I replied. I called Anton onto the stage and told him that his brother Marvin was with us. Naturally he was stunned, I asked him to sit next to me and I explained that it was his decision as to how much information I shared with the audience. He told me that he wanted everyone to know what happened to him. I explained to Anton that it was Marvin who I had shook hands with in the dressing room earlier.

"I thought so I could sense his presence," he told me.

"Ok, so bear with me, as I need to ask him what he wants to tell you." Everything Marvin told me I passed onto Anton. Marvin explained that they had grown up with just their mum and had never known who their father was, they were non-identical twins. Marvin had gone off the rails as a young boy and had run away from home at 16. He'd lived on the streets for a couple of years, got into drugs and stealing to feed his habit. Then 3 months ago he'd overdosed on a bad batch of heroin and died in a disused factory. Obviously Anton was in tears and explained that his mum was always hopeful that one day her son would walk back through her front door.

Charles being Charles asked Anton if all this was true. I just looked at Charles, how could he know all of it was true, I'd just told him his brother was dead.

Anton told Charles what I thought; I apologised to Anton and suggested we meet up after the show to finish off. Anton agreed and was helped away from the stage by one of the crew. The audience was stunned into silence which was broken by the unannounced arrival of Richard Brown.

"What a load of rubbish, how much did it cost you to get him to agree to your little story, Gary?" was his opening statement. The man was very tall and overbearing, it was obvious his approach was going to be aggressive, in your face and challenging from the start. I was happy to let him shout his mouth off in front of everyone, unknown to him I had an ace up my sleeve. His behaviour was typical of someone who refused to believe in spirits, I'd seen it before. It also told me that he had something to hide, I was sure of that.

He carried on his attempt to ruin our reputation as a paranormal team for what seemed like an age, he reminded me of one of those American preachers you see on TV, the venom and spite from the man was incredible. Molly stood up to say something and looked at me, I smiled and shook my head, thankfully she sat down. I wanted him to finish his rant first. Finally he seemed to run out of breath or crap to spout. Charles did his best to lighten the mood in the studio with a belated introduction about Richard Brown, the audience certainly didn't seem too happy with him judging by the abuse he was receiving. I just sat there and smiled at him, I knew he wanted a reaction from me and I also knew smiling at him would piss him off even more. Having confirmed he'd calmed a little Charles asked Richard why his lack of belief was so strong towards people like me; surely I gave comfort to the bereaved he asked. Richard took a deep breath and I thought, here we go again, but he took a second breath and decided to change tact. He explained that in his experience people like Mr Channing preyed on people who had lost someone for their own gain; hence me being on the show to raise my appearance and then start to charge people once I was 'famous' just like the others. True there had been examples of supposed mediums who decided to line their own pockets after becoming popular, so he had a point that needed answering.

I looked at Molly and nodded, it was her turn to get involved as we had discussed pretty much how things would go and the battle plan was working just as we had guessed it would.

So she explained that when we had agreed to come together as a team then the main agreement was that under no circumstances would we charge people for what we did. Richard went to interrupt her but in true Molly style she just placed a finger to her lips and carried on, she was great. She continued to explain that in fact we had only paid out money, for example for the equipment and to allow us to investigate the Hilltop Arms. Also we had been offered money from satisfied clients as shown on the website in the reviews section.

"You could have written them yourselves," was Richard's spiteful reply.

"Feel free to ask them yourself, Mr Brown, their email addresses are available," was Molly's snappy reply. And she sat down; using Molly at this time had been a good decision, I was extremely proud of her. We were doing well but I knew he wasn't going to give up that easy so I wasn't prepared to let my guard down.

Charles then asked me if there was anyone else here who wanted to make their presence known. I looked at Richard and the young woman from earlier was stood to his right.

"Possibly," I told him. I asked her what her name was. She told me it was, "Megan Harris." I always repeated what they told me so when I repeated her name I thought Richard was going to fall off his chair.

"Now wait a minute," he blurted out.

"No, you wait a minute," I told him. "You've had your say and you'll get a chance to respond but this is Megan's time now shut up." He obviously wasn't used to being spoken to like that but thankfully he sat back down.

I asked Megan to tell me some more about herself, so she repeated her name and told me she was 22 years old, or had been when she died. I asked her how she had died; she explained that she had been walking home from her part time job in a supermarket one evening when she had been dragged into the back of a van. I was shocked by what she was telling me and I hadn't repeated any of it yet so I asked her if it was ok to repeat what she was telling me.

"Yes, he needs to know."

"Who needs to know?" I asked her.

"My dad, Richard." It was my turn to nearly fall off my chair. Charles asked me if I would like to share what I was being told. I wasn't sure; this wasn't what I had expected to hear. I didn't like Richard Brown but at the same time I had no desire to humiliate him either. I told Charles that I needed to hear more first. I asked Megan to tell me more about what had happened to her. She told me that she had been drugged whilst in the back of the van and had woken up in a small room with a bed in it. There were no windows or lights and the door was locked, food was pushed through a small opening at the bottom. I decided to leave out the bit about Richard being her father but explained to everyone what she was telling me. Megan continued to explain that she had no idea how long she had been there when the door was opened and two women came in and told her to undress and put on a white robe that they handed to her. She was sure the food had been drugged as well, just enough to make her compliant. They then took her out of the room and down a long corridor into a large room that was lit with loads of candles. She was told to lie down on a table that was covered by a red blanket or cloth. She explained that at the time she couldn't make sense of what was happening because of the drugs. Then the chanting started and a man appeared in front of her, he had a black mask on and a black robe, then I started to feel scared. I then realised that my hands had been tied to the table, I tried to struggle but I felt so weak." This was heartbreaking to hear, you could hear a pin drop in the studio as I continued to relay what she was saying. I asked Megan if she wanted to stop but she said she needed to tell her story. She carried on explaining that the chanting kept getting louder and louder, also the man had come closer and it took her some time to realise that he had penetrated her, he was raping her. The drugs were starting to wear off as the adrenaline started to increase in her body, she could feel the man's movements speeding up and at that moment she was fully aware of what was happening.

She felt him come inside her and at that moment she also felt the knife plunge into her chest. We were all gobsmacked by what Megan was telling us, Richard's face was as white as a ghost, excuse the pun. I could feel this woman's pain; it was overwhelming and actually painful. My dream from the other night came to my mind; Megan's description was similar to what had been in my dream. I asked her to carry on; she continued to explain that at that moment she knew she was dying. The next thing she remembered was hearing a female voice telling her they needed to leave and being pulled. She remembered being surrounded by darkness for a long time and then the pulling stopped, the darkness disappeared and she was stood in a room that looked 'old fashioned'.

"There were lots of people in the room looking at me and smiling." I thought to myself, this sounds familiar. "It was a different feeling, loving, safe, different to the other room." The penny had dropped for me; I just needed to hear her say it. "I looked at an old man in front of me, he told me his name was Henry and that I was safe and not to worry, all would be explained." I bloody knew it, I looked at Sue and she looked at me, she knew too. But I still didn't understand the connection between who had raped and murdered her and Henry. Megan looked at me and said, "Henry told me to tell you to get ready." She disappeared and all the lights in the studio started to flicker, I could feel the hairs on the back of my neck stand up.

I looked at Mitch and said, "Get ready, Mitch, I think it's time."

The air seemed charged as the lights flickered and then some of them started to pop and explode, covering the audience with glass. That was the cue for panic to start in the studio, then all the lights went out and there was silence. I grabbed Sue and told her not to let go of my hand under any circumstances, I also told Molly to do the same with Mitch.

There was some light from the exits which allowed me to see Charles hiding behind his chair and shouting to someone, "How the fuck am I supposed to know what's happening, you fools?"

I looked for Richard and saw him stood in front of his chair, he looked at me and I told him, "Get this idiot out of here and I'll explain later." He went to protest but I said, "I don't care or have the time for your opinion, I'm not asking, I'm telling, now leave." Thankfully that's exactly what he did.

Some of the lights came back on and the studio was empty, the audience and the crew had gone. It was just the 4 of us, I had no idea what was happening but I was soon to find out. I noticed movement out of the corner of my eye, at first it was just shadows but then I could make out features. It was Beth followed by black eyes, the black mass was just behind them but this time it had a more human shape to it than before.

"Mr Channing, we meet at last," was black eyes' opening statement.

"And you are?" I asked.

"That's of little importance, Mr Channing, or may I call you Gary?"

I laughed, "Does it matter?"

"No it doesn't, so let's get to the point, where's Megan?" Now that shocked me, finally the connection made sense. "I see you've finally connected the dots, clever boy." *Patronising prick*, I thought. He was obviously waiting for an answer from me and when one didn't come his polite tone disappeared. "Where the fuck is she, she's mine?" At that moment his voice sounded familiar, it was the man from my dream. Finally my brain was catching up, Daddy, Elizabeth, and Beth, fuck, it wasn't a dream it was reality. Beth was his daughter; the look of realisation on my face must have been obvious.

I looked at Beth, "It was you, you saved Megan." Beth looked at me then her father.

"What the fuck is he on about, Elizabeth?" he roared. The black mass behind him changed shape and increased in size, it was getting ready for something, I could tell.

I grabbed the cross around my neck in my hand and called, "Jenny, Mum, I could really do with your help now."

"Already here," was her calm reply from behind me, I almost jumped out of my shoes. "Follow my instructions, Gary," she told me. The lights started to flicker again and the hairs on my arms were stood on end.

"Everyone hold hands with me and Gary," Jenny shouted. Sue was already holding my hand so Mitch grabbed Jenny's hand and Molly was already holding his. Instantly I could feel a surge of energy around us. Black eyes started to look confused at what was happening and the black mass seemed to shrink in size. Megan appeared in front of us and Jenny shouted, "Grab her hand, Megan."

Megan grabbed Beth's hand and pulled her towards us, but before she reached us something shot out from the black mass and latched onto Beth, it was like tug of war with Beth in the middle. Jenny shouted at me to grab her, I moved forward still holding Jenny's hand but I had let go of Sue's but she had already grabbed Molly's and we stretched out like we were trying to save someone from the water. I was able to grab Megan's hand; it was solid like a real person's hand. But the power of the pull from the black mass was incredible, so powerful, but I couldn't let the same thing that happened to Irene happen to Megan and Beth.

All my focus was on saving them and I felt another surge of energy flow through me and the connection between Beth and the black mass snapped like elastic and we all tumbled back into a heap. There was a massive roar from black eyes, he was well pissed.

"You haven't seen the last of me, Channing, you might have won this battle but the war is still on." The lights went out again and we were plunged back into darkness.

After a couple of seconds some of the lights came back on again and we started to untangle ourselves. Megan and Beth were stood to one side; there was a very different look in Beth's eyes from our last encounter.

"I'm sorry, Gary," she told me.

I looked at her and said, "We saved you, that's all that matters, Beth."

Megan said, "We have to go, it's not safe here."

I asked Megan, "What about Richard, don't you want to say goodbye to your father?"

"He never knew about me, he left Mum when she told him she was pregnant, his career was more important, so no I don't need to, after all we have never said hello," and with that they were gone. I looked around and Jenny had vanished as well.

"Where did Jenny go?" I asked. Sue looked at me and said, "She told me to tell you to keep up the good work and all in good time." What did that mean, "all in good time?" My thought process was broken by Paul Lockhart returning.

"What the fuck just happened?" he said. I couldn't help but laugh. It was such a stupid question considering he had been hiding in the control booth whilst everything had happened, which I found out later. Molly told him to bugger off and he disappeared to another part of the studio. Anton then appeared and we sat down whilst I explained in more detail what had happened to his brother and where the police could find his body, at least they could get some closure from being able to have a funeral for him. Anton thanked me and hugged all of us in turn. As he was leaving I shouted,

"Anton, no you don't look like a makeup artist but keep doing what makes you happy."

I turned around and Charles Boyd was stood in

the middle of the studio with Richard Brown, he looked like he had been dragged through a hedge backwards. I walked up to him and said, "Well that was more than you expected, wasn't it?" He was still in a daze and just nodded, his PA appeared at his side and took him gently by the arm and took him out of the studio. I looked at Mitch and said, "He's going to have nightmares about this."

Molly said, "He's not the only one."

"Sissy," was my reply which was swiftly followed by the bird from her.

Finally Richard Brown approached me. This is going to be interesting, I thought.

He held his hand out and looked me in the eye, "I'm sorry, you were right."

I shook his hand and said, "We've not finished yet, let's have a seat and a chat."

I told him everything Megan had told me, he was certainly taken aback by what I told him. "In case you have any doubts, Richard, remember, spirits have no need to lie." I got up and walked towards Sue, Molly and Mitch.

"Let's go home, it's been a long day," I said, and without so much as a look back we got into the car and drove home.

THE END (Possibly)

Printed in Poland
by Amazon Fulfillment
Poland Sp. z o.o., Wrocław

32304535R00166